PORCH LIGHTS
AND
Promises

TERRY W. WESTER

Paperback ISBN: 979-8-218-87649-4

Ebook ISBN: 979-8-218-87650-0

Library of Congress Control Number: 2025922103

Cover Design: M. Waqas
Author Photo: Courtesy of the author
Interior Design & Formatting: Jennifer Laslie
Printed in the United States of America.
First Edition: March 2025

10 9 8 7 6 5 4 3 2 1

For Vanessa, my love.
The porchlight will always be on for you.

SUMMARY

In the quiet town of Tanner, Alabama, Elizabeth "Beth" Miller is doing her best to rebuild a life for herself and her young son, Jupiter. After escaping an abusive marriage to wealthy contractor Denny Miller, Beth finds solace in an old yellow house with a red front door and a porchlight she keeps burning—part warning, part hope.

When firefighter Berry "Flex" Harlan visits her classroom for a safety drill, his easy charm and kindness toward her students—especially Jupiter—begin to break through her guarded heart. But Flex carries a past of his own, one he's not sure small-town gossip will let him outrun.

As Beth's family sides with Denny, and her sister's betrayal cuts deep, whispers and manipulations tighten around her. Flex becomes her refuge, their connection growing from cautious glances to late-night conversations under that ever-burning porchlight.

But in Tanner, old wounds don't stay buried, and some promises carry a price. When a fire threatens to consume more than just a home, Beth will face the ultimate test of love, loss, and the light that guides us through the dark.

Poignant, deeply Southern, and achingly romantic, **Porch Lights and Promises** *is a slow-burn love story about second chances, family ties, and the courage to open your heart when the past still smolders.*

PROLOGUE
THE LOCK CLICKS TWICE

The roll-up door on the yellow box truck clunked shut with a hollow finality, after the last of the boxes thudded into place beside a plastic laundry basket full of bedtime books and mismatched socks.

Beth stood in the narrow patch of shade beside the porch, arms crossed loosely over her chest, watching her sister haul down a lopsided box labeled **JUPITER'S ROOM** in thick blue marker. It was already bleeding through the cardboard from the sweaty arms that moved the boxes and the ever-present Alabama humidity.

"You labeled this one like five times," Maddie said, huffing as she set the box down. "We get it. Kid's got a room."

Beth smiled faintly, but it didn't reach her eyes. "I needed the reassurance."

The cicadas hummed like static in the late August heat. Somewhere behind the tree line, a dog barked once, then again, slow and bored. The new house, hers now, sat on the edge of a sleepy road just outside Birmingham. It was an old one-story home with faded yellow metal siding. The white shutters, newly painted, stood out from the building like band aids, there to cover old boo-boos, or to hide old damage that the house flipper did not want to get into. The front door was old but shined from the glossy new coat of red paint. Next to the door, completely out of character with the home, hung a large cast iron lamp with a yellow filament bulb pointing down. The light flickered on and off as you walked on the porch in a manner that made you question whether it was inviting you in or waiting for you to leave.

Inside, the house smelled like old wood and lemon cleaner, the scent reminded Beth of her grandmother's home, old but clean. The new keys jangled in her pocket, and her chest still hadn't unclenched since turning them in the lock that morning.

This house gave her a feeling that she needed, a feeling that was hard for her to pinpoint. The house provided a sense of safety, of the feeling that she could close her eyes and not be on edge. This feeling did not come from reinforced doors or bars on windows, but from distance. Distance from her past and the man that haunted her dreams and sent spasms of fear racing across her core in the middle of the night.

There were other houses, other apartments, but this old house spoke to her. It spoke of opportunity and new beginnings, but mostly it spoke of distance. It was far enough away from her past, but close to something else. Right around the corner stood a small building, painted white with one door in and a chain link fence that surrounded the perimeter. On the front of the building a sign hung that read 'Tanner Police Department'.

Jupiter darted past them racing into the front yard, barefoot and with the speed of youth, chasing something only he could see, a butterfly, maybe, or a sunbeam. His little arms windmilled as he spun and laughed and tripped into the grass.

Maddie watched him fall and bounce back up like rubber. "He's... okay," she said slowly, rubbing the back of her neck. "He really is."

Beth nodded. "I hope so."

They stood in silence, watching him.

Then, Maddie asked softly, "Do you think he remembers it?"

The question drifted between them like smoke.

Beth didn't answer right away. Her arms tightened around her ribs as the memory rose unbidden, the sound of shattering glass, of a bottle thrown too close to her head. Denny's voice roaring from the hallway. And Jupiter, crawling under the kitchen table, whispering, *"I don't want Daddy to be scary."*

Just yesterday, she'd slammed a cabinet door too hard while cleaning. Jupiter had flinched.

He hadn't said anything. Just stared for a second too long.

"He remembers something," Beth finally said. "But kids... they press things down. Hide them. Like seeds."

Maddie looked over at her, brow creased. "And what if it grows crooked?"

Beth stared at her son, now crouched beside a patch

of dandelions, blowing fluff into the wind with pure delight.

"I don't know," she said. "I just know he deserves better than what I let him see."

"You got him out."

Jupiter was up again and ran past them into the kitchen sliding in on his knees and stopping at a box with 'kitchen' written on its side.

The kitchen was beautifully remade and modern, with white lower cabinets and a black compressed marble counter top. The walls were white subway tiles with a thin black band that traced its way around the room. This along with the new stainless-steel appliances were nice touches, but the thing that Beth loved the most was there were no cabinets on up top, just beautifully waxed rough-cut floating shelves. The openness is what she loved, the lack of cabinet doors meant everything was open, this kitchen held no secrets, what you saw is what you got.

Beth nodded. "It should have been sooner, I let him see... things. Now, I have to teach him what *safe* feels like."

Jupiter came sprinting back toward them, beaming. He held a long red tube with a yellow conical cap on top in one hand and waved with the other. "Momma! I found my lamp!"

Beth moved toward him, leaned and gave him a strong hug. "It wouldn't be home without it."

She stood straight and walked past her sister letting her hand reach out and lightly touch the side of her arm. She walked out past her shiny red door and flickering porch light and stopped resting her hands on the painted porch railing. The wood was cracked, a little tired, but it held. She liked the idea of that, it spoke to her.

She smiled.

It wasn't much, it wasn't the grand house she left, but it was home.

I

THE QUIET BELL

The alarm was set for 5:30 a.m., but Beth's eyes opened at 5:14, the same minute they always did. Her body didn't need permission anymore. It had trained itself to rise before the day could take control. She liked control, she craved it.

The room was dimly lit with light in the early morning sun sending a pale glow as it cast through the thin dollar store curtains. A single bird chirped announcing its intentions, and somewhere outside, a rooster crowed like it regretted being alive. It was too early to think deeply, but she needed to figure out where that rooster was, she was living in the center of town, and while rural, it was definitely not a farm. She could not bring herself to move yet. She just lay there and listened.

She listened to the quiet hum of the box fan. The settling creaks of the house as the sun began to warm its old wooden bones. She listened to all of these sounds, but the sound that she listened to and loved the most was the sound of the rhythmic breathing of a six-year-old boy in Scooby-Doo pajamas and wrapped in the old quilt her grandmother had made before her hands gave out.

Jupiter crawled into her bed sometime around two, she guessed. No nightmare, just... instinct. He did it more often lately. Like he needed to make sure she was still real.

His little hand rested on her stomach, thumb twitching in a dream. She didn't move it.

At 5:17, her phone vibrated on the nightstand.

She reached for it without jostling him. The screen glowed with a message from her mother:

Remember that GOD has a plan for us all.

Read the bible with Jupiter and learn his plans.

Love, Mom.

Beth stared at it for a moment, then locked the screen and turned it facedown. It was definitely too early for that nonsense.

By 6:00 a.m., the kitchen smelled like coffee and vanilla cream from the pot brewing and the pale yellow candle burning in a clear jar on the stove, a welcome gift from her sister. Jupiter's lunchbox sat open on the table, ham sandwich, no crust, dinosaur gummy snacks, the last juice box from the fridge.

Beth leaned against the counter, barefoot, flipping through her lesson plans for the week. With a cringe she read, Fire Safety Week. She and the children would be treated to a full unit of songs, crafts, and the return of the cardboard flame mascot, Sparky, who'd met a watery death in the copy room last October when the upstairs boy's restroom was flooded in a juvenile prank involving inflated condoms, plastic cling wrap, and toilets.

Outside, the cicadas buzzed like static. Inside, the ceiling fan clicked every fifth rotation. To some, this repetition would drive insanity, but for Beth, it was like a concerto written to sooth her soul.

"Momma?"

She turned. Jupiter stood in the doorway, hair wild and one sock on sideways.

"Hey, baby."

He walked to her, half-asleep, and leaned into her body like a branch finding its tree. She wrapped her arms around him, kissed the top of his head.

"You want cereal?"

"Do we got the T. rex one?"

She sighed with mock drama. "I think the T. rex ate it all."

He groaned against her hip. "Mean ol' lizard."

By the time they got to the school parking lot, the morning heat was already starting to rise, the Alabama heat was no joke in August. They walked across the blacktop parking lot and Beth used her teacher's badge to beep her into the side door. Jupiter slid past her and started skipping down the hallway, his backpack thumping up and down as he moved. She smiled as she was reminded of an old cartoon where a small man rode on the back of a camel bopping up and down on its hump as they made their way across the desert.

"Morning, Miss Beth!" Ray the custodian called, sipping from his enormous thermos. "Big week. I heard Sparky's back in action."

"Let's hope he doesn't drown again this year." Beth gave him a fake smile as she passed. He was friendly enough, but the past two years had taught her that friendly does not always mean friendly.

Inside her classroom, the smell of dry erase markers and pencil shavings greeted her like old friends. Paper sunflowers and phonics charts lined the walls. On the bulletin board above the reading nook, a string of stars fluttered with crayon-written answers to the question:

"What Makes You Brave?"

Jupiter's was taped low, near the corner and his precious handwriting read:

When Mommy holds my hand.

Beth pressed her fingers against the edge of the paper, gently, as if afraid it might vanish.

At 7:33, her email pinged.

Subject: FIRE DRILL SCHEDULE – PLEASE READ

Reminder: today's fire alarm test will occur around 8:15.

Officer Sandridge and a local fire station are taking part in walkthroughs.

Expect a visit to your room later this morning. No surprises, we promise.

Beth stared at the screen.

She didn't delete it, her finger hovered over the delete key but just minimized the screen and set her mug down a little harder than necessary.

The sound of the alarm always put her on edge, it was loud, not a 'this is necessary' loud, but the type of loud that instilled panic in her soul, the loud of sirens while in the back of an ambulance loud.

She hated it.

Jupiter was already coloring at his desk with three other early arrivals. He was chatting about how fast a cheetah could run. She watched him for a moment, chin resting on her hand.

She knew she was lucky, that her son still laughed, still played, still bounced like rubber, but she also knew how deeply children absorb things. How memory didn't always scream, sometimes it whispered, slow and quiet, until you thought it was gone. Then, unbidden, it came back dressed as something else, something grown, something angry.

"What if it grows crooked?" Maddie had said.

Beth didn't have the answer, but today she would keep the kids calm, keep her voice steady, and smile through the alarm. The smile she always made to put on the brave face, the brave face that hid her trembling inner self from the world and anyone that would try to hurt her.

The fire engine always made a different kind of noise when it rumbled through school zones, like even the machine knew to lower its voice.

Flex leaned against the window frame in the passenger seat, sunglasses cutting the glare of early sunlight as Engine 2 coasted up to Tanner Elementary. The red paint, the chrome, the men smiling out of the windows glinted in the morning sun. Seeing a fire engine pass always drew the eye, but in an elementary school parking lot you got more attention than usual, and not just from the kids, from the ladies in the rider lines. The ladies driving their mini-vans and SUVs who looked through their sunglasses like starving people standing in front of a buffet.

His captain, Grady, grunted as he killed the ignition. "Ten bucks says the PTA president tries to hand you her number again."

Flex smiled without looking away from the windshield. "Make it twenty and I'll pretend to blush this time."

Grady barked a laugh. "You ever think about taking a job that's not half calendar pinup, half babysitter?"

"Sure," Flex said. "But then I'd have to wear a tie, and we both know how that ends."

He hopped down from the truck in one easy movement, the soles of his boots thudding against the pavement with practiced grace. Flex carried his inspection clipboard in one hand and the weight of old reputation in the other — invisible, but familiar.

He'd volunteered for this school visit.

Grady had teased him mercilessly. "What, you get tired of grown women slipping you notes in the grocery store? Now you want to impress their kids too?"

But that wasn't it.

Flex liked kids.

They didn't judge. Didn't pry. Didn't ask what *Flex* stood for, or how many times he'd pulled off his shirt on stage during undergrad school. They just wanted to know if you were strong enough to carry a hose and fast enough to beat a fire to the front door.

He could do both.

The lobby smelled like lemon cleaner and Elmer's glue. A woman at the front office window pointed him toward the administration wing, where he'd start his walkthrough. His route would take him past a few classrooms, then through the second-grade hall, and finally to the new addition by the gym, apparently remodeled after a lightning strike a few years back.

Flex took it slow, checking extinguishers, noting signage, jotting down reminders to remind someone else.

When the fire bell test began at 8:16 on the dot, it didn't catch him off guard.

But the sound still hit sharp, a mechanical scream meant to rattle.

And somewhere down the hall, a child screamed back.

When the fire bell screamed at exactly 8:16, it sliced through the classroom like a blade.

She'd prepared herself. Told the kids. Went over the drill. But the sound still made her jaw lock tight.

Little Tasha Jenkins immediately dropped to the floor and crawled under her desk, hands clamped over her ears. Beth crouched beside her, keeping her voice calm and low. Tasha was special and was considered highly functional on the autism scale. Beth felt for her, this sound was a trigger that they both shared.

"It's okay, sweet pea. Just a drill. Remember what we practiced?"

Tasha didn't budge. Her eyes were wide and glassy.

The rest of the class followed procedure well enough. Some looked nervous, others excited. Beth stayed with Tasha, not pushing her to get up, just being there.

A shadow moved across the doorway. Then a voice, warm, deep, gentle.

"Hey there. You okay under there?"

Beth looked up.

The firefighter wore his helmet, dark navy pants, and a department T-shirt. He held clipboard in one hand, his other already holding out a cartoon sticker of a

Dalmatian in boots. He knelt beside Tasha, his tone friendly, not intrusive.

"You know," he said, "I used to hate sirens too. I thought they were ghost alarms. Real loud ghosts."

Tasha blinked at him.

"Loud *and* rude," he added, eyes wide like it was a secret.

She giggled. A tiny one.

Beth watched, stunned, as Tasha slowly slid out and took the sticker from his hand.

He gave her a nod, then stood and offered Beth the faintest smile. Not cocky. Not charming. Just... human.

"Nice work," she said quietly.

He shrugged. "Kids are the best people."

He turned to the rest of the class. "Sorry for the disruption, folks. Sparky says you passed."

A few kids cheered. One clapped too hard and, jumping, knocked a bowl of crayons to the floor with a crash sending a chill down Beth's spine.

Flex nodded at her, "Ma'am." And turned to walk out.

Beth straightened and brushed her skirt, watching as he stepped into the hallway without saying another word.

Something about his presence, the calm in it, lingered.

Outside in the hallway he exhaled.

He had seen her before, but something about her

today, the way that she looked at him after he spoke to the little girl made his mind race.

He didn't know her story, didn't know the kid under the desk, or the little boy wearing a name tag that said Jupiter, the boy that stared at him in awe. He didn't know anything, but somehow the way she looked at him made him feel like he was a part of their world.

"Momma?" Jupiter stood by her desk.

She knelt. "Yeah, baby?"

"That man... he had big arms."

She snorted softly. "He did."

He tilted his head. "Was he real? Not pretend?"

"As real as they come."

"Like... real-real?"

"Yep."

He nodded, satisfied, and returned to his seat. With that commotion over, Beth turned to the class and started the process of returning little ones to order.

Ten minutes later, the firefighter reappeared at the door. Knocked politely. Beth turned, already speaking as she approached the door. "Ok, we have had enough excitement for one day."

She stopped. He was closer now, and taller than she'd thought. Sunglasses tucked in his shirt collar. Clipboard in hand.

"Sorry. Just need a signature for the inspection log."

She stepped forward, took the pen. His hands were large and strong, and there was a white scar along one knuckle. She chided herself and told herself internally to stop it, stop looking, they were all trouble.

"Everything pass inspection?"

He grinned, crooked. "You're running a tight ship."

She nodded, expression unreadable.

Behind her, Jupiter popped up again. "You really fight fires?"

The man turned. "Every week."

"You ever save a cat?"

"Three. One from a roof. One under a porch. One that climbed a tree with zero exit strategy."

Beth bit back a smile as Jupiter burst into a giggle.

Then the firefighter took off his helmet and offered it to Jupiter.

"You wanna try it on?"

The boy's eyes widened. "Can I?"

Beth hesitated for half a heartbeat, then nodded.

Jupiter staggered under the weight of it, laughing. For a moment, Beth saw it, the kind of life other families must live. One where trust wasn't a risk.

She took the helmet back gently.

"Time for math," she said, steady again.

The firefighter gave her a polite nod. "Thanks for letting me drop in."

"Thanks for... earlier," she said, looking sternly up at him. "With the student, with Tasha."

He shrugged, "Kids are the best people."

Beth studied him for a moment longer than she

should have, just enough to register the of scarring along his knuckles, the steadiness of his eyes, and the way his polo seemed to be painted to his chest. She didn't thank him again. She just handed back the clipboard.

Their fingers didn't touch, but the proximity sent electricity racing up her arm. In her mind she again told herself to stop.

"Back to your seat little boy." She turned and went back to the center of the room and got back to her business of building little lives.

Later, on her way to the copier, Beth passed the front office and looked out the window.

The fire engine sat at the edge of the lot, door open. The firefighter, Flex, she thought she'd heard someone call him, was loading a hose back into the side compartment. They took it out at recess to show the children how far it would spray.

He paused and looked up, drawn to her without knowing.

He saw her and through the glass, through the glare, their eyes met.

He didn't wave and she didn't smile but something passed between them. A flicker, a recognition of something special.

Beth saw in that moment a flash of comfort, she was reminded of her safe place and the flicker of the porch light. Was he safe...

"Stop it." Beth growled under her breath and walked back to her classroom.

Flex finished putting the truck back in order, climbed in and rumbled away.

"So how many?"

"How many what?", Flex replied.

"How many numbers you dog."

He stared ahead as he drove the truck. "Three."

"Damn, that is above average even for me! I bet you got some serious action when you were swinging your dick back in the day!"

"Well captain, that was back in the day, so you will never know." Flex bit his cheek to keep from saying more. He spent the rest of the drive tuning out the ramblings of his boss as he rambled on about his many sexual conquests. In the back of his mind, he could not shake the thought of the stern woman he locked eyes with.

2

THE FIRST LAUGH

The sun wasn't even over the pine trees yet, but the parking lot at Tanner Elementary was already busy with minivans, blurry eyed children, and parents who needed to be about their day. Beth sat in her car, door open, one foot on the pavement, listening to the soft whoosh of traffic on the nearby county road.

She was musing over a thought that went through her mind over breakfast. She thought it was a silly thought, something that did not deserve her time, but still, it was there. All of this internal noise was over the porch light. She never left it on at night as she was not a fan of bugs, and in Alabama a porch light means bugs, big ones. Why had she left it on, and more importantly why was she wasting time thinking about it?

"Enough," she chided herself. She twisted in the seat of her little sedan and twisted the rear-view mirror so she could see herself in the mirror. Beth was not a vain woman and normally walked out the door, hair in bun and a 'who the hell cares if I am not wearing make-up attitude', but today she woke up feeling special. She showered, dried her hair, picked out a vibrant sundress with blue floral print, and went ahead to apply her full arsenal of cosmetics. She looked good, felt good, and was ready to start her day with pride.

With a final glance at herself, she fixed the mirror, stood and almost fell. "Oh yeah," she spoke out loud, I forgot about the heels. Instead of the normal flats that she wore as part of her daily school attire she had pulled a pair of heels, not just any heels though, the pair that her sister called her "fuck me" heels. As she started to walk across the hot pavement, she at once regretted her decision in footwear, but damned if her calves didn't look good in them.

Inside the school, the building felt cooler than usual. Maybe it was the little sundress that allowed the cool air to hit quickly, but it was partially due to the way Mrs. Johnson looked at her. Patricia Johnson was a volunteer mom who worked at the front entrance desk. She had a child in the 4th grade and was a modern-day helicopter mom, if her baby was at school she would be too.

The look Patricia gave her told a story. The story being that she obviously disapproved of her choice in clothing for the day. She glanced Beth up and down several times, lingering a little too long at the hem of her dress and left thigh, the area where a small sunflower tattoo was playing peek-a-boo.

"Good morning, Patricia."

With a frown Mrs. Johnson replied, "Good morning, excuse me I am on dress code patrol, someone has to make sure all of these kids are given good instruction on proper dress, and... see a good example of modesty." She turned abruptly and walked away to a group of 5th grade girls huddled around a locker in the hallway.

Beth stood for a moment, watching her walk away and mouthed quietly under her breath, "Bitch." She made the journey to her classroom with her stoic face, smiling at children whenever they looked up. She noticed the janitor and Mr. Helms, a third-grade teacher, smile as she walked by and felt their lingering gaze on her ass like laser beams burning through a wood tree as her back was turned.

The one thing that no one told her when Beth decided to become a teacher was how much of a paper craft decorator the day entailed. There were always holidays, birthdays, and special events like fire week that needed crepe paper, corrugated cardboard, and laminated do-dads. She was halfway through hanging construction paper flames around the whiteboard when Jupiter came skipping in when the final bell rang.

"Guess what, Momma!"

She turned from the wall, staple gun still in hand. "What?"

"Flex said he's gonna do Fire Week with us!"

Beth blinked. "Who said what now?"

"Flex! The firefighter! The one with the cat stories. He said he signed up!"

23

Jupiter beamed, like this was Christmas and birthday rolled into one.

Beth felt the ground shift beneath her just a little. "When... when did he say that?"

"Just now. He was talking to the office ladies. They laughed *so loud.*"

Of course they had, those ladies were worse than the janitor and Mr. Helms combined when it came to a strong set of buns, especially when they were on a man in uniform. The things that came out of their mouths could make a sailor blush, and she had already heard stories about what they wanted to do the very same Mr. Berry, AKA Flex.

Beth set the stapler down and knelt in front of Jupiter, brushing a crumb off his shirt collar. "Baby... Flex, Mr. Berry, is busy. Sometimes adults sign up for things but don't always come, okay?"

"He said he would," Jupiter insisted. "And he winked!"

Beth stilled. "He winked at you?"

"No. At the office ladies. But I was *there.*"

Of course he did, just another player. She bit back a sigh and said, "Well we will see, hopefully he will be there."

She went back to her business and dove into her thoughts while the children chattered at their desks. Who cares if he is a player, he can wink at whomever he wants to. Still, he was a handsome man, and that polo did stir feelings in her. Not emotional feelings of course, but more of a basic, primal feeling. She stopped and walked over to her desk and opened a small notepad taken from her purse. The first page had notes scribbled, a shopping list, and at the bottom she added "AA Batteries." She looked at the note one more time, tapped her pen to the side of the notebook and put it away thinking, "batteries are more dependable than men these days."

Thirty minutes later, during recess, Beth ducked into the main office to grab a printer cartridge. Sure enough, a clipboard sat on the front counter with **FIRE SAFETY WEEK VOLUNTEERS** scribbled across the top.

There were five names listed.

Number four read:

Berry Jackson – Firehouse 2

Available all week except Thursday (training)

Happy to help however's useful :)

Beside the signature was a phone number written in perfectly neat print, too neat. His penmanship did not match his physique, it was the practiced effect of a man who had not grown up in the age of text messages and snap chats.

Beth stared at the clipboard for a moment too long.

Behind the counter, Mrs. Campbell raised an eyebrow. "Something wrong, honey?"

Beth snapped out of it. "No, just... checking if we had enough hands for Friday."

"Oh, we've got hands," Mrs. Campbell said with a smirk. "Mr. Jackson said he's good with groups, and glue sticks."

Beth smiled tightly. "Terrific."

Back in her classroom, Beth closed the door and locked it, even though no one ever really bothered them during her recess downtime, this was a precious moment for all teachers, and it was respected across the board to not bother another teacher during the daily, "why the fuck did I become a teacher" time slot.

She leaned against the whiteboard, her arms crossed. Her heartbeat ticked up a notch she had not noticed a very important fact when she closed the door, her son was inside and not at recess.

Jupiter sat at his desk drawing a firetruck, tongue poked between his teeth.

"He's funny," he said casually, without looking up.

"Who?"

"Flex."

Beth didn't respond right away. She crossed to his desk and crouched beside him.

"Do you like him?"

Jupiter shrugged like it was obvious. "He's nice. He talks to me like I'm big. Not like a baby."

She nodded, eyes stinging unexpectedly. "That's good."

"Can he come to my birthday?"

Beth paused.

Jupiter's birthday was in six weeks. They hadn't even planned anything yet.

"Well, I don't know. Wouldn't you rather just have your friends?"

Face crunching a little, one eyebrow raised he said, "I asked Peter, Sam, and Laura and they don't want to come. They said I wasn't it."

"It?"

"Yeah, I am not it."

Her heart broke a little at this, Jupiter had a close circle of friends at their old home. A forty-minute drive might as well be across the ocean when it comes to arranging time with old friends. She felt a strong pull of guilt at having uprooted him, she had to, but that did not ease her feelings or give him time with his old friends. She pressed the nails of her right hand into her thigh to keep the tears inside her eyes.

"Maybe," she said, brushing his hair off his forehead. "We'll see."

When she stood, she almost fell. She caught herself on the small desk and Jupiter looked at her excitedly, "You ok mommy?"

"Yes baby, I just tripped."

Jupiter giggled a little and started back on his firetruck work of art.

Her ankle hurt a little, but she was glad that it did. It took the focus away from her guilt and feelings that she was failing her son. Walking back to her desk she reminded herself to tell her sister that her "Fuck Me" shoes almost fucked her up, but... damn did her calves look good in them.

That night, after Jupiter fell asleep watching a nature show, Beth sat on the porch steps with her second cup of tea and stared at the porchlight again as it flickered it dance of welcome and go away.

The sky was clear, and you could faintly see stars, the large streetlamp in front of her house partially hid the night sky, but its glow gave her comfort as it kept the night from hugging her home, she hated the dark. She was amazed at the sound here, it wasn't quiet, but there were no cars rumbling past, or the wails of sirens from emergency vehicles, just the sound of crickets, and the gentle hum of the streetlamp down the road. She rubbed her hand on the railing post, it was warm to the touch and though cracked, smoothed over from the passing of countless pairs of pants that rubbed on their way down the stairs. This place was magical.

Her thoughts moved back to a troubling thought, Berry. She could not get him off her mind. Inside her head she could hear her mom chiding her, "you have a son to raise...you don't have time to date, that is the past...your decisions have been terrible so far, why would you trust yourself now?" All noise, all troubling, all in her damned head. The fact of the matter is she is a woman, women have desires, and desires need to be dealt with. Hell, it was fire week, and this was just another fire to put out.

Flex had signed up for the week. Had stepped directly into her world. It was probably harmless and probably had more to do with the cute girl with perky tits and perfect skin working in the front office for administrative credit to finish her degree than Beth, the woman in her thirties with a painful past and child in tow.

He was good with kids. Charming. Stable. He was also... complicated. That much, she could feel even from the few minutes they had spent together.

Still.

She hadn't turned off the porchlight after seeing him in her classroom, and something about that bothered her more than she wanted to admit. Taking the last sip of her tea, she walked back inside, past her shiny red door. Locking up she reached up to turn off the porchlight but stopped. She moved her hand over and picked up the small yellow bag laying on the white homemade shelf in her entry, the family heirloom that was marked over by she and her sister as children and more recently by Jupiter. She opened the bag and took out dollar store purchase. A new pack of AA batteries.

She turned and went to her bedroom, closed the door and left a quiet house alone with itself. Outside, the flickering light stopped its dance and stayed luminated. She left the light on, she was breaking her own rules.

Flex didn't usually get nervous walking into a classroom. He was good with kids, had the sticker stash to prove it, and his charm worked on parents, teachers, administrators, hell, even a few fourth-graders who'd called him "Captain America's tired cousin."

But standing outside Beth's door on Tuesday morning, second day of Fire Safety Week, clipboard in hand, boots tracking a line of red dust from the recently visited softball field, he hesitated.

She didn't smile yesterday.

Not really.

She'd said thank you, sure. But it had the weight of something trained, not given. Like maybe she didn't trust people who stepped in and fixed things too easily.

He got that.

So, he raised his hand to knock, and the door opened before he touched it.

Beth blinked at him, startled. "You're early."

Flex cleared his throat, already smiling. "Overachiever. Can't help myself."

She stepped aside, expression unreadable. "We're in the middle of math."

"I'll be quiet."

A little girl with pigtails pointed. "That's the cat firefighter!"

He gave her a wink. "Guilty."

Jupiter lit up from his desk like a flashlight. "Flex!"

The sound of his name from that kid's mouth did something weird to his chest.

Flex crossed to the well-used reading rug where the fire safety materials were laid out. He crouched next to the cutout of Sparky the Flame, tapping it on the nose like it was an old friend.

"Did you know Sparky's terrified of spaghetti?" he said in a whisper-shout.

The class leaned in.

Beth raised an eyebrow.

"He says every time he sees it he nearly pastas out!"

A beat of silence.

Then Jupiter cackled.

Not just laughed, full-body, head-back, nose-snorting cackled.

Flex grinned. "You're gonna get me fired."

Beth covered her mouth, but not before he saw it.

The laugh and smile, a real one, fast and sudden like it has snuck out her before she could catch it. They were both gone just as quickly, swallowed behind her neutral teacher face, but he'd seen it. The sight made him happy and sent a tingle through his chest, a tingle that turned to something warm.

His smile did not fade, and he let his eyes linger on hers for a few more heartbeats- for a few more brief moments he looked into eyes that betrayed the hard-outward appearance she presented. He was definitely attracted to her, but more so, he felt drawn to her.

Later, while the kids were busy crafting for the classroom bulletin board competition, Flex helped Jupiter tape a poster back to the wall that had come loose. The boy leaned against him like it was the most natural thing in the world.

"My daddy never helped me with stuff," Jupiter said casually, looking up at him.

Flex froze mid-tape.

He glanced toward Beth, she was tidying stacks of paper on her desk, back turned.

"What do you mean?" he asked gently.

Jupiter shrugged. "He was mad a lot."

Flex knelt to the boy's level. "What do you mean?"

"Daddy didn't like mommy, he would yell and one time he threw his plate on the wall."

Flex paused before asking, "Does your dad still throw plates Jupiter?"

"No, daddy doesn't live with us anymore. My grandma said he is a guest of the State of Alabama now."

"I see," Flex put on his best smile, "look little dude, big people can be hard to understand sometimes. I want you to know something though, something real important. Can you listen and see if it makes sense?"

Jupiter, face lighting up from Flex's infectious smile, chirped, "You got it Flex."

"Big people stuff is not because of little people. Sometimes it might feel like that, but you need to know that. When I was little the big people in my life were scary sometimes too. Like you, it wasn't because of me. Does that make sense?"

Jupiter didn't reply, just gave a shy nod and offered him the roll of tape.

Beth appeared a moment later, eyes flicking between them. If she'd heard, she didn't show it.

"Thanks for stopping in," she said. Polite. Guarded again.

"Anytime," Flex replied, standing.

Their eyes met.

She didn't look away this time.

Didn't invite him in but didn't close the door either.

And for now, that was enough. Flex waved to the kids and moved on to his next fire week task.

The hallway was quiet, the kind of quiet that only came after buses left, chairs were stacked, and pencils stopped rolling under desks.

Beth stood on a step stool at the front of her classroom, staring at the shredded remains of her fire safety display. One side had come unstapled during dismissal and folded like a wet newspaper. Construction paper flames now drooped sadly toward the floor.

"Of course," she muttered, yanking at a corner. It tore straight down the middle.

She exhaled through her nose, hard.

It had been a good day, better than expected. The kids were engaged, Jupiter was relaxed, and even the principal had complimented her for "bringing the sparkle back" to Sparky.

But somehow, standing alone in this space, with paper flames falling apart in her hands, it all suddenly felt like too much. Too fragile.

Like maybe everything only worked because she held it together hard enough not to let it fall.

"Need a hand?"

She turned, startled.

Flex stood in the doorway, no clipboard this time. Just him, muscled arms crossed, helmet under one arm, a quiet expression on his face.

33

Beth straightened. "I'm fine."

"Looks like Sparky's going down in flames again."

Beth let out a soft, unplanned laugh. "Maybe he deserves it."

Flex stepped into the room, slowly. "You really hate asking for help, huh?"

She tilted her head. "You really don't take hints, huh?"

He grinned. "Takes two to keep a conversation that dry."

She smiled despite herself. "Fine. If you want to re-staple that side, I won't stop you."

They worked in companionable silence for a few minutes. He held the paper while she re-aligned the flames. Their shoulders bumped once, neither of them commented.

"So," Flex said casually, "how long you been teaching?"

"Eight years."

"All here?"

"No. I moved around a little."

He nodded, like he didn't need more.

Beth glanced at him. "You?"

"Firefighter? Five years. Before that..." He trailed off, suddenly adjusting the stapler in his hand.

She waited.

He cleared his throat. "Before that, I worked nights, Bartending, and some other stuff."

The silence that followed was short but charged. Beth felt the hairs on her arm rise; this was not a conversation of Shakespearean prose, but the simple fact that he was not being over intrusive or telling her "How Pretty" she was gave her a sense of relief. She still felt like he was not there for her, better grounds to hunt, but this small attention felt good, and she felt bad for that. She was disturbed by this mix of emotions, but his lack of intrusion was nice, there was an honesty in that fleeting feeling.

When the last staple clicked into place, she stepped down from the stool.

"Looks good," he said.

"Better than before."

He nodded, adjusted his helmet under his arm. "Alright. I'm gonna get out of your hair."

Beth followed him to the door. "Hey."

He turned.

"Thanks," she said softly.

He gave her his best smile again, the big perfect toothed grin that pushed his cheeks back. Revealing that even his face had muscles on top of muscles, "Anytime."

Then, for a moment, they just stood there, not speaking. The classroom behind her still smelled like markers and glue. The hallway behind him held nothing but air and fading light.

Beth opened her mouth, maybe to say something else.

But Flex beat her to it.

"You always leave your porchlight on?"

She blinked.

"What?"

"Your porchlight, do you always leave it on?"

"How. How do you know where I live?

He lost his smile, and his face took on a look of panic, "Oh hey, yeah, that sounds bad."

Beth crossed her arms, all emotion gone in her face, and a growing tension building in her chest. Inside she thought here it is, here is the creep.

"I had to drop off a fire report at the police station last night, I saw you on your porch, nothing cringy, just me doing my job and seeing someone I know."

The tension dropped a little, she believed him but inside her nerves were tensing for a fight, "Well, it is cringy." She tried to give a partial smile to ease the situation.

He smiled gently. "I am sorry, really. I just saw you and when I came back from the station the light was still on, thought maybe you were waiting on someone."

Her mouth went dry.

"I leave it on for Jupiter," she said quickly. "He gets nervous."

Flex nodded, easy. "Makes sense."

Then he tipped two fingers in a mock salute and turned down the hall. Without turning to face her and not pausing his steps he said, "Sorry about being cringy, I will do better!"

Beth watched him go until he turned the corner, boots echoing in quiet rhythm.

She stepped back into the classroom and looked at the newly stapled wall, then at the window where southern sky was dotted by patchwork rows of fluffy cumulous clouds lined up like skipping stones in the sky.

She didn't know why she lied about the porchlight, maybe because part of her *was* waiting for something.

She just didn't know what yet.

3

STRUCK MATCHES

Beth stood at her mother's sink rinsing casserole dishes, her fingers wrinkling in the too-hot water, while the sound of Jupiter's giggles echoed from the back porch.

The Sunday routine hadn't changed since high school, roast chicken, cornbread, mac and cheese from scratch, and two hours of mild tension dressed up as polite conversation.

Maddie sat at the kitchen table thumbing through a church bulletin, still in her floral dress. Their mother stood behind her, refolding the same dishtowel for the third time.

"You look tired," her mother said gently in her not so subtle way of striking up a conversation where none existed.

Beth gave a tight smile without turning. "It's been a long week."

"You should take more naps. Jupiter's old enough to play by himself."

Beth let the silence speak for her and tried not to let the exasperation show on her face.

Her mother tried again. "I saw you had volunteers at the school this week. I stopped by the office to drop off that donation bag. The ladies were *buzzing*."

Beth kept her back turned and said bluntly. "Fire Safety Week."

"I know." A pause. "One of them mentioned someone from the fire department. Said he was tall. Real polite."

Beth said nothing.

"Goes by Flex, I believe?"

Maddie looked up from the bulletin.

Beth turned off the water and dried her hands slowly.

"He's one of the station's outreach volunteers," she said, measured. "He did a safety demo. That's it."

Her mother didn't nod. Didn't frown. Just folded that towel again like it held secrets.

"I'm just saying," she said softly, "just because someone wears a uniform doesn't mean they are safe."

"I know that. I don't know why you think I need to hear it?"

"Well, I spoke to Patricia, and she mentioned that you had eyes for him."

"Mama, Patricia is a mean bag. The only thing that comes out of her mouth are polite insults and drama."

"She," her mother began but was quickly cutoff.

"I know what you think mama, I know that you are disappointed in my... decisions."

"Baby, I am not disappointed, I just worry about

Jupiter. He doesn't need men coming in and out of his life."

"There are no men coming in and out. I have not dated anyone since... since we moved out."

"Now baby, that is not what we heard. You know I spoke to pastor about Denny. He said that he has been visiting him, and he is really making amends, for, well for his indiscretions."

"Mama, I know you are not saying.

"Look, I just want the best for you. Look at you living here now. Do you really think this is a good home for Jupiter, a good school system? You had such a good life with Denny."

"A good life, mama, he almost killed me. Did you forget about that?"

"I am not saying he was an angel, but Jesus tells us to forgive and turn the other cheek."

"The last time I turned a cheek to that man I lost two teeth!" Beth opened her mouth and pulled her cheek back revealing the back to molars missing on the right side of her lower jaw.

Flushed, Evelyn looked down at the floor, "Baby, sometimes men just, well they are just not always themselves."

"I cannot believe you would even... do you hear yourself mama?" Beth's eyes were full of tears ready to roll down her flushed face. She wanted to run, to get away from this conversation and leave. She wanted to go anywhere that was far enough away that no one would know her or the asshole who owned Denny Complete Construction Solutions.

"I only mean...I love you baby. I just want the best for you and Jupiter"

She knew she was not going to win this battle, her mother respected wealth and status over personal happiness. She knew retreat was the only choice, "I know, Evelyn."

The silence that followed was interrupted by Maddie, "So, that was awkward."

Beth and Evelyn stared daggers at her. Beth turned to walk away, "Shut up Maddie."

Later, on the porch swing, Beth sat with Jupiter curled against her side, his belly full of cornbread and ice cream, his shirt had smears of chocolate from his chin to his navel. His flip-flopped feet dangled just above the floorboards, rocking slightly with each creak of the weathered and slightly rusted chain.

The heat had started to break, a rare softness in the late summer air and the hummingbirds were busy fighting yellow jackets blocking them from getting their fill of red colored sugar water from the strawberry shaped plastic feeders handing from hooks on the eaves of porch.

Jupiter looked up suddenly. "Can Flex come to my birthday?"

Beth blinked, startled from her deep thoughts of nothingness. "What?"

"My birthday party. At the jump place. You said I could pick someone."

She hesitated. "I meant a classmate. One of your friends."

"He *is* my friend." Jupiter crossed both arms high on his chest with his chin up. God, how he looked like his father when that stubborn streak came out to play.

Her chest tightened.

"You only met him last week."

"So? I like him. He's nice."

Beth didn't respond.

Jupiter turned his face into her side, with the flowing shoulders of her dress riding over his head and said, voice muffled. "He laughs at my jokes. Daddy never did that."

A slow ache bloomed behind her ribs, and she held him closer, brushing her fingers through his hair. How much did he know, remember, or allow himself to remember what happened? He was there the night she went down, he saw his father hurt her, but his little mind just went to jokes. This angered her and she wondered how long it would take him to forgive and forget. These thoughts rushed in and out of her mind in the time it took to take a deep breath.

She felt an immediate pang of guilt over this thought. She had no right to control how he processed the past, but she worried, would it be forgotten? What would happen if he did? How much control would Denny have over her if he did.

"We'll see, okay?"

"But..."

"We'll see, Jupiter."

He fell quiet, and she rocked him gently until his breathing slowed.

Her mother watched from the kitchen window; Beth could feel her gaze without looking. The feeling of heat on her neck, of judgement dressed up as love.

Flex sat on the edge of his bed with one boot already stripped of dust, the other still waiting on the floor beside him like a patient soldier. The air in his apartment smelled faintly of saddle soap and cedar, clean, dry, masculine.

His apartment above the old feed store was small, a single bedroom. It had a kitchenette and a window that overlooked the back alley where he parked his truck. It was quiet, empty, and every surface inside was too neat, too still.

He picked up the horsehair brush, worn and fitted his palm after years of use. He swept the surface clean in long strokes, listening to the sound: a soft hiss, like static, like radio snow.

He liked that part most.

It reminded him of old mornings with his grandfather. Of spit-shined Sundays and unspoken lessons. Of what it meant to look put together even when your life wasn't.

He rolled the polish tin open with the edge of his thumb, the black wax glinting like oil under the warm bulb of the bedside lamp. A small square of T-shirt, ripped from something old and too tight, sat folded beside him, its edges dark with prior use.

He dipped the cloth gently into the tin, not too much, just enough to cover the leather, and began rubbing small, deliberate circles into the toe of the right boot. His wrist moved with unconscious rhythm. Left to right. Shift. Circle again. He didn't rush. There was no need. This wasn't about time.

The act grounded him.

There was a precision to it, the way the polish darkened uneven scuffs, the way the leather took to the pressure, as if it remembered him. The boot's surface, dulled from long hours at the station, slowly began to drink in the light again, like something breathing after a long sleep.

He paused, turned the boot in his hands, examined it under the lamp's glow. Not perfect, but better. Alive again.

As he polished, Flex thought about Beth.

About her eyes, guarded but deep.

About the way she said "thank you" like it cost her something.

And about Jupiter, who smiled at him like he was invincible.

Flex set the boot down and started on the other.

Same rhythm.

Same care.

A quiet war with scuffs and grit.

Because sometimes, the everyday routines mean more than words.

Sometimes, all you could do was polish your boots

until they shone, and hope that when the world looked at you, it saw a man worth keeping clean.

Fire Safety continued and he was soon to be in her class again, tomorrow in fact. Another round of bright eyes and wide grins and tiny hands asking if he'd ever flown a helicopter.

Flex had done half a dozen of them over the years, most were fun and harmless. Some flirtatious teacher would joke about climbing a ladder, he let a few of them try over the years, not the ladder on the truck of course, that would not be safe. The ladder up his abs was the true place these ladies wanted to experience.

Early on, that was exciting, the attention made him feel alive. Flex was a "healthy" boy as his mother described. He came into his own during his first year of college, the attention that he craved from the girls as a child was foreign to him as a young adult. It was a drug and the changes to his body made it easy to turn ladies' eyes, hell there were a few guys whose stares made him feel like a rib roast ready to be bought.

The nights with these ladies were empty, the attention was great but lacked the substance that his soul truly craved. As the years passed by, he slowly started dating less as he came to grips with only being wanted for his physical being. He accepted the comments from ladies around town and in the school office, but he no longer acted upon the opportunities.

But this career day had the potential to be different?

This one had Beth, and it made him uneasy. She just felt different. Yes, he did catch her looking at his chest and he recognized the hungry look that showed in her eyes, but it still felt different from the other ladies' attention.

He stood up and stretched, boots gleaming like they meant something.

Across the room, the closet door hung slightly open. Inside hung his fireproof station jacket, two spare uniforms, and an old black duffel bag shoved into the back corner.

He hadn't opened it in years.

Didn't need to. Everything in it lived in muscle memory.

He stepped closer anyway.

Knelt.

Unzipped the top slowly.

The plain canvas bag held a folded silk vest, a crumpled pair of worn dress pants, knee pads because the stage had been cement, and a tangle of gold cord once tied to a fake fireman's axe.

His stomach turned.

Flex pulled the zipper closed again.

It wasn't that he was ashamed. He knew why he did it. Knew what the money had paid for; books, tuition, rent, protein powder when he could barely afford tuna.

But still, there was a difference between surviving something and being strong enough to tell the people you love about it.

Especially someone like Beth. She seemed so conservative and put together, what would she think of his past?

He stood and placed the duffel back into the corner.

Then he pulled on his boots and grabbed the helmet off the hook by the door.

If he was going to walk into her classroom again tomorrow, he'd better look every bit like the man she thinks he is.

Because God help him, he wanted to be that man. He was not sure why, it was a just a look, but deep down he knew that her conservatism was less about being proper and more about survival. This drove a desire to be a better man.

At least for her.

Career Day was chaos, the sweet, buzzing kind filled with cupcakes, paper badges, and the screech of folding chairs dragging across the multipurpose room floor.

Beth stood near the back with her clipboard, watching the first-grade cluster file in, herding their favorite stuffed animals and questions like a parade of tiny executives.

Flex was already there, leaning against a table near the red plastic cones that marked off his "demo zone." His station helmet sat on a folding chair behind him. He wore the dark navy uniform today, crisp and clean, and the kids swarmed him like he came with a siren.

"Do you really drive the truck?"

"How hot is fire?"

"Have you ever rescued a puppy *and* a grandma at the same time?"

Flex knelt beside a boy in a dinosaur hoodie. "Buddy, that's exactly how I start every Thursday."

The room erupted in laughter.

Even the teachers chuckled.

Beth didn't.

She just watched, arms crossed, clipboard held a little too tightly, like she was guarding herself from her own reaction.

Flex spotted her near the back and gave a small nod with pursed lips, not flashy, not cocky. Just... acknowledgment.

Beth nodded back.

But her pulse betrayed her, her heart beat a little too fast. "Stop it," she told herself. This did not stop the reaction, the warming of the side of her neck and the flush on her cheeks. It absolutely did nothing to the tingle below. It had been a long time since a man had given her that tingle.

It was not just his looks, well maybe a little, that drove this reaction. He was good with the kids, with the other parents and most importantly, with Jupiter, who stood near the front, glowing.

When it was time for Flex's segment, he pulled out a cartoon poster titled "The Flame Game." It featured three scenarios: one safe, one risky, one just plain wrong.

He held up flashcards.

"Okay, team. You tell me, is it a flame, a shame, or a safe game?"

The kids howled in response, pointing at a picture of a toddler playing with matches.

"SHAME GAME!"

Flex winced. "Yeah, that's a no from Sparky."

Beth bit the inside of her cheek. She hated how good he was at this. How *effortless* he made it look.

It made her suspicious, people that good usually came with a price. She remembered Denny in his charismatic youth. The Denny that she beamed over as a young lady whenever he entered a room.

Then she looked at Jupiter, raising his hand, eager, smiling so hard his cheeks pushed his eyes half closed, and that made her chest ache.

She thought biting the inside of her right cheek, "Oh this man is going to make us hurt."

After the assembly, the kids crowded the hallway to line up for dismissal. Beth lingered by the door as Flex packed up his props into a gym bag.

He looked up as she approached.

"Hey," he said, careful.

"Hey."

She didn't say thank you, didn't compliment him, but she did pause.

"You were... good," she said at last.

He tilted his head with a look of fake awe on his face. "That sounded almost like praise."

"Don't get used to it." She scowled back at him before relaxing her face into a smile. Not a public, I am smiling because social convention demands that I do, but a real and genuine I am actually happy smile!

"Noted."

They stood in silence for a beat.

Then Beth surprised herself and blurted out words that were just a little too quick and she cringed inside, "You made Jupiter feel seen today."

Flex's smile softened. "He makes it easy."

Another pause.

She glanced toward the hallway, where the kids were beginning to shuffle toward the buses.

Beth opened her mouth to say thank you again, something safe and routine. Instead, her voice caught in her throat.

She hesitated.

What the hell was she doing? Asking a man like him to coffee? What does that even mean anymore? Was it a date? Was she ready for that? She barely trusted herself to pick out shoes that didn't leave her limping.

Then, she thought of Jupiter, of how the boy's face lit up when Flex walked in the room. Of how she felt when he smiled at her like she wasn't broken, like she was still something worth discovering.

Her fingers curled slightly around the clipboard by her side... screw it.

"I, uh, listen, would you maybe want to buy me a cup of coffee sometime?" She again cringed as she felt like an adolescent girl trying to get the attention of a boy she was crushing on. She thought to herself, maybe I should punch his shoulder and tell him boys are gross like I did when I was 10, with this kind of smoothness, she might as well give it a try.

"Yeah," he said standing, "that would be great." His face was warm, and she knew that he was truly interested, but for just a moment, could he be just a little shorter, she was eye to nipple with his chest, and it was making her hungry.

"I mean just as friends."

He cocked his head to the right and slightly dropped his eyebrow, "Ok, sure."

"I mean I want to get to know you, but I am still in a weird place. Recently divorced, you know kind of a train wreck."

He smiled, "Well, if that is a train wreck it doesn't look like there were many injuries."

Her smile faded a little with that comment, "Just coffee, just friends. I am still trying to figure out what the lines are in my life. I just want to be honest with you."

Flex reached out and patted her on the right shoulder, "Got it, I understand. Friends."

"I mean I have a child, well you know, you have met him... I just have to be careful on who I let close, he, we have been through a lot."

"I get it."

"Do you?"

He didn't answer.

He just nodded, slinging the gym bag over his shoulder.

"I'll see you around," he said gently.

"Yeah."

Then as he started walking away, he looked over his shoulder, those broad shoulders, and smiled, "Just coffee with my friend Beth."

Without looking back, he said aloud, "By the way

friend Beth, I wrote my number on your desk calendar. Let me know when you want that coffee."

She watched him walk away, watched the rise of his pants as his hamstrings and glutes moved in perfect rhythm, up and down, extend and retract. That feeling, that electric tickle, the warmth. She shook her head and turned back to the classroom and the chair from his station.

Beth stood there a long time after he had gone, staring at the folding chair where his helmet had been.

There was a part of her who wanted to run after him. To run to him and feel his arms around her and feel his warmth, to smell his scent.

Then, part of her wanted to run *from* the part of herself that wanted that. She could hear her mother's voice, the chiding sound of derision in her voice.

In the end, she didn't do either, but that night, back in her safe space, in the well-used and loved home she had adopted, she left the porchlight on again.

She told herself the lie that she told Flex, that it was for Jupiter, but deep down she knew better. The porchlight was for a vacancy and need that she held in secret. The porchlight was left on for him.

4

FAMILY SMOKE

The front porch creaked as she walked, paced was the better description. She held her cell phone in her hand, the screen cracked from a very bad night, a night that she tried not to remember. She paced back and forth past the shiny red front door, the wrought iron porch light, and dragging her finger tips on the cracked porch rails.

She stopped, took a deep breath and moved to sit on a new addition to the porch, a gift from her father. She sat on the gift, a cedar swing that almost glowed in red intensity with its newly varnished finish. He had driven to Tennessee a few days earlier to visit the Amish and told her that when he saw it, he knew that she needed it.

She tucked her right leg under her left that was lowered, toes touching the floor. Her bare foot allowing her big toe to gently push her back and forth. The night before she had painted her toe nails, a vibrant pink that accentuated her tanned skin. In the past she would have sat in a massaging chair every other week relaxing and getting pedicures every other week, but money was tight, so a trip to the Dollar store and an evening brushing while Jupiter sat on the floor fixed the problem.

She was typing a text to a number that was scrawled in immaculate handwriting on her calendar. This text had been typed, deleted, and retyped a dozen times with the ultimate and final version being a simple 'How are you?' With a sigh she pressed send and shook her head.

She stared at the screen and stared as the text changed to 'Delivered' and then waited for it to change from 'Delivered' to 'Read', or to see those three little dots appear.

She waited for five minutes and then laid the phone down.

"Breath woman, take a breath and stop this nonsense."

She stared out into the yard over the old porch rails and was studying the red blooms on the old crape myrtle planted just at the corner of the house. This massive specimen was not pruned in the proper cropped manner. It was tall and wild, unlike the neighbors that was cut at head height with all of the lower branches removed. The neighbors tree reminded her of a chicken leg while hers danced wildly with each passing breeze.

Her phone screen lit up and starting vibrating, she looked and saw four letters on the screen. Four letters that she had input in her contact list. Flex.

She tapped the screen to answer and a half a second later said "Hello."

"Hey Beth, this a bad time?" The sound crisp and clear through the white bud tucked neatly in her ear.

"Hey, no, I, people normally don't call."

"Sorry, I have a habit to not text whenever possible. I like to talk."

"I think you might be the only man on earth that would call instead of text."

"Sounds like I am special then." He laughed, she smiled.

"Maybe not, but let's keep the cockiness down."

"Yes ma'am, duly noted and all cockiness will be stored for a later date."

Beth ran her teeth over her bottom lip. She would realize later that was a silly thing to do after putting on fresh lipstick.

"So, I texted."

"I am aware, that is why I called."

She rolled her eyes. "I wanted to see about that coffee."

"Oh yes, the coffee that you invited me to buy you."

Mocking offense, "I never asked you to buy me coffee, just to have coffee with me." It felt good to be a little silly after being wound up tight for so long.

"I know, just easing the tension a little, it would seem that I am a little nervous right now."

She again bit her lower lip, why was he nervous, she had seen the attention heaped upon him be every woman that looked his way.

"Nervous, you? No."

"Yes ma'am, to be honest I feel a little shy right now."

"Well, how about it? Are you going to buy me coffee or not?"

"So, I am buying, would that be a date then?

"I already told you, just friends getting coffee." She flushed at this little lie.

"I see, well then I think that we should probably meet up soon and have this friendly coffee."

She paused, this was really happening, "How about Sunday afternoon?"

"Works for me, what time and where?"

Tapping her freshly painted pink toe on the porch she replied, "I have lunch with my family Sunday, how about we meet up around 5:00pm at Wester's Coffee Bean?"

"Is that the place on 3rd?"

"That is the place, my friend owns the place, her coffee is always perfect."

"Roger, Sunday. 5:00pm. The Bean. I will be the guy in the gray t-shirt. See you there... friend."

Eyes rolling, "Good, and... ok."

"Talk to ya."

"Bye now."

She ended the call and stared at her phone for a few moments and then leaned back in the swing and pumped her legs back and forth arms swinging. When she stopped, she heard a noise behind her. Turning she saw the top of a little head that was hanging out next to the porch. She wondered how long he had been there, and how much he was able to understand from the one-sided conversation he could hear.

It was the kind of Alabama Sunday that felt more like

July than mid-September, thick air, and ice sweating straight through every glass on the table.

Beth sat across from her father at the small oak table in her parents' kitchen, Jupiter between them swinging his legs under his booster cushion. The ceiling fan in the living room ticked like a clock with one tooth missing, just off rhythm.

Her mother had outdone herself, as usual, roast chicken, mashed potatoes, gravy, collard greens, cornbread, deviled eggs, and the real star of the show, a banana pudding still chilling in the fridge.

The food didn't help Beth's appetite, not today.

The conversation on this trip was pleasant, but she could feel it coming, the pause. The moment her mother would reach for a refill, take too long, and drop the first little barb in her usual calm, sugared voice.

She had casually mentioned that Maddie would be watching Jupiter after dinner so she could meet a friend for coffee. She knew it would come eventually.

And there it was.

"I ran into Tessa Glenn at the bank on Friday," her mother said, pouring sweet tea into her husband's glass. "Said the fireman from Career Day was very... *charismatic.* Rumor is that you have been seen paying quite a bit of attention to him"

Beth didn't respond.

"She said the teachers were passing around photos of him on Facebook."

Beth looked down at her plate.

"She said they're old photos," her mother added gently. "From his... younger days."

Maddie coughed into her napkin.

Jupiter didn't notice. He was too busy sculpting mashed potatoes into a mountain with a gravy moat.

Beth's voice was low. "I don't care what they're passing around."

Her mother tilted her head, slicing her cornbread in half. "It's not about caring, sweetheart. It's about being aware. A man with that kind of past attracts a certain attention."

"He teaches kids how not to burn themselves alive. I think we can manage a little attention, and I have a past too, mama. Everyone single my age does."

Her father cleared his throat. "All I'm saying is, it doesn't look great. You've worked hard to move on. People remember what happened with Denny."

Beth froze.

There it was. His name. Spoken out loud at the dinner table like it hadn't been blacklisted for two years.

"I *have* moved on," she said slowly. "And what Flex does in his personal life, or did in the past, has nothing to do with me. We are just friends."

"Pfft, Let's put the cards on the table." her mother said sternly. "I mean... why are you willing to risk a future with Denny over a firefighter? That man can barely afford to live in an apartment. You know Denny will be out soon, and like I already told you, Pastor said he has made great progress. Why don't you let the past be the past and move forward with a man that can take care of you and Jupiter?"

Beth stood, collecting her plate and Jupiter's. Her hands moved with clipped efficiency.

"Momma, I love you, but if you think that I will ever be back with that man you have lost your ever-loving mind!"

Jupiter stared up at her, his eyes wide with little tears building up around the corners.

"No one is telling you that you gotta get back with Denny," her father added. "But he took good care of you, Beth..."

"I don't believe what I am hearing," she snapped. "Do you know that every night before I go to sleep, I turn the T.V. on? I look in the closet. I look under my bed and check every door and window in the house to make sure they are locked!"

She stomped to the sink and laid the plates down a little too harshly. The clunk making everyone at the table jump a little.

"I lay in bed every night and dream of being hurt, of seeing my head bounce off the wall, and I wake up, sometimes screaming. And you, you think that there is some kind of magic button that will erase the past, that I am going to walk back into that house and pretend that the fresh paint on the wall is not from my blood staining it."

The room quieted.

Jupiter looked up at Beth, brows drawn. "Are we leaving?"

Beth forced a smile. "Not yet, baby."

She walked around and patted him on the shoulder, "Why don't you run outside for a few minutes and see if you can catch that squirrel."

He turned to look at her and slowly stood up and moved out, tears just starting to roll down his cheeks.

When he was out and in the yard, Evelyn spoke, "Beth..."

"Mama, daddy, I am only going to say this one time. If you want me and Jupiter to ever walk through your door again. If you ever want to see us again, don't you ever bring up his name. I will not hear it, and the next time you are with pastor tell him I said he can kiss my ass."

She looked at Maddie, "You still good?"

Wiping a look of shock off of her face Maddie nodded. "I am going to run Jupiter to the Dairy Barn for a shake and then over to the park. We will be back at my place when you are ready."

"There is banana..."

Beth held up her hand, "Enough." She turned and stopped by the table by the front door, picking up her purse, she dug inside and pulled out a beaded bracelet that held her keys. "Good night." She walked out the door not looking back and started to slam the door but paused when she saw Jupiter looking up at her.

"Hey baby."

"Hey momma." His lower lip trembled as he spoke, eyes still welling up with tears.

"Aunt Maddie is going to take you for a shake and to play while I run over to see a friend."

"Flex."

Pausing before she spoke, "Yes baby, I am going to see our friend Flex."

"Can I come?"

"Not tonight baby, you play with Aunt Maddie, you will have fun."

"Momma..."

Leaning down, she wiped a tear away with her thumb. "Yes baby."

"Daddy was bad wasn't he."

Her breath caught, she was not expecting this, "Your daddy...he has problems." She could not get anything else out, she wanted to scream why does anyone had to ask that question. The only thing that stopped her was the innocent gaze of a loving little boy, a little boy who was not physically hurt by his father, but was wearing scars, nonetheless.

She leaned in and hugged him, "I love you baby, you go with Aunt Maddie, y'all have fun, and don't worry about that big people stuff. Can you do that? Can you have fun and send mommy some pictures?"

He buried his face in her chest and sucked air in through his nose, "uh-huh."

"Be good baby, I will see you in a bit."

Flex stood in front of his small mirror, running a hand through his thick hair and studying the fit of his gray T-shirt. It hugged just enough to show the work he put in but wasn't tight enough to look like he was trying, faded jeans, clean boots, and a leather cuff he'd worn since college.

He picked up a cologne bottle.

Held it.

Set it down.

Picked it up again.

"Come on," he muttered to himself, giving the glass bottle a gentle clink on the edge of the sink. "It's just coffee."

He spritzed once into the air and walked through it. Not too much. Just enough to whisper, *I tried.*

Grabbing his keys, he headed down the stairs and out the back of the old feed store that housed his apartment. The sun was starting to dip behind the awning of the storefronts on Main Street, casting a warm gold over Tanner's narrow sidewalks. He checked his watch twice before even starting the engine.

He arrived at *Wester's Coffee Bean* ten minutes early.

Inside, the place was small but charming with worn wood floors, bookshelves filled with old paperbacks and plants, handwritten chalkboard menus hung behind the counter. The scent of cinnamon and roasted beans hung thick in the air. There were a few couples inside, some waiting for their orders, others sitting at café tables sipping coffee and ignoring each other as they stared into their phones.

Flex ordered a black coffee and found a corner seat near the window. Not dead center not tucked away. Just enough distance to watch the door without seeming like he was waiting.

From his back pocket, he pulled out a dog-eared paperback: *A Canticle for Leibowitz.*

The spine was cracked, and the pages yellowed.

He lost himself in it just enough that he didn't notice

the time passed, until the door jingled and Beth stepped in. The late afternoon sun glowed in her hair, and he swore he saw a halo around her head. Her red floral sundress flowed gently off her shoulders, revealing just enough of her breasts to catch a man looking, but covering enough for modesty. The fall of the dress off of her hips stopped halfway up her thighs, she was toned but not built like an athlete. She was beautiful and Flex had to force himself to pick up his jaw, smile, and not stare.

She spotted him instantly and warmed at the sight of his eyes, the stress and trauma of the afternoon at her parents temporarily forgotten.

She approached slowly. Her hair was half-up, loose around the edges like she hadn't tried too hard. That somehow made her even more stunning.

"Hey," she said.

"Hey," he replied, setting the book down.

She looked at it, tilting her head. "You're reading?"

He smiled. "You sound shocked."

"I just... most people scroll their phones while they wait."

"I like pages. Smell of old paper. Besides, phones don't have dog-ears."

She laughed softly, then caught herself and cleared her throat. "I didn't expect that."

He took a sip of his coffee. "I get that a lot."

Beth ordered a vanilla latte and returned to sit across from him. For a moment, they didn't speak. The quiet was filled with clinking spoons, grinding beans, and acoustic guitar through the ceiling speakers.

"You read a lot?" she asked, curling her hands around the warm ceramic mug.

"When I can," he said. "Keeps me out of trouble."

She smirked. "Is that hard for you?"

Flex chuckled. "Used to be. I was a bit of a wreck in my twenties."

"Let me guess," she said, raising a brow. "You were the bad boy with the heart of gold."

"More like the broke guy with too much muscle and no backup plan."

Beth stirred her latte, trying not to smile too wide. "Well, you turned out alright. Fireman. Role model. Reading sci-fi in a coffee shop. That's some serious reform."

Flex shrugged. "It's a work in progress."

She nodded, looking down into her drink. "Aren't we all?"

That silenced them again. Not out of awkwardness, but because there was weight in that truth.

Their pasts didn't sit at the table with them, but they hovered just over each shoulder.

Beth picked at the corner of her napkin. "I haven't done this in a long time."

"I'm guessing you don't mean coffee."

She shook her head. "I mean... sitting across from a man who doesn't want anything from me."

Flex leaned back a bit, watching her. "What makes you think I don't?"

Beth met his gaze. Her eyes were glassy, but strong. "I'm trying not to think."

Another silence, but this one had warmth. Like both

were quietly thankful the other was there but didn't know what to do about it. The evening passed in talk, not small talk, but with the comforting speech of two people genuinely interested in each other. She would talk about teaching, he, surprisingly, about things that most men would avoid. He spoke of his love of science fiction, the smell of hardware store, and his dreams of one day owning a business of his own.

One crucial thing was missing from his part of the conversation, one thing that truly intrigued Beth. He did not coo and awe over how beautiful she was, he just spoke to her. That is all, spoke, looked her in the eyes, and smiled. He exuded warmth and comfort. Everything in her heart told her that this was a dangerous man. This was a man that could hurt her without laying a hand on her.

Eventually, the sun dipped further and painted long shadows through the windows.

Beth stood first. "I should go."

Flex stood too, and as they reached the door, their arms brushed. Just the barest graze of skin, wrist to wrist.

Both felt it.

The silence that followed wasn't awkward but charged.

Beth turned to him. Her lips parted, her eyes softening.

Then she leaned in, instinctively, for a hug.

Her arms lifted, but stopped halfway.

"No," she said suddenly, stepping back. "I can't."

"Beth," he said, quietly.

"I'm sorry," she whispered. "I... I just need to go."

And like that, she turned and stepped out into the evening.

Flex stayed behind, one hand on the doorframe, watching the curve of her back as she disappeared into the parking lot.

He didn't follow.

He just stood there, breathing in the space where she'd been.

And behind him, the forgotten paperback sat open on the table, a single dog-eared page waiting for someone to return.

Later, on the drive back home, Jupiter dozed in the back seat with his head against the window, and Beth gripped the steering wheel like it might bolt from her hands.

Where there's smoke.

She hated that line.

Because part of her believed it, too.

The simple night of conversation erased the prior fears from earlier, the pain inflicted by her parents. How was that possible, she walked into that coffee shop fighting to hold herself together, but his smile... it just made that go away.

And that touch, oh my god that spark. The hair on her arm stood up as she thought about it, even now. It sent a tingle down her spine that ended in a place of warmth and in a way that made her thighs squeeze together. That man, that good looking man, that interesting man who spoke to her like a human but set her on fire at the same time.

He was trouble, maybe not in a get arrested sort of way, but trouble in the heart. She did not feel ready for this. She was afraid, but that tingle, oh god she was hungry.

She pulled up in her driveway and carried her sleeping little man inside and to bed, she left him in his clothes and covered him up. Walking through her house she listened to the creak of wood until she reached the front door. She turned all of the lights off and started to her room, paused, went back and turned the porch light back on.

Inside, she felt silly, but that little light made all the difference right now. She turned and went to bed, thankful to be away from a monster, to have her baby safe at home, that she was brave enough to try and evening out, and most of all that she had bought those batteries. She was very hungry after all.

5

SILT AND SUGAR

B eth stared at the watermarks on her classroom ceiling like they held secret meanings, shapes that twisted themselves into clouds and ghosts. The hum of the air conditioner clicked off mid-cycle and left her alone with the sound of dry markers in a cup on her desk shifting against each other, a hollow reminder that school was out for the weekend and she had no more excuses to linger.

It had been five days since the coffee.

Five days of catching herself smiling at random times. Five days of second-guessing every glance, every laugh, every near hug that had fizzled into awkward air. Five days of kicking herself for leaving without saying anything more than "I have to go."

And now it was Friday.

She looked at the desktop calendar lying in repose. It was well used with several stained rings from coffee pours that just missed the target and scribbles of ideas for classroom activities. There, scribbled in pristine, confident handwriting, was his number, in her mind the number. She was tempted to scratch through the number, better to walk away now than get her heart broken, she rationalized.

It had been five days and neither of them had broken the silence, no text messages, no calls, nothing to show that he, nor she, got anything more out of the night at the coffee shop. Probably just playing it cool, being a player, and earning that nickname "Flex".

Beth pulled her light denim jacket from the back of her chair and stepped into it, brushing chalk dust from her sleeves with a flick that carried more nerves than grace. Outside, the sun was still baking hot, and the cicadas were already tuning up their evening symphony. She really liked how she looked in the denim jacket, but just as she opened the door of the school, she was assaulted by the bane of Alabama living, humidity.

Just as she reached the front steps of the school, a deep voice called her name.

"Beth."

She turned, and there he was, Flex, standing with one hand tucked in his jeans pocket and the other holding a brown paper bag that smelled faintly of cinnamon and warmth.

He didn't wear his uniform today.

Just that same gray T-shirt and faded jeans. And still, with the fall of the t-shirt over his chest and the strong, sturdy thighs pressing the jeans out in just the right areas, well, he looked like he belonged on the cover of something. Beth caught her breath and a primal part of her wanted to tackle this man.

"I, uh... I didn't want to text," he said. "Again. Thought maybe I'd just show up with a little snack, I hear that ladies like to be fed."

He held out the bag, tentative but smiling.

"What is it?" she asked, not reaching.

"Apple fritters. From Ella Mae's. Still warm."

Beth blinked. "You bribing me with sugar?"

"I'm bribing you with nostalgia," he said. "And carbs."

She took the bag finally, letting her fingers brush his. "Tanner boys don't play fair, do they?"

"I'm not from Tanner originally," he said. "Moved here after I got hired full-time at the station."

"Hmm," she hummed, peeking into the bag. "Still smells like a small-town boy move to me."

They both chuckled.

He leaned against the stair railing, not too close, giving her space. "I wasn't sure I'd see you again."

"I wasn't sure either," she replied. "The other night... I got scared."

Flex nodded slowly. "That was a real moment. And you walked away. I respected that."

Beth looked down. "You didn't follow me."

"I wanted to. God, I wanted to. But I knew you needed space more than you needed me running after you."

She nodded, appreciating that.

"You want to walk?" he asked suddenly.

"Now?"

"There's still sunlight."

Beth hesitated, then tucked the bag under her arm. "Alright."

They walked down the gravel trail behind the school that led toward Mill Creek. It wasn't fancy, just packed earth and stretches of stubborn grass, but the water moved slowly and clear alongside them, and that helped settle something in her chest.

Flex reached down and picked up a pebble, tossing it into the stream. It skipped across and landed in the grass nearby sending a small group of grasshoppers out from their hiding spaces.

One of the grasshoppers flopped into the creek and started thrashing around.

"Poor thing.", Beth cried.

She moved over to the edge and leaned over to rescue it. She overextended on her lean and fell forwards to the water. Flex, on point caught her by the waist, but not before she splashed both arms into the water.

With a pull he got her back on her feet, "That must have been one heck of a grasshopper!" He laughed and she grimaced as she realized that as she fell, so did the apple fritters, now there was a drowning grasshopper as well as a sweet treat in the water.

"Well shit!"

Flex laughed, "Now, now, language Ms. Teacher lady."

This snapped Beth back to normal behavior and she said blushing, "Sorry, I just..."

"All good, you want to get that jacket off?"

Flex held his arms out and offered assistance, and she stuck her left arm out. Sliding the cuff back and forth until the sleeve gave way. He then repeated on the right arm leaving her in a satin tank top and jeans.

As she turned around to retrieve her jacket, she caught Flex wide eyed looking directly at her chest. She understood the reason why, she only wore the damned jacket because she picked a satin top and could not be bothered with a bra today. Either the cold water, or the hands of the man helping her, had caused her nipples to become fully erect and they were poking out for all the world to see.

She quickly crossed her arms and cupped her breasts. To his credit, and her surprise, Flex looked down modestly. He turned beside her and looked ahead. She did not know whether she should be embarrassed, aroused, or amused by this little turn of events. Based on the flushed cheeks Flex was sporting, she decided to go with amused and have a little fun.

Beth glanced sideways. "So, that was embarrassing, so how about you tell me something embarrassing."

"Embarrassing?"

"Yeah. I don't know... level the playing field."

He thought for a moment, then grinned.

"In college," he said, "I once stripped at a bachelorette party thinking it was a paying gig. Turns out it was a prank. I danced for the bride's 92-year-old grandma."

Beth burst into laughter, loud and sudden. "Oh my God!"

"She gave me a ten," he said solemnly.

That made her laugh even harder. She nearly tripped on a tree root.

"You're terrible," she gasped.

"Hey," he said, holding up his hands. "You asked."

The laughter rolled between them until it settled into a quiet warmth.

"So, the rumors are true, you really were a stripper?"

"...yes. I had to pay the bills, and, at the time, the attention felt good."

"At the time?" Beth asked, biting the inside of her lip thinking, oh God don't go too far man, please tell me that you out of that life.

"Yeah, I was a big boy growing up, I didn't have my first girlfriend until my sophomore year of college. That was the year I discovered the gym, and how to control my eating."

"And."

"You are an attractive lady, and I am willing to bet that you were always getting attention, and you know, that probably helped you deal with lots of problems, you know, knowing that not all attention was good."

"OK, I get it."

"See, I didn't have that, so when I, and I don't mean to sound cocky, but when I got a six pack, pecks, and delts I found myself getting attention from a lot of ladies. And look, men can be animals, but I have met some ladies that could give the man with the least class in the world a run for their money."

Laughing, "Yeah ladies can be rough sometimes."

"I needed money, I had the ability to get attention,

and I used that to get by. I actually made more dancing that I do now as a fireman."

"So... how far did your dancing go."

His face hardened a little as he spoke, "You mean how much of my clothes came off?"

"Yes." Her reply was swift and gave no doubt that she wanted a direct answer.

"Never fully nude, just to my dancing outfit."

She felt a little sick from hearing him speak but wanted to move on and she decided that a little humor would help.

"By dancing outfit, I assume you mean banana hammock?" This was delivered dryly but she followed with a small sly smile.

Laughing, "Yes, that is one way to describe it. Yes, I danced in my purple banana hammock."

"Oh lord, purple, I have the full mental image now!", she laughed and placed her hands over her eyes in mock surprise and shame.

"Careful with that mental image, remember I used to get paid for that."

They stared at each other for a moment and then in unspoken unison turned to continue their hot and humid stroll around trail.

They stopped at a wooden bridge that crossed the shallowest part of the creek. It was the kind of place kids might have dropped sticks off of, playing races against the current.

Flex leaned on the railing. "Can I ask you something?"

Beth leaned beside him. "Depends."

"Why did you really ask me to coffee?"

Beth stared at the water. "Because you were kind. Because Jupiter adores you. Because for the first time in a long time, I saw someone who wasn't trying to control me."

"That's a good reason," he said.

She turned to him. "Why'd you say yes?"

"Because you looked at me like I was a person, not a fantasy."

That made her pause. Then she softened. "You ever going to tell me about the photos?"

He didn't flinch. "Probably not tonight."

She nodded. "Okay."

A pause.

"But I'll tell you this," he added. "That part of my life, it helped me survive. But I'm not that guy anymore."

"I don't think you are either."

They walked back in silence, Beth brushing her hand lightly against damp denim jacket laying over her left arm, she was still walking arms crossed. On a normal day, in this heat, her areolas would have been as flat as pancakes, but today they were still fully erect and reminded her that even if she had been able to eat the fritter, she would have still been hungry.

The trail ran its course and came back out at the parking lot. He walked her to her car, and they lingered.

Flex looked at her, his eyes tracing the worry lines in her brow. "I know that you have heard rumors about me, but... there are rumors about you as well."

The smile left her face along with the color, "Oh yeah, people talk."

"That they do. Listen, if what I heard is true, if it is..."

She reached out and placed her hand on his arm, "I think we have reached my comfort level for the day." Her face portrayed no emotion, not a hint of anger, acceptance, just a wall of no emotion. It was a mask, a mask that kept everyone at bay and allowed no one to see her truly felt.

"Ok, just, let me say this. You're safe now, you know that, right?"

"I'm getting there," she said.

And then, without thinking, she stepped into him, not a hug, not quite, but just enough to let their shoulders touch, her head near his chest.

He didn't move.

Didn't push.

Just stood steady.

The warmth of his body next to hers was not fire, but it was heat, and it reminded her that she still wanted, still needed, still could *be* wanted without fear.

"I'll call you," she whispered.

"I'll answer."

She pulled back, gave him a brief smile, then turned to her car.

He watched her go until her taillights disappeared around the corner.

Back home, Beth sat on the swing again, this time with a fritter on a plate beside her and Jupiter asleep in his room. She nibbled at the edge of the pastry and tasted brown sugar, cinnamon, and something like comfort. She had to make a little stop on her way home, her little treat was sitting on the bottom of Mill Creek, and she could not get the thought of it out of her head.

The porchlight glowed gently, flickering, overhead.

She leaned back, tucked her feet under her, and stared into the quiet street. She thought about the day, about her unexpected little walk and the honesty that they shared. She liked him, god help her, she liked this man.

She also thought about a question, and answer, that she had put off. Would she allow Flex to come to Jupiter's birthday party? She wasn't sure.

After a long relaxing spell of crickets battling out the war for sound supremacy with the cicadas and the relaxing creek of the porch swing chain she called it a night. She went to bed with high hopes of sweet dreams, dreams filled with apple fritters and the eyes of a man that looked at her with compassion, not lust.

She was denied those dreams. That night her mind regressed, it went back to those long nights of sleep deprived by a drunk man, a man who was supposed to be her partner. A man who swore to love and protect her. A man who ultimately injured her body and soul.

If life was fair these terrible remembrances would be locked in the past, never to be opened or revisited. Life, however, is not fair and tonight she was lost in her own hell.

She awoke screaming, her bedding twisted, and her body covered in sweat. Next to the bed stood a little man, her little man who stood there with a look of deep concern.

"You ok momma?"

She sat wiping the damp from her face, "Momma is ok baby, just a dream."

"You said daddies name."

"Did I? I am sorry baby."

"He won't hurt you momma, I want let him."

"Baby, that is... I am ok, here, climb up and let's get you back to sleep."

He climbed up on the bed next to her and snuggled in quickly falling into a deep sleep. She held him and stared at the ceiling with silent, hot tears rolling down her face. No more noise escaped her lips, and sleep did not return for her. She just lay there, trapped in her mind, and reliving those terrible nights.

Maddie lay on her couch in a pair of satin pajamas, the T.V. was on with a show that she was not interested in. She was scrolling through social media on her phone, watching one silly video after the next.

A notification popped up. She received a new message on SNAP. She thumbed over to it and read the simple message, 'Hey girl, what's up?' that overlaid a selfie of a man with dirty blond hair and stark blue eyes and wearing an orange jumpsuit with a white t-shirt showing through.

The message was from "Big D".

She looked up and at the T.V. still not focused on the show. She stared at the screen for a minute before she sat up, fluffed her hair, unbuttoned the top button of her pajamas, and pushed her breast up showing a hint of cleavage. She held her phone out, up and high, and took a selfie of her own.

She smiled while she typed a message over the picture in the app, 'Hey baby, missing you.'

6

ASHES OF FORMER THINGS

The porch swing creaked rhythmically beneath Beth as she nursed her second cup of coffee, elbows resting on her knees. The morning light filtered through the trees in dappled patches, turning her chipped nail polish into flecks of rose gold. The screen door behind her squeaked once and slammed lightly, followed by the pitter-patter of small feet.

Jupiter stood at the edge of the porch in a T-shirt two sizes too big and dinosaur pajama pants. His hair stuck out in every direction. A juice box sloshed in his hand and the crumbs of his cherry Pop Tart were clinging to the corners of his mouth.

"Mama," he said, squinting. "Can Flex come to my birthday party?"

Beth looked over her shoulder and blinked. "That's not how people usually say good morning."

He shrugged. "I dreamed about the fire truck again. He let me sit in the seat and I pushed the buttons."

She gave a tired smile. "It wasn't a dream, baby. That really happened at school."

"I know," he said, flopping beside her on the swing. "But in my dream, he had a robot dog."

"Well, maybe he'll bring one next time," she teased. "But listen... I was thinking. If you want, we can invite Flex to your party."

Jupiter's whole face lit up, juice forgotten.

"Really?" he asked. "Like for real, for real?"

Beth nodded, rubbing her thumb over the rim of her mug. "For real, for real, but only if he says yes."

Jupiter launched up and ran inside, shouting, "HE'S COMING TO MY PARTY! I GOTTA TELL SPIKE!"

Beth chuckled and leaned her head back against the porch post, letting the early sun warm her eyelids. She hadn't even told Flex yet, but the excitement in Jupiter's voice made it worth the internal panic bubbling in her stomach.

She picked up her phone, opened her messages, and typed:

Hey, want to come shopping with me later? Party prep. Could use some strong arms and good taste in frosting colors. 😊

She stared at it for a second, then hit send before she could think twice.

The dots showed up right away.

Strong arms, check. Frosting expertise... debatable. What time?

She smiled.

Thought you didn't text? Noon? I'll pick you up.

A few moments passed and she almost put down her phone.

Looks like I have man an exception. I'll wear my best aisle-walking boots.

The organ groaned to life like a tired old mare as the congregation stood for the third verse of *Just as I Am*, their voices more dutiful than joyous. Ceiling fans rotated slow as molasses overhead, pushing the warm, perfumed air around. The scent was a blend of Aqua Net, baby powder, and old hymnals that hadn't been opened since the Carter administration.

In the third pew from the front, seated between Evelyn and Maddie with a too-tight collar and a forced smile, sat Denny Latham. His hair was trimmed close, his hands folded like a choirboy's, and his starched shirt clung to the sweat gathering under his arms.

"Good to see you back where you belong," Evelyn whispered, her hand patting his thigh in a way that was both maternal and proprietary.

Denny gave her a closed-mouth smile, just enough to keep up the illusion. Maddie, seated on his other side, leaned in a little closer, the edge of her thigh brushing his. Her sundress was modest, but her perfume wasn't.

"You clean up really good, Big D," she murmured behind her church smile.

Denny didn't answer. But his smirk said enough.

From the pulpit, Pastor Carlton Jenkins cleared his

throat with a dramatic pause that echoed like thunder in a room full of farmers and homemakers.

"My brothers and sisters," he began, gripping the edges of the podium like he was trying to hold the weight of sin itself, "we are gathered here today not just to worship, but to witness the miracle of *forgiveness.*"

A few mumbled *amens* rolled from the right side of the room like tired tires over gravel.

Pastor Jenkins continued, "Some among us have walked through fire—literal and spiritual. They have been burned. Broken. But the Lord... the Lord has *brought them back.*"

Heads nodded. Someone shouted, "Preach it, Brother!"

"I'm reminded of Luke fifteen," he went on, already halfway to a sweat, "the story of the Prodigal Son. You all know it well. A man who ran from his father's house, who spent his days in filth and disgrace, but when he returned? His father didn't scorn him. No, he *ran* to him. He *embraced* him."

Evelyn dabbed the corner of her eye with a lavender handkerchief.

Denny swallowed hard. Not from guilt. From the heat. From the performance.

"And today," Pastor Jenkins declared, voice rising like a revival tent, "we welcome back one of our own. Brother Denny Latham."

Gasps fluttered in the sanctuary. A murmur of recognition moved through the pews like a chill breeze, one part curiosity, one part suspicion.

Denny stood slowly, hands trembling only slightly. He gave a short nod to the congregation, humble, grateful, calculated.

Maddie smiled sweetly as Denny rose for the congregation. She'd played the doting sister long enough. When the cards were right, she'd claim the life Beth threw away.

Pastor Jenkins smiled, the kind of smile you give when you've rehearsed the altar call three times in front of a mirror.

"He has walked through darkness," the preacher said. "He has *paid his debt*, and he stands before us today a *changed man*."

Evelyn clutched Denny's hand and looked skyward, as if she'd just delivered him from Gethsemane herself.

"He's asked for forgiveness," Jenkins said, voice thick with reverence. "And who are *we* to deny him that grace, when the Lord Himself does not?"

A scattered applause rose from a few pockets of the congregation. Not enthusiastic, more awkward, politer than believing.

Maddie leaned over, whispering with honey on her tongue. "You were always good at standing in front of people."

Denny sat again, slow and stiff, eyes forward. A few eyes lingered on him from the pews behind. Some of those eyes held skepticism while others poured open pity. One or two, women with tight perms and tired wedding rings, gave him soft smiles.

When he sat, Jenkins stood quietly for a moment, pacing back and forth, looking up and down, like he was searching for divine inspiration for what to say next. Then, jumping and holding his hands above his head he shouted, "WE CALL ON THE LORD TO EASE THE HEARTS OF THOSE TROUBLED BY A RETURNED SON! WE CALL ON EACH AND EVERY PERSON TO PRAY FOR OUR DENNY AND HIS ELIZABETH! WE PRAY THAT GOD WILL INTERVENE AND LAY HIS HAND ON HER HEART AND EASE HER PAINS AND HELP HER FIND FORGIVENESS!"

The congregation was split with silence and amens. Denny did not look around to see from who, but he felt the hair stand on his arms.

Pastor Jenkins moved into his closing remarks with gusto, launching into a chorus about redemption, and "how no soul is too far gone to be called home."

And still, through it all, Denny didn't close his eyes during the final prayer. He didn't bow his head.

He watched.

He watched the people who wanted to believe in him. He watched Evelyn beam as though her prayers had singlehandedly rewritten history. He watched Maddie preen like a cat with cream.

And he waited.

He waited for Beth to walk in and see what they had done.

But she didn't.

She wouldn't.

And that stung more than he expected.

When the service was over and the mulling crowd made its way out to enjoy the various joys of Sunday afternoons in the south, Denny hung by the front door.

The last to leave was Evelyn and Maddie, each shaking the pastor's hand and giving their best side hug.

They approached Denny and Evelyn said, "Don't worry, Hun, she will come around. Just give her time. We women can be temperamental things."

"I know mom, and I know that I made a big mistake, I am so sorry for what I did. It was the booze, but the last six months in the county hit me with a life lesson that I needed."

"Yes dear, I know it had to be rough."

"I just couldn't believe it when I got served with divorce papers."

Maddie patted his arm, "She was mad, and she had a right to be."

Evelyn frowned at this, "God doesn't like divorce. I am not saying what you did was right, but I was there when you both vowed for better or worse."

"I miss her, and I want to see Jupiter." He said this looking down, with a look that would melt the heart of the most skeptic soul. It was a fake look, one that he had practiced many times in the past. People were easy to manipulate, you just had to be sincere in your manipulation.

Maddie's lips curled at this, "I am sure you will get to see her soon."

"Look, you go back to Chelsea, and we will see you soon, maybe have you over for Sunday dinner."

"I am not going back to Chelsea."

Maddie looked up, "Oh."

"I had my attorney buy a house here in Tanner, I still

have the other place, but I wanted to be here. I wanted to be close."

Evelyn's face lit up like a candle in the dark at this, "Well isn't that grand! I am sure she will see that as a true act of love."

"I hope so, either way, I know I have a long road ahead to forgiveness, but I have my walking shoes and am ready to do my part." Inside his thoughts were a little different, inside he said 'That bitch will get back in line.'

"Ok dear, I have to go, we are raising money for the youth group over at the General. I will see you soon."

Maddie and Evelyn left, and Denny walked to Pastor Jenkins, "Got a minute?"

"For you, I have two!" Both men laughed and Jenkins guided him back into the little church hand on back.

Denny stopped halfway down the aisle said, "Pastor, you really moved me today, that speech, it was inspired!"

"I believe you mean sermon."

"You are correct, sermon. That last time I heard something that good was when we were in that little bar in Cancun on our senior trip. You remember that."

Laughing, "You know I remember a little of it, but it is a little hazy."

"Half way through your second fifth that evening you convinced three girls from Mountain Brook to come back to our room. Now that was inspired."

"Yes, it was!" Jenkins crossed his arms. "Now I believe you wanted to speak to me about something?"

"Right to business, I like it." He reached into his back pocket and took out an envelope and handed it to the pastor. "I believe this will help your congregation and thank you for our talk last night."

"We will certainly put it to good use, and anything for my old pal."

Denny shook his hand and walked away. Jenkins opened the envelope to retrieve the contents. Inside was a check made out to Tanner First Baptist Church for ten-thousand dollars with a memo line that said "Youth Group". It also held twenty crisp one-hundred-dollar bills held together with a paper sleeve, in the sleeve was a separate handwritten note that read, Thank you for the show!

Pastor Jenkins smiled and took out his wallet, he put the cash in his wallet and then went to his office to place the check in the donation fund. That cash would be helpful, he might use it for his day job, renovations on the small retirement home he owned, or maybe what his true goal is, to start his political career. Either way, the return of Denny will be good for business.

Walking away from the church to her old sedan Maddie held out her phone for a selfie. She was sending a snap to "Big D" that read 'You have been locked up for a bit, you want to do those things you were snapping me about?"

She waited for a reply and sat in her car, when Denny walked out of the church, she saw him reach for his phone. He stopped and held his phone out and then her phone dinged.

It was a picture of his winking face, and the snap

read, "1509 Carter Way, garage code 1543". This was followed by another snap, 'There is one bed, be in it, naked, wet, ready.'

She grinned, she was tired of the game, she had not slept with he nor any other man since he was locked up. The charade was getting old, she was ready to tell everyone about their relationship held in secret over the past two years. She was tired of being the doting sister living in a small house while her sibling got the full advantage that Denny's wealth brought with it. She was not in love with Denny, but she wanted that life. She wanted that life and she secretly hated Beth for throwing it away, she would take a few hits for that life. She would take a few hits to be able to stay home.

She looked in her mirror and checked her makeup and thought, he did have other benefits besides the money, his snap ID "Big D" told the truth, and after six months of celibacy she could use some of that action.

Beth pulled into the parking lot of the Tanner General Market, which was really just a glorified Piggly Wiggly with a fancier sign. Flex stood near the carts, holding a reusable grocery bag filled with other reusable grocery bags in one hand and a grin on his face. He wore navy cargo shorts and a T-shirt that said "TREKKIE" with a little cartoon spaceship on the front. His hair was damp like he'd just showered. She caught herself biting her lip and at once released it.

"You look..." she began.

"Like a man ready to get judged for his sprinkle choices?" he offered, holding out the bag like a knight presenting his sword.

"Something like that," she said, sliding her keys into her purse.

Inside, they headed straight for the party aisle. Beth tossed in paper plates, a pack of balloons, and a banner that said "HAPPY BIRTHDAY!" in glittery letters. Flex held it up and inspected it like it was a legal document.

"This glitter feels like a trap," he said. "You sure about this?"

"Jupiter loves shiny stuff," Beth replied. "He's eight. The entire world is still made of magic and sugar."

Flex placed the banner carefully into the cart like it might explode.

"Speaking of sugar," he said, steering them toward the cereal aisle, "Jupiter got a favorite?"

Beth sighed. "He goes through phases. Right now, he's into that one with the marshmallow monsters."

"Classic," Flex said. Then he turned, eyes suddenly mischievous. "Wanna play a game?"

Beth raised an eyebrow. "In the cereal aisle?"

"Cereal personality quiz," he declared, stepping back and gesturing grandly. "You point to a cereal. I'll guess your entire romantic history based on it."

She laughed. "Okay, fine. Lucky Charms."

Flex crossed his arms and tapped his chin. "You're whimsical, love too quickly, cry at commercials, and once dated a musician who wore more eyeliner than you."

Beth doubled over in laughter. "Oh my God, that's... weirdly accurate."

"Your turn," he said.

She looked up and down the shelf. "Frosted Mini-Wheats."

Flex smirked. "You tell people you're no-nonsense and mature, but secretly, you're just waiting for someone to bring out your inner child. You've definitely written poetry, but you pretend it was just 'lyrics' for a band that never formed."

Beth wheezed. "Are you a psychic?"

"Nope," he said, snagging a box of Cinnamon Toast Crunch. "Just a man who spent way too much time eating cereal alone in his twenties."

They kept walking, cart slowly filling with streamers, candles, cake mix, and juice boxes. The weight of recent weeks had lifted somehow, as if laughter acted like helium, raising her inch by inch above the pit of tension she normally lived inside.

"Jupiter is impressed with you."

"Is that so? Well, he is a cool kid."

"I mean it, he said that he dreamed you let him press buttons in the fire truck and had a robot dog."

"Wait, did you tell him that I am a secret nerd?"

"No, why?"

"Hmmm, robot dog. That does sound cool." He smiled and they moved out of the cereal aisle.

They were walking toward the checkout when they passed a table marked "Sunday Bake Sale - Support First Southern Baptist Youth Trip!"

"Oh Lord," Beth muttered.

Flex paused. "What?"

She gestured toward the table. "Evelyn's church. If she sees us shopping together, there's going to be a prayer circle started by sundown."

Flex glanced over and saw the stern, helmet-haired women behind the table, including a particularly sharp-eyed figure in a floral blouse who was mid-slice on a sheet cake.

"That your mom?" he asked.

"Yep."

"She looks like she could spot sin from a hundred yards."

"Don't test her," Beth warned, tugging his elbow. "Quick, detour to produce."

They slipped behind a pyramid of cantaloupes like a pair of spies ducking enemy lines.

"So... do you go to church? Flex asked.

Beth shook her head, "No, not since... not in a while."

"I see," He absently placed a bag of oranges in the buggy.

"That church in particular, the preacher is one of my ex's old running buddies. I don't trust him."

"Really, and your mom is ok with that?"

Beth nodded, biting her cheek. "They preach forgiveness. She thinks it means second chances."

Flex didn't reply immediately, but she could see the thought flickering in his eyes.

"You don't think he's changed?" he asked gently.

Beth's face hardened. "I think some men don't need

second chances. I think some people mistake forgiveness for forgetting."

Flex nodded. "I won't press."

She looked at him then. "Thank you."

They exited without incident, and when they reached the car, Flex opened the trunk and started loading bags. The sun was overhead now, casting heat lines off the pavement, but neither of them seemed to mind.

"Hey," Beth said, arms folded loosely, "you were good in there. Really good."

"Years of grocery training," he said. "I'm certified in aisle flirtation and checkout efficiency."

"I mean it, would you maybe consider coming to Jupiter's party? He asked for you."

Without missing a beat, he smiled and said, "Sounds like fun."

She stepped closer. "You sure you want to come to a party with screaming kids and cheap pizza?"

"Jupiter asked for me," Flex said. "I'm not about to disappoint that little guy. Besides, who can pass up cheap pizza"

Beth hesitated, then stepped in and hugged him, fully, this time. Her arms wrapped around his waist, her face brushing his chest.

He froze for a beat, then melted.

His arms circled her, strong and steady, and for a moment, they simply stood there in the heat and hum of a small-town summer.

She pulled back slowly. "Thanks for coming with me today."

"Anytime," he said, brushing a piece of glitter off her shoulder. "This stuff is everywhere already."

She got into the car, started the engine, and paused before pulling out.

"See you soon, Flex."

He tapped the roof gently. "Count on it."

That evening, Beth lit candles on the kitchen counter while Jupiter doodled invitations with crayons. Her phone buzzed once, then twice, photos from Maddie showing different cake designs, and then a message from Flex.

I had fun today. Tell Jupiter I'm working on robot dog plans. Top secret stuff.

Beth smiled, tucked the phone into her back pocket, and turned on the porch light as the sun dipped below the trees.

The porchlight was on, and she noticed it had changed; it no longer flickered on and off.

The glow of the porchlight wasn't just safety. It was permission. A soft promise that it was okay to hope again, just not too loudly.

And for the first time in a long time, Beth let herself lean into that glow, into the idea that maybe, just maybe, the worst was behind her... and something better was inching closer with every step.

Maddie lay in bed with a sheet pulled up over her bare breasts. She was in a plain room whose only contents were a bed and small dresser. The walls were painted with a builder tan with cream moldings. You could still smell the paint, and it was obvious that this house was just beginning its service.

She was sending pictures on her phone of baked goods to her sister, "You need some furniture." She spoke to a man in the other room who was peeing with the door open, she could tell by the sound that he was only on target 75% of the time.

"Yeah, I will have my assistant take care of it."

She tapped her fingers on her thigh, "Assistant? Let me handle it."

"Sure, get my card, do what you want."

Maddie ran her hand up her thigh and cusped her breast, "What I want is to do that thing again."

A man looked around the corner with a devilish grin, "Oh yeah."

"That is...if you can get it up again." She said this while moving her hand up to her lips in mock surprise.

He walked over to her, wearing nothing but the fading perspiration from their last session. He grabbed the ankle of her left foot and pulled dragging her down flat on the mattress, threw back the sheet and crawled up and in between her thighs. He grabbed her phone, tossed it to the floor and pinned both of her wrists down behind her head.

"IF, IF I can get it up again. You are going to need an ice pack when I am through with you."

Her face twisted with desire, "Big talk, care to put a little action behind those words?"

He leaned in and kissed her deeply, grinding his groin into hers, she moaned, and he leaned his head back, "I will prove it."

The look on Maddie's face changed and she stopped moving and looked at him sternly, "Why do you want her back while you fuck me?"

He didn't move for a moment and then let with his right hand and gripped her jaw firmly, his thumb pressing under her chin, eyes full of warning, "Because, I say when it's over. Now, don't question me like that again. Got it?"

She ran her tongue over her lip and nodded. He relaxed his hand and sat back, she leaned forward and ran her hand down his chest and wrapped her hand around his testicles, she squeezed and with her other hand slapped his face, "Got it, now you don't forget what you promised. When you are done, you are mine."

He held a look of shock and panic on his face that turned to a mischievous grin, he removed her hand and leaned in for a kiss, they lay back into what they were there to do.

Evelyn kissed Franklin lightly on his lips, the same ones that she had kissed every night for the past 42 years. The held each other's hands, closed their eyes, and Evelyn spoke, "Father, we thank you for your wonderful lesson today. We thank you for the redemption you provided by the giving of your only son. We ask you to look over our family and continue to bless us with your joy and compassion. We ask that you keep us healthy and free from sin. Tonight, Lord, I ask one more thing, please heal the rift between our Elizabeth and Denny so they can move forward in the spiritual blessing of marriage. We ask that you bring our family back together in whole. We ask this in your holy name." They both spoke "Amen" at the same time.

As they lay together in bed Franklin asked, so tell me again about that sermon.

7

BROKEN SPOONS

T he cake was in the oven. The dinosaur-themed balloons were half-inflated on the counter. And Jupiter had fallen asleep with one shoe on, and a crayon still clutched in his hand.

Beth stood barefoot in the kitchen, swaying slightly to a soft hum that didn't come from her lips. It came from the house. The kind of murmur that only old homes offered, wood stretching, a pipe clicking, wind rustling against thin windowpanes. It should have made her feel safe. Should have reminded her that she was somewhere new.

Tonight though, it only reminded her that walls remember. And ghosts don't stay buried just because you change the locks.

Her phone dinged, she walked to the kitchen table, an old diner styled table with a red Formica top, polished chrome trim and four little stainless-steel chairs with red sparkle padded seats. She picked up the phone and saw a text from Flex.

Want me to bring ice in the morning?
Gonna be hot, even for a birthday party.

She smiled despite the weight in her chest.

That would be perfect. And Flex...

She paused, deleted the second part. Then wrote:

Thanks for showing up.

No response came at once, but she didn't need one. Flex was the kind of man who answered with action, not emojis.

She turned to the oven, set a timer, and reached into the drawer for the wooden spoon. Her fingers brushed the edge of the handle and suddenly her stomach twisted. The spoon itself was nothing special, just a wooden spoon that did not make her skin crawl when it stirred in a pot, or bowl, like the metal and hard plastic spoons do.

This spoon was old, a utilitarian piece of kitchen equipment found in any other home. The only thing that stood out was a large chip, better described as a crack, in the cradle of the spoons bowl. She hadn't used that spoon since they moved. It had come from the old house, the house she brought Jupiter home to from the hospital, the house shared with a man from her past.

When she picked it up she got more than just a spoon, something uninvited came roaring back into her mind.

A memory, something suppressed that made her pause. The chipped wooden spoon tugged at something buried, an echo, a bruise of memory. Three years ago...

She'd barely shut the kitchen cabinet before Denny's voice slammed into her like a wall.

"You spend two-hundred and fifty damn dollars at Target and forgot the goddamn beer?"

Beth froze.

"I didn't forget it," she said quietly, "You didn't write it down."

Denny moved across the kitchen like a super charged storm cell, like a towering anvil full of electrical potential and the tornadic activity that all Southerners fear. There was thunder in his shoulders, lightning in his eyes. His boots clomped against the tile like the drum of cavalry riding into battle.

"You think I have time to babysit your ass with a list?" He reached around her and yanked open the fridge door. "No beer. Just fucking yogurt and kale shit."

Beth stepped back, palms out. "Denny, I can go back..."

"Oh, now you'll go back," he mocked. "Like hell you will. Your dumb ass will probably spend two-hundred more of my hard-fucking earned money!"

He reached behind her and yanked open the utensil drawer. She thought he was just slamming it shut out of frustration. But instead, his hand wrapped around the thick wooden spoon, the one her mother had given to them as a house warming gift. The one she used to stir gumbo in the winter.

He slammed it into the counter with a crack, like a carpenter driving nails.

He repeated this and cracked it again.

And then, he turned, his blues burning red. This was the look he gave when she knew she was going to take a hit from the man she loved, from the man who swore to love and care for her. She did not flinch, she learned over the years not to react, reacting made things worse.

"You ever fail at the only goddamned job you have, which is spend my money and shop," he growled, lifting the spoon slightly, "and I'll show you what it's good for."

Beth didn't run. Not yet. Not until Jupiter woke from the noise. Not until he whimpered for his momma. Not until Denny hurled the spoon across the room where it slammed against the pantry door like a shotgun shell. The spoon left an indent in the door and cracked; it cracked like her will to continue.

Beth clicked back to the now and opened her hand. The wooden spoon she'd just touched clattered onto the counter. It lay there like an accusation, like the reminder that she knew then that she should leave, like the physical representation of her inability to stand up for herself, like the embodiment of fear.

She backed away like it had burned her. Her chest rose and fell in sharp, staccato breaths. Her face felt cold with the loss of blood to her face.

She whispered, "Don't you dare ruin today, too."

As if speaking to the memory.

As if daring the past to stay in its goddamn place.

She grabbed a towel laying on the table and tossed it onto the spoon, it hit and knocked the spoon from the black stone countertop and onto the white floor. She left the kitchen, not caring that the spoon lay there, she would throw the thing away later, now she had to run.

The next morning, the birthday chaos began early with the sounds of roosters. She reminded herself that she had to find those chickens, who had chickens in town?

Jupiter was up by six, screaming joy into the rafters and begging to wear his firefighter costume even though it was ninety degrees and was made from a full polyester jumpsuit. Beth let him deciding that it was not worth the battle. She figured he'd pass out from heatstroke eventually or decide that it was in fact just too damned hot to wear it.

Flex showed up exactly on time, a bag of ice in one hand and a small mystery box in the other. He was wearing a pair of faded boot-cut blue jeans, brown square toe boots, and a blue and gray Henley t-shirt, she was wearing a pale-yellow sundress with blue forget-me-not flowers and thong sandals. They both looked at each other briefly appraising each other and said in unison, "You look great/fantastic." They both grinned and had a brief pause to look into each other's eyes.

"What's in the box?" she asked, taking it with curiosity.

He winked. "Top secret."

Jupiter ran up between them and tried to wrestle it from her hands.

"It's for later," Flex said. "You've got to earn it."

"Like with pushups?" Jupiter asked, immediately dropping to the porch and counting as his rear end dipped lower than his shoulders.

Beth laughed, genuinely, and Flex handed her the ice. "We can do intervals. Party games first, then boot camp."

The yard was filled quickly with family, friends from school, and children. Jupiter was quick to make friends, and it showed, with fourteen children running around. Each child embraced the theme of the party and wore the paper dinosaur face masks she picked up for the day.

Paper plates clapped in the wind. Streamers wrapped around porch beams. Two folding tables buckled slightly under the weight of off-brand sodas and the homemade volcano cake Beth had painstakingly frosted.

Children screamed, sugar crashed, and somewhere along the way Flex had become the star of the show. He taught the kids how to unroll a fire hose using streamers, held a marshmallow-stuffing contest (Jupiter lost proudly), and led a wildly unsafe dance party with his Bluetooth speaker blaring 2000s pop.

Beth stood to the side watching it all.

Watching her beloved son but also watching *him*.

Watching how the children orbited him like he was the sun. How her son lit up when Flex so much as knelt beside him. He was the sun, he radiated warmth and an inviting openness that everyone could feel, and something in her heart cracked open. Not in a painful way, but in a terrifying way. *The what if this could last way? The am I ready to allow this way?*

Then a voice interrupted her thoughts like a sudden blast of wind that comes before a thunderstorm.

"Well, well. Somebody went and brought the whole town out."

Beth turned.

Denny stood just outside the gate, dressed in clean khakis and a pale blue polo, holding a gift bag like he'd just stepped out of Dad Magazine.

Her stomach twisted.

"You weren't invited," she said, loud enough for the nearest parent to glance their way.

"I called Evelyn. She said it'd be a sin to miss my own son's birthday."

Beth stepped forward, blocking the view between Denny and Jupiter. "That wasn't your call to make."

"Look," he said, all gentle smiles and soft words, "I just want to see my kid blow out his candles. That's not too much to ask, is it?"

Beth didn't answer. She looked at Jupiter. Then at Flex. Then back at Denny. Finally, she looked at her mother, her mother who stood with a joyous look of expectation and who was tapping her father on the arm to look.

She wanted to scream, but not here. Not with neighbors. Not with children. Not with cake cooling under a fly net.

Evelyn started to approach but was halted with a

single point of the finger by Beth. Even her mom could tell that this moment was going sour. So, her mother stood there and slowly started moving back to her husband and Maddie who were taking advantage of the shade tree.

"Fifteen minutes," she muttered.

Denny gave her a slow, grateful nod. "That's all I need."

From where he stood by the drink table, Flex could feel it, a shift in the air.

The party buzz had lulled into the mid-afternoon warmth: kids half-drunk on sugar, moms fanning themselves with napkins, a country song warbling through his Bluetooth speaker. It should've felt like a win. Like the kind of moment, he'd tuck in his back pocket and carry home.

But then *he* showed up.

Flex clocked Denny the moment he stepped through the gate, clean, polished, with that artificial softness that didn't match the eyes. Beth's reaction told him everything: the stillness in her spine, the flicker in her gaze from side to side, like someone bracing for a blow even if one never came. Her face tightened and he noticed a slight wrinkle at the corner of her eyes.

He didn't move immediately. He watched. Waited.

Denny circled like a politician at a cookout. Flex hated those types, the hand shakers, the bless-your-heart-smilers. He knew men like that. Had pulled them out of house fires more than once, watched them cry in one breath and manipulate in the next.

But it wasn't until Denny approached him directly that Flex felt the knot fully tighten in his chest.

"Fireman, right?"

Flex shook his hand, more out of reflex than welcome. It was a calculated grip, too soft, too rehearsed. The man had rehearsed this whole damn thing.

"Big shoes to fill," Denny said. "Jupiter's had some good role models."

Flex gave him nothing.

"Just don't get too comfortable," Denny added, his smile dropping a fraction. "Kids are impressionable. But blood runs deeper than hero worship."

And there it was.

Flex stared at him. His mind raced, to Beth's eyes when she talked about her past, to the slight flinch she gave when someone touched her arm too quickly.

"Only if the blood doesn't come with bruises," Flex said, cool and quiet.

He watched Denny's expression freeze.

And then Beth was *there*, grabbing Denny's arm like she'd done it a hundred times before, with urgency, not tenderness. The kind of grab that told the story of covering up and hiding the indiscretions of others, of standing between a man and his consequences too often.

"Inside. Now."

They disappeared through the front door, and Flex stood there, every nerve on high alert.

He hated not being able to hear what was being said.

Hated being stuck outside while *that man* was alone with her, even if just for a minute.

He kept his eyes on the windows.

Watched the curtains sway in the breeze created by Beth's frantic movement in the living room as she was followed in circles by the man. The man who followed her like a shark to its prey.

He watched and the sound of the sound around him disappeared, the noise of children playing, Jupiter squealing, and balloons popping gone as he zeroed in on the moment of risk that was before him.

His hands curled into fists. He knew better than to storm in, this wasn't his house, not his call, but if he *heard* anything, *anything*, he wouldn't hesitate.

Ten minutes felt like an hour.

When the front door opened, Beth's voice rang out like a gavel.

"Jupiter! Your father's here and leaving now."

Flex watched the boy run over, watched Denny crouch down and hand over the bag like some returning hero.

It made his stomach turn.

When Denny left through the gate, Flex stepped forward, but Beth met him halfway.

Her hands were shaking, just slightly.

Flex didn't ask.

He walked over to the half collapsed folding table and poured a glass of water on her. The only thing he could offer in that moment that didn't feel like pressing.

"He's poison," he said as he watched Denny stroll away.

"I know," she answered, voice raw.

"You okay?"

"No. But I will be."

She looked at him then, really looked at him. And for the first time since he met her, he saw it, not just the pain, but the fire beneath it. The grit. The refusal to let that man break her again.

And Flex felt something deep inside him shift, settle, root itself in place.

He would stand between her and any storm she asked him to.

Even if she never asked.

Moments earlier.

She closed the door behind them and turned to him, seething.

"You *don't* talk to him. You *don't* show up here. And you *sure as hell* don't get to pretend to be Father of the Year."

Denny held up his hands. "Beth..."

"No!" she snapped. "You get *fifteen minutes*, and that's because I didn't want my son's eighth birthday to be the one where I finally told the neighbors what a monster his daddy really is."

His mouth opened, then shut.

She stepped closer. "You remember that spoon?" Her voice shook. "The one you broke across the wall because I forgot your goddamn beer? It's in this kitchen. Still tainted. Still chipped. Still *mine*."

He paled, slightly, but didn't back down.

"You don't scare me anymore," she whispered.

"I don't have to," he said quietly. "Because your mama still thinks I'm the one worth saving."

Beth felt it like a knife twist.

Denny leaned in, so close his breath touched her cheek. "And the whole church? They're praying for you. That you stop being so bitter. That you come back to the light. They think I'm redeemed, Beth. And you? You're just angry."

She stared him down.

"I'd rather be angry than trapped."

Then she opened the door and said loud enough for the entire yard to hear, "Jupiter! Your father's here and leaving now."

Jupiter came running, confused but smiling.

Denny knelt, hugged him quickly, and handed him the gift.

"Happy birthday, son."

Jupiter cringed at the touch and looked at his mother, he did not say thank you, he did not say goodbye. He just stood there holding a bag from a man that he did not really know.

Then he stood, nodded at Beth, and walked off through the gate.

Beth watched him go, trembling with adrenaline.

She didn't turn until Flex walked up and gently handed her a glass of water.

116

Later, when the sun had dipped and only glitter and cupcake wrappers remained, Flex walked Beth to her door.

Jupiter was inside, playing with a toy robot dog from his mystery box.

"I have to ask," Beth said, smiling tiredly, "where did you *find* a robot dog?"

"Technically," Flex said, "it's a Bluetooth speaker shaped like a robot dog. But it barks when it plays music, so... pretty close."

Beth laughed and the creases, those tiny wrinkles at the corner of her eyes reappeared, earlier they were the mark of fear, but now they drew him in.

"Thank you," she said. "For everything today."

"You don't have to thank me."

"Yes, I do. I need to."

She hesitated.

Then said, "You saw him. You *heard* him. And you didn't flinch."

"I know what fear looks like," he said quietly. "And I know what courage looks like, too."

She leaned in and kissed him. She placed her lips on his and lingered there with her eyes closed, it was not deep, not desperate, but real. He placed his hand on her lower back and breathed; he drank in her scent and started a fire within him.

He held her for a moment and thought he could taste frosting with a hint of salt, it was beautiful.

When she pulled away, he smiled. "That a thank you?"

"That's a maybe."

"I'll take it."

They stood by the door for a few lingering moments longer and little passed in the way of words, but volumes worth of passionate love stories passed between their eyes. It was a moment in the now and neither of them were willing to spoil that moment with the vulgarity of small talk.

He reached out his hand brushed the side of her cheek with the back of his fingers and sensually allowed the tips of his fingers to grace the top of her ears. He turned and walked away.

She turned a few moments later and walked in through the shiny red door and sat cross legged in the floor with her little man and she laughed as he laughed with enthusiastic but tired eyes and recounted his special day.

Across the street from the faded yellow house with red door stood an even older house, it was currently not occupied and being rejuvenated by an ambitious husband and wife duo. It had a small cinder block garage that sat near the property's edge, far away from the streetlight that lit up the faded yellow house.

A red light glowed by this building watching a man kiss a woman in the doorway. The red light glowed and released smoke. The holder of the cigarette watched the kiss and flicked the cigarette into the yard and turned to walk away. He walked in the dark around the corner to a parked car.

He entered into the car and picked up his phone, snapped a picture and typed, 'take your panties off and put the cuffs on, I will be home in 10.'

Denny started his car and drove home as his phone lit up with a new snap. It was a photo taken beneath silk sheets, teasing, revealing just enough to provoke and disturb. The caption in the snap read, "Already started without you."

The sender, Maddie, laid the phone down and reached over to the new nightstands that she purchased the day prior for the formerly empty room and took out a pair of handcuffs and closed the drawer, she stopped halfway through, reopened the drawer and took out a blind fold and said aloud, "Hurry up Big D."

Jupiter fell asleep in the floor with his robot dog still in his hand. Beth picked up his tiny frame and carried him over to the couch, covering him with a brown crochet throw that she made with her grandmother and started her routine and cleaning up the beautiful mess.

She stopped short in the kitchen and looked at the cracked wooden spoon in the floor. She bent to pick it and stared at it coldly. She stood with it and mouthed quietly, "Fuck You." Followed by a swift walk to the trash can where it went to rest, a part of her life that she was ready to move on from.

She left to go to bed and caught a detail that she had missed earlier. In the corner, next to the table that sat by the door was a little bag. It sat there in the floor unopened, tossed aside by Jupiter. The bag that was given to him by his father, and it lay there alone, unused, and forgotten a perfect representation for the relationship that its gifter tossed away.

That night, Beth lay awake staring at the ceiling. Her breasts rising with each deep breath and the feeling of the weighted blanked sent spasms of joy as it moved over gently over her bare nipples. Her eyes closed as her hand moved to find her spot, while she replayed images of a first kiss and the feeling that his nearness enamored. After bringing herself to climax and the sensation of relief washed over her body she thought about her life and how to go ahead.

The splinter was still there, in the spoon that was lying in the trash, and in her memory.

But the light on the porch glowed steadily.

And for the first time in years...

She wasn't waiting for the storm to return, for the heavens to fall, or tumultuous wind to blow her life asunder.

She was preparing for the promise of spring, for the potential of the rebirth of passion in her life, for the welcoming of a new lover.

8

COLD ASHES AND BRIGHT LIES

Beth found herself watching the porchlight again.

It was early evening, the cicadas hadn't quite given up the day, and the sky had turned that warm bruised lavender that always made her think of her grandmother's quilts, patchworked and uneven, stitched with comfort in mind, not symmetry. Flex had texted her earlier and asked if she wanted company, maybe a second shot at that coffee date that ended in a good-bye, not a kiss. She'd said yes and then panicked for an hour trying to figure out what "casual but not desperate" looked like in clothing form.

She settled on soft jeans, a white linen blouse, and the scent of lilacs dabbed just beneath each ear.

She walked through the house to her favorite room, the freshly renovated kitchen and popped a pod in the coffee maker, it made the familiar pop as she closed the lid and the familiar hiss as the water started to heat up. The cup filled and she watched it expectantly, thinking that she would enjoy the next cup with Flex, but for now, this would do.

She opened her fridge and took out a tall plastic bottle, the real reason that she enjoyed coffee in fact. She held the bottle and took a drew in the aroma deeply as she popped the top. The scent of hazelnut filled her nostrils, and she smiled as she poured just enough, too much for most, into her cup. She smiled as she remembered a joke made in the teachers' lounge that she liked her creamer with a little bit of coffee.

Walking slowly through the living room she found Jupiter entertaining himself with his collection of coloring books. "Hello, my little man." She sat down beside him and ruffled his hair. He gave her a little growl.

"Mom, stop!"

"Oh, are you too big for me to play with your hair?"

"You know I am, I am eight!"

Feigning shocked indifference, she held her free hand to her chest, "Oh, the shock and horror!"

"Look." He held up the coloring book, the picture was a truck rolling through a field. He had colored the truck blue. Looking closer she noticed a blend of another color around the fender edges.

"What is this?" She pointed at the second color.

"That is rust, I saw a truck like that yesterday."

She looked a moment longer and realized that his mind was developing and he had an artist locked inside him. She made a note to foster that.

"Baby, would you mind if I went out tonight? Miss Sarah said that you could play with Conner while I am out."

"OOOH, I like Conner, he has cool toys."

"I know you do, baby."

"Where are you going?"

"Well," she paused, "Mr. Berry, Flex, asked me to join him for coffee."

"Can I go?" He asked at once.

"I think that I need to see him by myself, is that ok?"

He paused, eyes rolled back processing, "Are you, his girlfriend?"

She almost spit her coffee at this. She swallowed and said, "Baby, Mr. Flex is my friend. We are just going to talk, I need a friends mommy's age."

"I saw you kiss him."

Her hand shook as she processed this, why was she worried? Partly it was due to her fear of hurting him, of letting anyone close to him, but mainly it was due to her thinking that she had pulled something over. That she had gotten her kiss but in a way that he was kept away, not seeing this new side of her.

"Well, yes I did."

"Doesn't that make you, his girlfriend? I kissed Sara on the slide, and she was my girlfriend."

"You kissed a girl?!" Beth's eyes were wide at this revelation, she thought she knew everything about her little man.

"Yeah, really she kissed me, right here," he pointed to his cheek, "and then we were boyfriend and girlfriend, not the holding hands kind, but we dated."

"Is that dating?" She smiled at his innocence.

"Yeah, but her friend told her that she was too young

to be tied down and we should see other people, so we broke up."

"I see, and how long did you date?"

"We started on the slide and decided to just be friends at lunch."

Laughing, "Well, it is a little more involved for adults, but Mr. Flex and I are friends, and I think I might like to see him more. Would that be ok with you?"

"Yeah, I like Flex. He let me press the buttons in the truck and got me a robot dog."

"He is sweet."

He looked up at her, "If you date someone and kiss them do you have to be mad and yell at them?" He asked this with all honesty and curiosity.

Her heart ached to hear this come from his mouth, and she panicked. This was not the, oh I am surprised panic, but the gut twisting kind where your stomach feels like it is in your throat, and you just want to run away panic.

She collected her thoughts and ruffled his hair again, he scuffed up his face and pushed away at his hands.

"No baby, if you date someone you should not be mad and yell at them. If you care enough about someone you should never do that."

"Is that why we are not living with daddy?

She wanted this conversation to be over, "Baby, your daddy and I..."

"Daddy hit you, I saw it."

"Baby."

She could not speak, she leaned over and squeezed

him, maybe a little too hard. They sat there, no more words spoken, she holding the little man and he being held. They had both been tested and experienced the worst. Was she really willing to let Flex in her life? He seemed like a good man, but she loved Denny once. That love cost her and exposed her child to the worst of adulthood.

She relaxed and he let the conversation go, it was clear, even to an eight-year-old that the time to talk was over. He slid back to his coloring book and started to create his next masterpiece.

She listened to the scratching of crayons on rough paper and the creak of the house, in the distance a rooster crowed. She absently thought, "where is that damned chicken?"

He was heading out from a long shift at the firehouse to get ready. Flex barely made it down the station steps before the alarm kicked in.

Structure fire. Miller Road. Single story. Unoccupied.

He shouted to the crew and jumped into his gear like muscle memory. Within minutes, the engine roared to life, tires squealing onto asphalt as they raced toward smoke curling up behind a rusted-out auto shop.

The fire wasn't big, but it was mean. Grease and insulation made it spit like a kicked mule. They moved fast, hoses, axes, coordination that came from muscle and trust.

It wasn't until he crawled out through a blown

window that he realized his jacket had caught on the jagged frame, ripping clean from armpit to waist and ruining the clothing underneath. It was crazy that he had snagged something strong and sharp enough to actually cut through the tough outer skip of his fire suit, but he had. If it had been that sharp, he had obviously dodged serious injury.

He stood in the smoke, panting, and looked down at himself, sweaty, soot-smudged, and now one coffee-date-worthy shirt short.

"Of course," he muttered, looking at his watch. This little fire detour had cost him dearly. He finished up his tasks and asked the chief if he could head out straight from the scene, it was only half a mile to his apartment. With a nod of approval, he handed off his gear and hit the road.

He tore off the fire jacket and wiped his face. Thirty-eight minutes to shower, dress, and get across town.

He sped home, leapt through the door, and cursed the dryer for still being full of wet towels. His one decent button-up, the blue oxford she'd complimented during Career Day, was in a wrinkled heap at the bottom of the laundry basket.

He yanked open his closet.

Nothing.

Too tight, too stained, too "shirt I wore when my cousin got arrested."

Panicking, he grabbed his wallet and keys and ran down stairs to Whit's General Store, still wearing no shirt, but a look of panic on his face.

Old man Whit looked up from the counter, squinting. "Boy, you look like you lost a bet with a raccoon."

"Date emergency," Flex panted. "You got any shirts that won't make me look like I teach archery at summer camp?"

Whit pointed at a rack near the cooler. "Flannel's all we got in your size. Clearance."

Flex stared at the heavy red-and-black plaid, sweat already pooling at the base of his neck. "Perfect," he muttered.

He grabbed the shirt and pulled out the tags, pausing only to throw on the flannel, and handed over a twenty.

"You sure you wanna wear that in this heat?" Whit asked, grinning.

"Better to be hot than late," Flex said, already jogging for the door.

He didn't know if Beth liked flannel, but he hoped she'd see the effort and maybe laugh at the chaos it took just to sit across from her and hear her voice.

As he sprinted home to finish up, he thought about her smile and the little wrinkles that formed at the corners of her eyes. He didn't know it at the time, but this was the exact moment that she had moved from a person that infatuated him to the woman he loved.

When he knocked three soft taps like he didn't want to scare the house, Jupiter answered the door, holding a tiny robot dog like a bouncer guarding his club.

"You smell like smoke," Jupiter declared.

"I am smoke," Flex said with a wink, then leaned in to whisper, "But I showered first. Mom check, okay?"

He leaned in and raised his arm. Jupiter laughed and leaned into sniff.

"Uh-Huh, smoke and stuff."

Flex laughed and ruffled his hair, it was not so bad having him do it, but not his mom.

Beth's laugh floated from the kitchen.

He stepped in, eyes finding hers easily. She smiled in that half-lidded way that meant she was happy but trying to pretend it wasn't obvious.

"Want coffee?" she asked.

"Only if we don't have to go out."

"I thought we were going to Westers?"

"It has been a day, if it is ok can we just sit, swing, and chat?"

She smiled at this, even though she was looking forward to an evening out, this would be fine too.

"How would you like your coffee sir?

"With too much sugar?"

"Well, I can do that, but I will make it with grace as well," she said.

She blushed and busied herself with the kettle. A car pulled up and Jupiter yelled, "Conner's here, gotta go."

She walked the little man to the car said her good-bye's and walked back to the kitchen, Flex was sitting on the swing in the heat, and she noticed the flannel shirt, odd choice.

They sat on the porch, mugs in hand, and chatted. He told her about his day, and the fire defeated, leaving out the part of dodging serious injury. He reached over and took her hand and it sent chills up her spine. This made her feel like a teenager again, and after years of being a mom, this felt amazing.

They sat swinging for three hours, chatting, laughing, and enjoying the moment.

Then her phone buzzed.

She glanced at the screen, her breath catching.

UNKNOWN NUMBER

Thought you should know what your hero looks like when the lights are off.

Attached: two images. One was grainy but clear enough, Flex, shirtless, dancing on what looked like a club stage, back when his hair was longer and the cocky grin of youth still lived on his face.

The second image made her stomach turn. A full nude shot, explicit and framed in a way that felt designed for humiliation.

Her heart raced. Her mouth went dry.

Flex saw her expression change before she could hide it.

"What is it?" he asked.

Beth didn't speak. She just turned the phone toward him.

He froze.

"That's not me," he said after a long beat, his voice low. "That one..." he tapped the nude image, "that's not real. The dancing photo? Yeah. That was me. Long time ago. I was broke. I needed money. But the second one's fake."

Beth felt a strange dissonance. She believed him, somehow, she knew instinctively he wasn't lying, but that didn't stop the nausea from creeping up her throat.

"Someone sent this to hurt you," he said. "And me."

She nodded slowly, the shock settling in. "Who would...?"

She looked again at the images, remembering his statement that he had danced, but never nude. She wanted to believe, but...

Beth's hands trembled.

Flex sat across from her on the porch, fists clenched on his knees. "I didn't lie to you."

"I know," she whispered. "I want to believe, but."

"But it changes things, doesn't it?"

Beth didn't answer. Because she didn't know.

She didn't want to doubt him, but the image was burned into her eyes, cruel and intimate, and she hated that something so vulnerable could be weaponized.

They sat there, not speaking, the moment of intimacy damaged beyond repair. They sat until a car pulled up and a little man jumped out, chattering about his day. Flex sat, listened, smiled. When it was time to leave, he stood before her.

"I know that I have a past. That is what it is, the past. I cannot change it, but I understand if it is too much for you."

She listened not speaking, dozens of scenarios rushing through her head. Who sent the pictures, obviously it was Denny, but how could she know? Was it really fake? Was he worth the risk?

"I, need to think."

"I understand," he looked at her deeply. "I really do, just... please know that is not me now. I own my past, I am ashamed of it really. I cannot change it though. If you want me, you have to believe that.

"I really..."

Flex leaned in and looked at her, "I want you to want me, you are the only lady who has looked at me as a man. I want that, but it is up to you. I really do understand if you don't, but it will hurt."

A moment of eternity passed with them locked in each other's gaze. She believed him, she really did, but this was a lot to process. She knew about his past, but to see it, to see the picture that he said was fake. It brought back memories of seeing a picture of another lady in Denny's phone and his denials. Tonight, it was just too much.

"I have to go inside." She said curtly and took a step back.

Flex looked at her and his eyes saddened. "I understand."

"I have to think."

"I am here when you are done."

He smiled a half assed smile and turned to walk away. Her heart broke at this, and a tear formed at the corner of her eye. She was letting Denny strike at her from a distance and this infuriated her.

"Flex!"

He paused and she ran to him and roughly grabbed

him by the arm spinning him around, before he completely stopped, she pulled on his flannel shirt and pulled him down, deeply kissing him and taking him by complete surprise. This moment was intense and over quickly.

"I still need to think, but I had to. I am in control here."

He looked at her in surprise and just nodded.

"I will call you, just let me think."

She turned and ran up the old wooden stairs and past the shiny red door and closed it without looking.

Flex watched and when the door closed, he touched his lips torn between the dueling emotions of shame and intense feelings of connection that the kiss created. He turned again and walked away.

That night both she and he would lay awake, thinking of the possibilities that their relationship could create. They lay there and silently wished that they were holding each other, that the past would die, the past of shame that he held and the past of regret for being treated like a possession that she could not seem to shake.

Maddie pulled up to pick up her mom at 8:45 a.m., just in time to get her over to Sunday School. Her father was not attending today, his back was sore from his Saturday honey-do-list that was laid out to "while away the hours."

Evelyn walked out dressed in a black dress that sat

just at the shoulders and a black sheer cover that ran the length of her arm. The cuffs, neck, and hem were trimmed in white with a crisp satin band around the waste. She was wearing black sheer panty hose and black flats carrying a white clutch purse.

"Damn momma, could you have picked a hotter outfit for September?" Maddie said quietly to herself just before the car door opened.

"Hey momma, you look great!"

"Why thank you! I felt good when I woke up this morning and thought to myself, Evelyn, you just get yourself together and go all out today." She said this laughing as she buckled in.

"Momma, we are going to stop for a little coffee before we go to church."

"I don't think we have time for that."

"The good lord always has time for a hit of caffeine, besides I am buying, and I know you like that iced coffee."

"Alright then." She scowled, but Maddie knew she was eating the attention up. She loved anyone buying anything for her, that was how you got her heart on your side.

"We... we need to talk too."

"Hmmm, I don't like the sound of that. You haven't gone and got yourself pregnant, have you? I told you God don't like loose women."

"No momma, it's not about me, it's about Beth."

"Oh?"

"Look, I know you are not going to like this but, oh, hold on let's get this order."

They pulled into a small coffee shop with burnt wood siding, it was the local favorite that was supported by the town, their coffee was not consistent, but it was a source of pride to not use the "Big Chains."

The car stopped at a window on the side, no drive through menu here, this was a personal touch establishment. The window opened and they were greeted by a smiling face, the owner of the store, Vanessa. She was in her mid-thirties but looked like she had just knocked on the door of thirty itself. Her skin was tanned, almost olive and she had a big bright blue eye draped with heavy black lashes that said hello before her mouth opened.

Vanessa leaned on the window seal, arms crossed, and just slight amount cleavage popped up from behind her chocolate colored apron. She greeted them warmly, "Maddie and Evelyn how are you! Mrs. Evelyn you look fantastic!"

Maddie replied for both, "We are doing good Vanessa, kids good?"

"Everyone is doing their best, we appreciate it. Now, what can I get you lovely ladies this morning?"

"I will have a double sugar free Irish Coffee, two Splendas, and momma will have her usual."

Vanessa smiled, "Non-fat white mocha, whip cream, and mocha drizzle?"

Evelyn beamed, "You are the best Vanessa!"

"Just give me a few minutes and I will have you ladies ready to go."

With a flourish of bouncing blond hair, she turned and got busy at her craft.

"Now Maddie, what is this you need to talk about?"

Maddie put on a face that she had practiced in the mirror for hours the night before. She frowned, "Momma, Beth is doing some bad things since she left Denny. I hate to even talk about it, but I am worried for her. More than that, I am worried for Jupiter."

A worried look came across Evelyn's face, "Oh my, what..."

Leaning out the window Vanessa was handing out two drinks in her signature lavender coffee cups, they were embossed with a golden 'W'.

Evelyn feigned a smile, "Now dear, how did you get that done so quickly?"

"Trade secret, but since you are so nice... I saw you pull up and I got started on your favorite."

"What if we did not order that?"

"It's a risk I am willing to take. Really though, it's not a risk at all. If you did not order them, I would drink them." She winked and took a twenty-dollar bill from Maddie. She started to make change and Maddie just smiled, waved, and rolled her window up.

Evelyn, held the cup in both hands. "Tell me, what has she got into now?"

"Like I said momma, I hate to even get into it, but I just think it is right."

Lifting her cup to sip her coffee Evelyn sighed, "Go on."

"Momma, I did not feel that it was right to bring a new man to Denny's birthday party, not and leave his daddy out. So, I decided to check into this "Flex" and after asking around I found out he was... Well momma, he was a dancer, you know the kind that takes his clothes off."

Eyebrows creased, "Maddie, what did you say?"

"He was a dancer, you know screaming women and G-strings."

"I thought he was a fireman?"

"He is now, but he used to get up on stage and dance. I called an old friend, and he did a little digging. He found pictures. I can show you momma, but I don't want to."

"I don't need to see sin to know it is there."

"Look momma, it wasn't just dancing, he did other things."

"Like what?"

Maddie pressed her right hand to her chest, "Momma, he took all of his clothes off, from what we hear, he was a sex worker."

Evelyn turned sharply, "A what?"

"Gigolo, prostitute, he had sex for money."

Coffee almost spilling Evelyn looked up, "Oh lord!"

"I know momma, and Beth has him around our Jupiter, you saw how he looked up to him."

"He did that with women for money."

"Well," Maddie looked away trying to hide a smile, "We don't know that it was all just women momma."

Both stared ahead in silence for the rest of the ride. As the vehicle turned into the church parking lot full of Sunday mornings finest Evelyn sniffed and said, "Lord knows what Denny is going to do when he finds out."

"He knows momma. I told him. He is Jupiter's daddy, and he deserved to know."

The vehicle came to a stop and Evelyn took a deep breath before opening her door, she then went about the Sunday morning ritual of hugs and small talk with a side of secretly judging the other ladies present.

The red velvet padded church pews were full. Pastor Jenkins stood tall behind the pulpit, thick leather-bound Bible in hand and sweat already forming at his collar. The Southern Baptist sanctuary smelled of old hymnals, lavender powder, and brewing coffee. Denny sat proudly beside Evelyn and Maddie, who looked down at her lap and chewed her lower lip.

The sermon was full of fire and brimstone, focusing heavily on sexual perversion and leaned heavily on Deuteronomy 23:17-18 that forbid both male and female prostitution and the six psalm warns the faithful against the seductive nature of prostitution. The crowd answer back with loud amens, but Evelyn sat with her head down, through most of the sermon.

During the recitation of the Psalm, Evelyn patting Denny on the leg and leaned in. "I am so sorry son."

He looked at her and smiled patting her hand in reassurance. He leaned over and whispered, "I need you to trust me."

She stared at him, searching his face for some hint at what he meant by that statement, in the end she just gave a faint smile and nodded.

At the end of the sermon the offering plate was passed, Denny tucked in a fat envelope with the exaggerated flair of a man who knows that he can toss around more money than most.

Pastor Jenkins cleared his throat.

"Brothers and sisters... today, we talk about letting go. About finding courage to walk away from sin, from deception, from being unequally yoked."

Evelyn beamed beside Denny, her hand resting gently on his.

"And sometimes," the preacher said, "God whispers. He whispers, 'Son, you tried. You reached out. You waited. But now you must protect your family.'"

Denny stood and interrupted, both hands raised to the sky palm up.

"I have a testimony."

The sanctuary fell to hush.

"You go ahead son, testify and let the Lord speak through you!" Jenkins punched the air as he spoke, spittle flying from his lips that was quickly followed by sweat from his meaty hands.

"I wanted to reconcile. God knows I did. But when the mother of my child brings dangerous men into her home, flaunts brokenness, and poisons a boy's soul with indecency..." he paused, letting the weight of his words settle, "I must act."

Murmurs.

Heads nodded, a few of the parishioners looked down at their phones, turning the screen to their neighbors. The images of Flex were on each of their phones. Not just the two that were sent to Beth, but many more, some showing dancing, but others him fully nude and engaging in sexual encounters.

Maddie smiled, her work with AI was top notch, those years of computer science at Junior College weren't totally wasted.

"God has shown me that the path forward is clear. I will pursue full custody. I will rescue my son from this den of sin."

Amens echoed. Evelyn clapped, tears forming.

Pastor Jenkins stepped forward, wrapped an arm around Denny.

"Let the church stand behind our brother in Christ," he said. "Let us pray for the courts to see truth and restore order to this family."

Beth wasn't there to hear it, but the echo would soon reverberate over the community soon enough. It would move with the force of a tsunami crashing over a beach stopping for nothing and taking down anything in its path.

The joint was halfway respectable, in the way that only places with roadhouse jukeboxes and booths sticky with old beer could be. Country music crackled from speakers overhead, not too loud to drown a conversation, just enough to make every truth sound like a lie and every lie sound like a confession.

Denny nursed a whiskey at a corner booth marked by shadow. Maddie sat beside him, silent, her hair curled and her dress too short for a Sunday evening. She stared at the tabletop, the corner of her lip red and puffy.

The door of the roadhouse creaked open. I let in a

summer breeze that stirred up the prevalent scent of beer, sweat, and urine from the men's room. Maddie hated this place.

Pastor Jenkins walked in first, suit jacket slung over one shoulder like a man who'd spent his afternoon carrying burdens he didn't ask for. Behind him came Judge Ernest Porter, slow-moving and meat-thick around the waist, his linen suit wrinkled like it'd been balled up in the back of a car.

"Well," Jenkins said, sliding into the booth across from Denny, "Ain't this a sweet little reunion."

"Like old times," Denny said, grinning.

Porter dropped into the booth beside the pastor and let out a low groan. "God, my back. You know we ain't twenty-two anymore, right?"

"We were devils at twenty-two," Jenkins said, chuckling darkly. "Drunk, horny, and fully convinced the world owed us something."

"No," Porter added, lighting a cigar, "we just knew the women did."

Denny laughed, leaning back like a man in full control of the room. "You remember that blonde from Delta Chi? The one with the braces and a pussy that smelled like bad decisions?"

"Which one?" Jenkins grinned. "You'll have to be more specific."

Porter let out a wheezing laugh. "Hell, we left a trail of regrets up and down that dorm. Whole sorority house probably got a few kids named after us." He slapped the table and winked at Maddie.

"World was simpler back then," Jenkins said. "No social media. No evidence."

"No consequences," Denny muttered, his tone shifting.

Porter narrowed his eyes. "Ain't that the truth."

Maddie shifted in her seat, but no one looked at her.

She was furniture to them, breathing, pretty, and disposable.

"You know," Jenkins said, swirling the ice in his glass, "this generation? They got too many feelings. Everyone's wounded. Everyone's triggered. Can't even touch a girl's waist without being accused of sin."

"Sin used to be fun," Denny said, smirking.

Maddie stood suddenly, muttering something about the restroom. No one stopped her.

"She's not gonna hold," Porter said once she was gone. "That one's soft. Pretty, but soft. You need to control her better."

Denny shrugged. "She is useful."

"That's what they're for," Jenkins said matter-of-factly. "Their purpose is in service, in obedience. Eve wasn't made with her own rib, after all."

Porter leaned in then, his voice a gravel whisper.

"You're sure about this court order?"

"Kid's mine," Denny replied. "She's running around with a dancer-turned-fireman. You really think a family court in Alabama's gonna let that stand once we put the right words in the file?"

"I've got the motion ready," Porter said, patting the envelope. "But I want it known, once I sign it, I expect favors."

"Same ones we always delivered," Jenkins said, raising his glass.

They clinked.

Porter leaned forward, "That one, Maddie. I want her again, tied up and blind folded. I want her for a night by myself, you two not there. I want some me time."

Denny smiled, "You got it Judge, a little piece of Maddie pie for the win!"

And for a moment, the laughter stopped.

Because they all remembered something.

Something unspoken. Something old. Something buried under years of handshakes and prayers and backroom deals.

"Remember spring formal, '06?" Jenkins asked quietly.

Denny looked down at his glass. "Yeah."

Porter blew out a line of smoke. "I do too. No one ever asked what happened to her. You know that?"

Jenkins leaned back, lips thinning.

"They don't ask," he said, "because the answers are ours. And that's how it's always been."

Maddie returned a moment later, mascara smudged slightly, smile forced.

"Everything good?" she asked, voice a little too high.

Denny looked up at her with lazy ownership.

"Everything's perfect, baby."

She slid beside him.

The pastor turned to her.

"You believe in forgiveness, don't you Maddie?"

She blinked, unsure.

"Yes, sir."

"Good. Then don't forget what we're all forgiving you for."

Her face fell as the men laughed and drank, their voices carried them through the night and into Monday morning.

None of the men looked at her again, she sat in private shame. She told herself she could manage this. She told herself that she would take a hit. There was no turning back for her, she had gone too far.

9

SPLINTERS IN THE LIGHT

The email came around 10 am, the children were at recess, and she sat at her desk, preparing for the final moments of the day. The message was simple, they'd asked her to come in after school hours, not in her classroom or the principal's office, but in the old conference room where faded portraits of Tanner's founding educators watched from the walls like somber jurors.

She messaged her sister and asked if she would be able to pick up Jupiter while she took the meeting. A simple thumbs up sealed the plans and she went about her day. After small talk with Maddie and a kiss on his cheeks she waved her son away and turned to find out what this last-minute meeting was all about.

She walked into the room to see the characters she would expect, principal, vice-principal, but the others she did not know. Beth sat on one side of the long table, hands folded, palms damp with nervous sweat. Across from her, Principal Givens, three board members, and a

PTA rep sat with neatly stacked folders and guarded expressions.

Givens spoke first, "First, thank you for taking this meeting last minute, we know that you are busy with your little man. Second, this meeting is not an ambush."

Beth squinted her eyes at that, announcing that the meeting was not an ambush was the definitive way to know that it was an ambush.

He continued, "We have been made aware of accusations of improper conduct by a regular at the school, firefighter Berry Wallace. We understand that he has spent more time with your classroom than others, and that there may be a relationship outside of work between you."

"Is that a question?"

"No, a statement. Parents are upset, Mrs. Johnson is leading the charge and we need everyone on the same page as to how to deal with this."

Beth clinched her jaw, "Get ahead of what, exactly? Let's make sure we are all on the same page her."

"Very well, to get ahead of the claims that a regular volunteer at our school, and the possible romantic partner of one of our teachers, is engaging in lewd conduct and may, or may not, be a prostitute."

"Are you serious!" She leaned forward and made eye contact with everyone in the room. "You believe that this man is... is... a prostitute?! I know exactly what you are talking about and to be blunt, what he did in his past in no one's business, and why exactly would my relationship with him be discussed in this room?"

"We just want to get ahead of... the optics," Givens

said, trying to sound sympathetic. "Of course, no one is accusing you of anything inappropriate, Elizabeth."

But that wasn't true. Not really. The implication hung in the air like the stale coffee someone had brewed an hour ago and forgot to drink.

"Someone anonymously sent the images to the board," one of the members added. "They were traced to a public Facebook group but then deleted before moderators could intervene."

Beth didn't ask what images. She knew. Flex, shirtless. Flex dancing. Flex in a photo she hadn't seen before, nude, artfully posed, but unmistakably him. The pictures were on her phone now, in a text message from an unknown sender.

"It has no bearing on his character, and he does not deserve to be judged by anyone, in this room or anywhere else." Beth said softly. "And it certainly doesn't reflect on me."

A pause. A shared glance between the board members.

"We understand you've developed... a relationship with Mr. Berry Wallace and from your comments this afternoon we believe that might be the case," another board member said. "Outside of school that is."

She swallowed, she could deny this, say that no she could say they are just friends, but if she denied him now... if she denied him now she would not be able to ever look in his eyes again. "Yes."

"The PTA is concerned that your personal choices might become a distraction in the classroom. Jupiter's...

situation, the local rumors, the church... it's all adding up."

Beth felt a flush crawl up her neck. Not embarrassment, anger. Quiet, aching rage. Her personal life was being dismantled, not by facts, but by whispers and people in pews who never once asked if she was okay.

"What exactly, do church rumors have to do with this school?"

"Look Beth, we don't like this any more than you do. The fact is we would rather not be having this conversation, but we are. There is large contingent of this town that are very religious and they have publicly stated that they want to see Mr. Wallace removed as a fire fighter, and to be quite frank, to remove you as a teacher."

Beth sat back, heart sinking and the air in her lungs feeling like lead dragging her down into the water. She did not say much for the remainder of the meeting. She listened as options for her to consider were laid out with one theme repeated, end any relationship she had with Flex.

When the meeting ended, they didn't fire her. But she left with something worse, an unspoken warning. Behave. Distance yourself. Quiet down by taking the focus away from the school.

She stepped into the late afternoon sun with shoulders hunched and vision blurred by unshed tears. The heat clung to her skin, and even the familiar sound of children playing at recess on the far side of the building couldn't break the heaviness in her chest.

That night, she tucked Jupiter in with less laughter than usual. He didn't act upset, but something in him seemed quieter, like he'd caught the echo of the adult world's cruelty.

She sat and brushed his golden blond hair off his forehead. "You want me to read you a story?"

"No momma, I..." His voice choked and the beginning of a tear welled up in his eyes.

"What is it baby?"

"Bryce came over to Aunt Maddie's this afternoon."

"Ok, well did something happen between you two. You seem to get along well."

He looked at her through watered eyes. "I hit him."

This took Beth by surprise, "Why did you hit him, that is not like you."

"He said something bad."

"What did he say baby?"

"He said Mr. Flex took his clothes off," Jupiter whispered as he pulled the blanket around him tighter.

Beth froze. "Where did he hear that?"

"Bryce said he heard his momma talk about it at the gas station. She told Bryce not to play with me no more, he came over to Aunt Maddie's house anyways, but he said he can't come to our house anymore. He said that he heard that you do bad stuff with Mr. Flex too"

Beth's breath caught. "Jupiter... none of that is true. Or it doesn't matter, not the way they think."

He nodded, eyes wide. "I still like Mr. Flex."

"I do too," she whispered, brushing a hand through his hair. "I really do. He has been nice to mommy and to you."

"I don't want my friends to be in trouble for coming to play." The wet eyes turned to streams as the damn broke and the fears of a child rolled down his cheek. "I want to play with Mr. Flex too."

She leaned down and squeezed him tight, "Look baby, I need you to do something for me O.K.? Can you do something for mommy?"

He nodded his head as the tears continued to fall, and a trail of clear fluid started its path out of his nose.

She used her thumb to wipe his nose and absently wiped it on his blanket, "This is big people stuff, you remember when we talked about mommy and daddy and big people things that little ones don't need to worry about?"

He continued to nod, lips pursed and face red in his attempt to stop the emotion.

"I need you to do what mommy said before, trust mommy. O.K., things like this happen and all you have to do is trust that mommy will take care of it, and you." She said this with a locked gaze on her little man.

He nodded and she lay down beside him, pulling him in as his body pushed the hot tears out. She lay there and wanted help, she wanted a partner with her to tell her this would be alright, to tell her to trust in them, but she didn't. Tonight, she was alone and had to be the foundation for this little man to stand on.

When he fell asleep, she quietly got up and walked to the front door to ensure that the porch light was on. She felt safe when that light was glowing, and it did glow. She crossed her arms over her chest and walked over to the little couch and sat down. She pulled her knees into her chest; arms wrapped around her legs and buried her head in between.

That is when her own tears came out, this day, this long fucking day had ground her down and she let the frustration flow. She knew who was ultimately behind this, she knew the man who was still trying to control her life and punish her for walking away. She knew and she hated.

She fell asleep this way, lost in tormented dreams of the past and haunted by the hurt that she saw in her son's eyes, the eyes of a boy who saw his father hurt his mother and now saw the shining glow of a new role model tarnish. She slept and the house creaked, adding its own pained sounds to her own.

She awoke the next morning to a call. The screen showed the familiar face and simple title, Mom. The call was not answered, but was soon followed up with text, *I am coming over.*

Two days passed and Flex had not called.

Beth told herself that was okay, that he was giving her space, like she'd asked in her rushed text the day before: *Things are a little crazy. Need to breathe. Give me a minute.*

But every hour that passed made her wonder if the rumors had reached him too. If the photos had torn something between them that even their truth couldn't patch.

She stood on her porch, arms wrapped around herself, staring at the swaying branches of the front yard Sycamore tree as if it might offer some sign. Evelyn's words still echoed from two days earlier:

"You've made a spectacle of yourself, Elizabeth. Men don't want damaged women, women who leave their husband and take up with deviant men."

Beth had laughed. Right there at the kitchen table, with a mug of cooling coffee in her hand and her mother glaring across the rim of her glasses.

"I'd rather be damaged and whole," Beth said. "Then perfect and hollow like you want me to be."

Franklin had been silent, as always. He fiddled with the sugar jar, stared into his cup, and refused to pick a side. He sat at her table and listened as his wife cut his daughter down to the core.

Her family was falling apart from the inside, and Maddie hadn't returned any of her texts. She was absent, and silence began to speak louder than any betrayal. She wondered if her sister believed that she was the harlot her mother made her out to be. Maddie had always been there for her, but where was she now.

She needed to sit, to think, to not be watched or judged or dissected.

The swing creaked as she lowered herself into it, and for once, the sound didn't comfort her.

She missed Flex. She missed his smile and the way

that his presence made her mind feel at ease. She wanted to see him and smell his scent.

But right now, she didn't know if missing him was enough. The swing brought no comfort; she had a desire to move. She stood up and went inside to get ready but thought "to hell with it" she did not care how she looked; she needed to walk.

Flex parked a half-block away from Beth's house and killed the engine.

The firehouse was quiet tonight, no alarms, no sirens, but inside him, a different kind of bell was ringing. Not the kind that sent you barreling through smoke-choked hallways, but the kind that warned you something tender might be burning just the same.

He hadn't heard from Beth in two days. Not really. Her last message had been vague, distant.

Give me a minute.

He'd given her two days. And now he was sitting outside her street, feeling like a teenager trying to guess if the porch light meant "come on in" or "stay the hell away."

He thumbed his phone. Still no response to the picture he'd sent, him holding a grocery-store bouquet of sunflowers and a silly card with a dinosaur on it. Something Jupiter would like. Something she would laugh at.

He wasn't laughing now.

Instead, he scrolled back through the images that

had been sent to him by an unknown number two nights ago.

A screenshot of him dancing; young, dumb, carefree, wearing less than he should've. Then another. Fully nude. Lit by stage lights. A photo he didn't remember being taken. And then one that had clearly been altered, his head photoshopped onto someone else's body. Too perfect, too clean. A fake. But it didn't matter.

Someone had dug deep. Someone wanted him gone.

He'd heard about the board meeting. Word travels fast in small towns, faster still when it's bad.

Flex leaned his head back against the truck seat and stared through the windshield, past the bugs gathering under the streetlamp, into the question that wouldn't stop echoing: "Is she ashamed of me?"

A loud knock on the driver's side window made him jump.

He turned and a lump caught in his throat, like some sort of magic his thoughts had conjured up the woman that he needed. There, knocking on his window was Beth.

She stood there in thong sandals, sweatpants, and an old university t-shirt with her arms crossed. Her face was unreadable. Not angry, not soft. Guarded.

He rolled the window down.

"You some kind of creep sitting out here on my street?"

"What, no, I just..."

She held her hands up palms out and a hard look on her face, "Save it."

He stared out her, confused at this interaction. "I.."

156

"I said save it, besides, I am just messing with you." She did not smile, but her face softened a little and those little lines at the corners of her eyes reappeared.

He sighed and smiled, "God, I thought I was in for it."

"Well, you might still be after you explain why you are creeping around out here. You gonna sit out here all night like some lovesick bloodhound?" she asked.

He managed a small laugh. "Wasn't sure I had clearance to land."

She tilted her head. "You could've knocked."

"You might not have answered."

They stared at each other for a moment. Her jaw twitched like she was weighing her next breath.

Finally, she stepped back. "Come on. But I'm not putting on a bra."

He killed the engine and followed her down the block and into the yard with the flowers of the crepe myrtle next to the porch blowing across the lawn and the leaves of the sycamore tree signing in the wind. Up the worn and creaking porch, past the light that glowed in the dark whenever he drove by.

She put one hand on the doorknob and reached back with the other, it was an invitation to come with her. The feel of their hands touching sent electricity up his fingertips that exploded throughout his body, her soft hand took his she led him through the door and his heart thrummed at the connection and potential of being allowed, not into her life, but to have a chance of a chance. She led; he followed.

The living room was dim, lit only by a table lamp and the blue glow of a cartoon playing on mute for Jupiter, who had fallen asleep sideways on the couch. One sock on, the other missing, as always.

Beth tucked a blanket over him, then walked past Flex without looking.

He followed her into the kitchen.

She turned and leaned against the counter, folding her arms. "So. Who dug up your Chippendales days?"

Flex smirked but shook his head. "I didn't even know that photo existed. The nude one's fake. The dancing... yeah, that was me. A long time ago. I was nineteen. Trying to keep food on the table and gas in the truck."

She stared hard at him, "I'm not judging you."

"Feels like everyone else is."

Beth picked up the coffee pot, poured herself a cup, and stared into the steam. "It wasn't the photo that got to me," she said. "It was the reminder."

"Of what?"

"That people will do anything to make me feel small. Make *you* feel dirty. Make Jupiter feel like he doesn't belong."

Flex nodded. "I think I know who sent them."

Beth arched a brow. "You do?"

"Don't you?"

She paused, "I think..."

"You know."

"Denny." Beth felt her stomach turn, she already

came to this conclusion but to say it out loud may it real, and the thought of her ex digging at Flex to punish her made her sick. "You must hate me"

Flex didn't answer immediately, "Why would you say that?"

Beth sat down slowly at the kitchen table. "He is trying to hurt me and the only way to do that is to hurt you. He knows that I care about you, and he will do whatever it takes to make me pay for leaving him."

He was lost for a moment, stuck on four words that she said, *"I care about you."* When he spoke it was soft, "You care about me?"

She looked up and looked at him, "You think a girl in sweats, and no bra is going to bring a man into her house and see her that way if she didn't?

He smiled and stared.

"He wants to do whatever it takes to bring me down, to make me pay. He wants a war."

"Yeah," Flex said ominously. "And he just fired the first real shot. This will get rough, he probably has more practice, you know a dog that bites once, has probably bit before."

That Sunday would come with fire and thunder in the pulpit, the type of noise that would stir the passions of the faithful and bring down the fabled Walls of Jericho.

Denny walked into Tanner Southern Baptist dressed in his best, blue-gray suit, crisp white shirt, and a silk tie the color of repentance. Evelyn clutched his arm like a trophy. Maddie walked behind them in a pastel dress that looked one size too small and wearing more makeup than a mannequin in a store front display, the kind of makeup that would hide a blemish, or a bruise.

The sanctuary was already full. Word had gotten out.

Denny was going to speak about the current zeitgeist rolling around town. By now, everyone had either heard of the dancing fire fighter, or had seen pictures of his escapades. All were split into two camps, either appalled that this despicable man was around their children at school, or aroused at his physique in the pictures.

Pastor Jenkins took the stage and offered his usual welcome, a few scattered verses, and then nodded to Denny who walked up with practiced humility.

Beth came today and sat frozen in her pew, estranged from her family and appalled that they arrived with this man, this monster who beat her in front of her son. Jupiter beside her coloring on a kid's bulletin. She hadn't told anyone what she suspected about the photos, that they were faked by the man who was walking like a pilgrim to the alter, and she sure as hell hadn't expected Denny to do what he did next.

"I want to thank the Lord for opening my eyes," Denny began, clasping the mic. "For revealing to me that it's time to let go."

A murmur rolled through the pews.

"I've chased the wrong things. I've prayed for reconciliation. For my family. For my son. But God has shown me that sometimes, we're called not to rebuild what's broken, but to protect what still can be saved."

He turned his gaze toward Beth.

"I cannot, in good conscience, allow my son to remain in a house of sin. With a woman who welcomes half-naked men into her home. A woman whose values now stand against this community, against the church, against God Himself."

A gasp.

Beth sat in place, burning, but too stunned to move.

"I have petitioned the court for sole custody to save my son so he can be brought up in a Christian home that values the love of our God and his son Jesus Christ!" he continued, "I ask this congregation to pray for that outcome. Pray that I may raise my son in the light."

Pastor Jenkins stepped up, nodding slowly. "We support you, brother. And we will stand with you. It is a brave thing to walk away from temptation and choose righteousness. We will also pray for another member of our congregation."

He pointed at Beth, "Will you allow this to continue? Will you allow your son to be exposed to this depravity! GOD KNOWS YOUR HEART!"

Beth sank, all eyes had turned to her, Jupiter sat fixated on his father standing next to Pastor Jenkins. A look of horror that was soon replaced with the aura of a decision made. He took his small hand and placed it on top of his mother's as she looked around in horror at the faces of the judgement that was being heaped upon her.

She watched but no longer heard, she felt like she did the night her head hit the wall and saw the same burning anger in Denny's eyes that burned that night. She was ashamed and she did not hear the members of the congregation demand that she be removed from the church, or that they should march to the firehouse and demand that this sinner be removed. The false cries of those she loved condemning her. The final thing that she did not hear, was that of her mother standing and walking up with Denny as she asked the church to pray for her and to ask God to forgive her for failing to raise her right.

She heard none of that. When blood returned to her face she stood quietly, with the sound of fire and brimstone being heaped upon her and she smiled. Gently, her hand wrapped around Jupiter's and walked him out of the church. They walked past the eyes and the looks of disgust through the double doors and out to her car.

She buckled Jupiter in and walked around to her door, opened and sat down. As she pulled her door closed a hand reached in to stop her. She looked up into the face of evil that was wrecking her world and that face smiled. Denny stood there and pulled the door open, stepped in, and kneeled beside her.

"I need you to know that this is not for show, this is personal, and you are my...project."

Anger flushed in her face and with a force she did not know was in her yelled, "GET THE FUCK AWAY FROM MY CAR!"

This surprised Denny, but only momentarily. He smiled like the Cheshire Cat, all teeth and no soul behind it. "That is what I like, a little fire, shame you didn't have that when we were married. Did you hear that, Jupiter? Did you hear Mommy's little tantrum?"

"Don't talk to him, you son-of-a-bitch! Don't you speak to him!"

Denny leaned in closer and said quietly, "He, like you, is my property. You might not understand that now, but you will. In the end, you will be begging me to take you back."

"Get the fuck out, before I call the cops, Denny. I will, so help me God, I will, and you will go back to prison."

"Well now, that is where you are wrong, you see I have taken care of all those little inconveniences and made sure they will never believe a little cunt like you. Did you hear that, Jupiter? Did you hear me call Mommy a cunt?"

Red-hot light was all she saw. She saw the red-hot light and heard nothing but her heartbeat. What she did not see was her right hand shoot out and slap Denny across the face. It was a clear shot that left fingerprints across his cheek and a trickle of blood at the corner of his mouth.

When her vision returned, she still saw that full toothed smile tinted red from the cut in his cheek. He smiled and said, "Thank you." Stood and walked away.

She shook as she put her car in reverse to back out. Looking in her rear-view mirror, her gaze fell upon Jupiter, and his bottom lip was shaking and tears were rolling down his cheeks. He did not whimper, or make any other sound, but his face said more than the greatest poet could write about sorrow. She saw this and her heart broke as her little man saw violence one more time.

That night, the honky tonk on the edge of town buzzed with the low thrum of bad country covers and cheaper beer.

Denny sat in a back booth, nursing a whiskey and coke and a sore jaw.

Across from him, Pastor Jenkins sipped sweet tea from a Mason jar. He didn't drink anymore, but he knew how to keep company, and next to them, grinning with too many teeth and none of them trustworthy, sat Judge Leroy Skinner.

The same man who'd presided over Beth's original protective order. The same man who'd once played safety on the same college football team as Denny and Jenkins.

"Still can't believe you quit the team after freshman year," Leroy said, slapping Denny on the back. "We were hell on wheels back then."

Denny laughed. "Still are, some days."

"Got that little envelope for me?" the judge asked, voice low, eyes sweeping the room.

Denny slid it across the table. It was fat and crisp and bound with a rubber band.

Skinner didn't count it. Just tucked it into the inside pocket of his linen coat. "I'll have that emergency order drafted Monday morning. You'll have Jupiter before the week's out. Let's not forget the other part to our little deal."

Denny chuckled, "You got it LeRoy, when do you want that little present?"

"No time better than now!"

Pastor Jenkins chuckled, slapped the table and said, "I always said the Lord helps those who help themselves."

"Damn right," Skinner muttered. "And women like Beth? They forget their place. Let them get too much freedom and pretty soon they're dragging half-dressed men into Sunday School."

"Beth always thought she was so fucking smart," Denny said, sipping his drink. "Time to remind her what happens when she forgets who writes the rules in this town."

LeRoy tapped his finger on his Rolex, "Aaannnnddddd."

Denny got out of the booth, walked over to the bar where Maddie was dutifully waiting and whispered in her ear. She turned and looked at the table and with a look of panic started to whisper back.

Denny shook his head and pointed to the table, she looked down at the floor, shook her head once again before she stood and walked to the booth. She looked at Judge Jenkins and in low breath, "I sure am tired Judge, would you please give me a ride home?"

"Well little lady, I would be happy to give you a ride." As he stood, he tapped a finger to his brow towards Denny who sat at the bar chatting up the new bartender. He paid no attention as they walked out. Maddie walked in front of the Judge and if you looked close enough you could see a faint tear forming in the corner of her eye. It only lasted a moment as she forced herself to hide within herself, this would be over quick enough, just another step on the path to the life she deserved.

Beth spent another night with little sleep, spending the majority of the night staring at the ceiling fan spinning overhead, its rhythm the only thing keeping her thoughts from breaking apart entirely. Each blade whispered a different fear. Denny's words from the church service still rang like hymnals twisted into threats.

The silence from Maddie was another issue that was louder than any scream, where her sister was and why was did she come with her mom and Denny. She knew the entirety of the history of domestic violence experienced, and still she stood by him.

Beneath both issues lay a photo, that damned photo to be exact.

It didn't matter if it was fake. It didn't matter if Flex had already explained it. In a town like Tanner, innuendo was a wildfire. Truth was just a branch in the path.

And she knew what was coming.

She felt it in her bones, in the way the very walls of her home pulsed with nervous heat, like they knew they might soon stop being hers.

She got out of bed just after 3 a.m., pulled a cardigan over her tank top, and wandered into the kitchen. The spoon was gone. The cracked one. She'd thrown it away.

But the ghost of it remained in the drawer like a phantom limb.

She made tea she wouldn't drink.

When the knock came at the door just before sunrise, she thought for a moment it was a dream.

But it came again, measured, polite, and completely wrong for the hour.

She opened it to find a man in a charcoal-gray suit and thick-rimmed glasses standing on her porch, holding a leather-bound folder.

"Bethany Keller?" he asked.

Beth pulled the cardigan tighter. "Yes?"

"I'm Marshall Keene, legal representative of the Jefferson County Family Court. I'm here to inform you that an Emergency Protection Petition has been filed by Mr. Denny Keller requesting temporary removal of the child Jupiter Keller into the sole care of the petitioner."

Beth's world tilted.

"No," she whispered.

"I'm afraid the order is already in motion," the man said, reaching into his satchel and handing her a paper. "A judge has signed off on an expedited hearing. You will have the opportunity to contest this within seventy-two hours."

Her hands trembled as she took the paper.

"I'm sorry," he said, with a glance at the porch light, still glowing above her like a fragile halo. "I don't like serving these kinds of notices. But it's the law."

Walking down the street, deputy in tow, was Denny. They approached the house and the world went dark; she did not pass out, but time passed in a way that she could not describe. When the world came back, it was a world gone wrong. Her little boy was in the backseat of his father's truck and the deputy was speaking to her about her rights.

Beth didn't speak as he turned and left. She stood in the doorway long after the hum of his tires faded down the road.

Inside, the tea had grown cold.

Later that morning, Flex was at the firehouse garage when his phone rang. One look at the screen told him it wasn't good.

Beth.

He answered quickly, wiping grease off his hands. "Hey..."

"I need you," she said, her voice hoarse. "Now."

He was already moving.

When he arrived, he found her on the porch, shaking. Not crying. Not breaking. But close.

He didn't ask what happened. She handed him the paper.

He read it, his jaw tightening. "He's making his move."

"He already made it."

Flex looked up. "We'll fight this."

Beth shook her head. "He's got Maddie. He's got Evelyn. He's got the church. And now, apparently, he's got the judge, and he took my little boy."

"You've got me, I am here, I will help."

"That's not enough."

He didn't respond to that. Instead, he placed a hand on her shoulder.

"Then we find the cracks," he said. "And we break him at the seams."

At noon, Beth drove to her parents' house.

The driveway was full, her father's pickup, Maddie's Civic, and her mother's ancient Lincoln parked at its usual angle like a ship run aground.

Beth knocked once before walking in.

The scent of fried chicken and Pine-Sol clung to the walls. Her mother sat at the table folding bulletins for next Sunday's service. Franklin read the newspaper like nothing had happened. Maddie appeared at the top of the stairs, in a black tank top and jeans, hair pulled into a careless bun.

Beth walked straight to the dining room.

Her voice was flat. "Did you help him do this?"

Evelyn looked up slowly. "I don't know what you're talking about."

"Don't lie to me, Mama."

Her mother gave a slow sigh and set the bulletins down. "Denny called. Said you were allowing a... man with an inappropriate past around Jupiter. Said he had photos."

Beth's lip curled. "And you believed him."

"I believe in redemption and I have seen the decisions you have made."

Beth took a step forward. "You believe in control. That's what this is about. He wants to own Jupiter. Own me. And you, both of you, are just happy to watch it happen if it means things go back to how they used to be."

Franklin looked up. "That's enough."

"No, it's not. Because this is my son. My goddamned life."

Maddie stepped into the room. "Maybe if you weren't so quick to act like the whole world's against you..."

Beth turned, ice in her voice. "Where the fuck have you been?"

Maddie's eyes narrowed. "I... I..."

"Doesn't matter, you stood with him, you know him, what he is capable of."

Maddie shrugged. "I'm just trying to keep Jupiter from growing up surrounded by scandal."

Beth's mouth twitched into a smile, cold and trembling. "Scandal?! You talk about scandal: how about we talk about your time living in Atlanta and how you made ends meet??!!"

Maddie went pale.

Evelyn stood abruptly. "That's enough! Both of you."

"No," Beth said, stepping back. "I just came to see how deep the rot went. Now I know."

She turned and walked out. No one followed her.

No one said goodbye.

That night, Flex found her sitting on the edge of the back porch, not in her normal swing on the front porch. The old wood creaked beneath his boots as he approached.

"You, okay?" he asked.

Beth didn't look up. "No."

He sat beside her.

"They think I'm broken," she whispered.

"They're scared of how strong you are."

A long silence followed.

Then, quietly, she asked, "Do you still want to take me out to dinner?"

Flex turned to her and nodded. "I want to do more than that."

She finally looked at him, and for the first time that day, the weight in her chest shifted. Didn't disappear, but loosened, just enough.

"Then help me fight," she said.

Flex didn't hesitate. "I already am."

Beth stood in front of her mirror, her fingers tightening the braid in her hair. The porchlight behind her shimmered through the bedroom window, throwing fractured light across her cheekbones. Her face looked different tonight, not because of makeup or exhaustion, but because of something deeper. Something recently born. She didn't look like a woman waiting anymore.

She looked like a woman preparing.

Downstairs, Flex was waiting in the kitchen, quiet but alert. The smell of reheated pizza filled the air, leftover from the night before, left sitting through the chaos of the morning. Even in the chaos, Flex had been there.

Beth came down the stairs in jeans and a blouse with small red birds printed over a white background. It wasn't much, but it was womanly, clean, real.

"Where we headed?" she asked.

Flex turned. His eyes flicked down her frame and softened. "Somewhere we won't get recognized."

Beth arched an eyebrow. "That narrows it down to about three places."

He grinned. "Then I picked the one with the strongest coffee and the most confusing jukebox."

They ended up at The Mended Bridge, a little restaurant just outside the town limits, tucked off Highway 31. It wasn't exactly hidden, but it wasn't on most people's radar unless they knew the smell of pecan-wood smoke or the way the owner's dog greeted every table personally.

Beth and Flex sat at a small booth in the corner; beneath an old black-and-white photo of the original bridge the town was named after. Half the lights in the place flickered like they were ready to give up the ghost.

They talked.

Not about court dates. Not about Denny. Not about custody or fake photos or betrayals with last names.

They talked about music, about how Beth used to pretend to be a symphony conductor with a stick in the backyard, and how Flex once tried to learn acoustic guitar but broke the strings with his dance moves. They talked about childhood pets and weird southern sayings their grandparents used, and how Flex once believed "don't let the bedbugs bite" meant actual monsters lived in mattresses.

At one point, Beth said, "I don't even know what I want anymore."

Flex replied, "Then let's find out together."

And she almost cried from the simplicity of it. She almost cried because she knew that she was using Flex tonight, using him to forget that her son was taken from her today. Using him to forget that tonight she would not be able to tell him goodnight. She thought about this and immediately regretted the thoughts. She was using him, but not as a user, as a woman who needed the support of a partner, and she was glad that Flex was there.

When they pulled back into her driveway, the light over the porch was still glowing. A child's drawing of a firetruck had been taped to the inside of the front window by Jupiter, now asleep in another home, not here where he should be.

Flex parked the truck, and Beth laid her hand on his leg.

"I want to show you something," she said.

He followed her inside, and she led him to a narrow hallway just past the laundry room. At the end of it, hung crookedly between two light switches, was a framed picture.

Beth lifted it off the wall and handed it to him.

It was a crayon drawing, Jupiter's handiwork. It showed three stick figures. One small, one tall with big muscles, and one with a big yellow sun for hair. The sun-hair woman was holding both stick hands. Above it, in capital letters: "MY SAFE TEAM."

Flex's throat tightened.

"He drew that last week," Beth said. "Said he wanted to put it by the front door so anyone who came in would know who lived here."

Flex traced the little figures with his thumb.

Beth looked up at him and whispered, "I want to believe this can be real."

He met her eyes. "Then we make it real."

She leaned into him. This kiss was not soft or curious like the one before. It was solid. Earned. It lingered, not as a question, but as a promise.

They didn't make love that night. They held each other. Skin to skin. Mouth to collarbone. Just breathing. And Flex whispered, "You don't have to carry this alone anymore."

Beth fell asleep with her head on his chest, Jupiter's drawing still in his hands.

The next morning, the first ripple of justice came from the unlikeliest place.

Beth opened her inbox to a message marked

"anonymous." No name. Just a single line and an attachment.

"He's done this before. And it wasn't just photos."

Attached were legal records, sealed, but leaked, nonetheless. A juvenile case. Denny's name on it. A file from his early twenties. A sealed complaint by a teenage girl alleging misconduct, intimidation, and coercion. Suppressed. Buried. Until now.

Beth read every word.

She went to the bedroom where Flex still slept and slid beside him.

"Flex," she said when his eyes opened, "we have something."

"We have what?"

IO

ASH IN THE ROOTS

The house was too quiet now. Not peaceful, but hollow, like something sacred had been carved out and left gaping. Beth walked through the kitchen on bare feet, tea gone cold on the counter, toast still sitting in the toaster. She hadn't hit the lever. The bread sat in its holder in a state of unmade, its purpose not being fulfilled much like this mother who sat without her precious son.

It had been thirty-two hours since Jupiter sat in Denny's truck driving away from his refuge of safety and into the unknown wilderness of chaos that was his father's trademark.

She hadn't spoken to him. Not heard his voice. Not seen the wild halo of his morning hair or had to remind him to brush his teeth twice because the first time didn't count if he just swished the brush around his lips like a paint roller.

Thirty-two hours without his smell. His weight on the couch beside her. His noise.

And now... silence.

Flex stayed most of the weekend. He didn't try to fix her. Didn't tell her to sleep. He was simply there doing the dishes, folding a load of laundry she didn't remember starting, standing by the door when she cried and needed the porch.

Today, though, he was at work. Another house fire on the north side of Tanner. She didn't ask for details. She didn't want to think about fires right now.

Her phone buzzed.

A text from an unknown number. But this one wasn't cruel, it wasn't another piece of sabotage. It was a link. No caption. Just a URL to a private Dropbox.

Beth clicked it before she could second-guess herself.

Scrolling through the files she saw photos, surveillance stills, emails, but more importantly an invoice from Dixson Private Investigations to their customer, Maddie Keller. Her sister had worked directly with a private investigator. She helped Denny gather the photos, the videos, the fabricated documents.

Beth's stomach flipped.

She sat down hard in one of the kitchen chairs and stared at the screen. A voice memo attached to one of the emails loaded automatically.

It was Maddie's voice.

"She's fragile. She thinks this guy loves her. But she's not thinking straight. Just get the proof. She'll thank me someday."

Beth didn't throw the phone. She wanted to. But she didn't.

Instead, she picked it up and called Franklin.

He answered on the third ring. "Hello?"

"I need you to come to my house," Beth said, her voice flat.

"Right now?"

"Yes. And bring Maddie."

There was a long silence.

"Beth..."

"Bring her, Daddy. Now."

Beth stood on her porch performing her now perfunctory routine of pacing, pacing and running her fingers along the smooth paint on top of cracked wooden railing. It was teetering at ninety-five degrees Fahrenheit, but the burning rage coursing through her made the air feel cool.

She paced and watched until a red SUV pulled up and parked in her front yard. She scowled as the occupants looked in her direction and stormed into her house. They would meet her on her terms. She sat in the kitchen, the kitchen with bread still in the toaster that was not toast.

The door opened and Franklin walked in first, he saw that all the plantation shutters were closed and lights off making the house, even though it was midday, seem dark and imposing. The only light on in the house was in the kitchen and its glow lit up Beth from above casting long shadows under her eyes, making her seem more imposing than normal.

Maddie followed behind her father, still wearing too much make up to hide the secret injuries that she was incurring by Denny and his friends. The makeup hid these injuries, but it was her stubborn will and idea that it would all be worth it to have a new lifestyle that hid the injuries deep down, the injuries to her soul from being used as a sex object by a man who should care about her, the disgust she felt at herself for allowing herself to be passed around by him to his friends. She stopped midway through the living room and stared at Beth with a sense of lingering horror at what would come.

Beth didn't speak first.

Franklin, "What is it, Elizabeth? Why did you need us so urgently?"

Beth still did not speak, instead she lifted a stack of freshly printed documents and laid them on the table. She stared at them and looked up at her sister with a fire burning in her eyes that would melt stone. She waved them forward and they came.

Franklin stood at the table's edge and looked down at the papers, sliding them aside one at a time and then paused at the last document, the invoice with his other daughter's name. It took a moment to process, and Franklin stood there.

Beth then held up her phone and pressed play on the saved audio file and played the recording between Maddie and the Private Investigator. When it completed a single tear rolled down her chin.

Franklin turned slowly to Maddie who still stood in the living room, who stood there with the look of a cornered animal, one who was caught and did not expect to survive.

Maddie mouthed a few worlds lowly with a sound

that barely competed with the normal creaking of the house, "I didn't know he was gonna do that," she said.

Beth, tear still wet on her face replied, "Why."

The silence stretched like a wire between them. In the kitchen, Franklin shifted uncomfortably and then sat in one of the glittery red vinyl seats, face white as his normally high blood pressure dropped as he felt the cracks in his beloved family and the bond of sisters being torn apart.

"He told me you were unstable. That you were losing Jupiter anyway," Maddie whispered. "I didn't know he'd take him like that."

Beth's hands balled into fists at her sides. "You think it's okay to send nude photos of someone to your sister because you believed a man who beat her bloody? You know who Denny is, you stood holding my hand in the god damned emergency room! MY SON, YOU HELPED HIM TAKE MY SON!"

"I didn't send..." She tried to reply and then faltered, trailing off and still staring ahead, still reeling from the shock of being found out. This was not how it was supposed to go, she was supposed to have the new life and then gloat over her sister, not standing here, on trial, and certainly not in front of her father.

"You hired the private investigator!" Beth snapped.

Maddie's eyes glistened. "He said you were gonna ruin Jupiter's life. That you were sleeping with someone dangerous. He made it sound like I was protecting him."

"You were protecting Denny," Beth said coldly. "Like Mama. Like half this town."

This sank in the air like a lead balloon for a moment

and she continued with a thought just formed in her mind, "Was momma part of this?"

Franklin cleared his throat. "Beth..."

"No," Beth turned on him. "You don't get to sit there and say nothing anymore. I'm not asking you to stand on a street corner and hold a sign. I'm asking you to look me in the eye and tell me you know what he is, what they did."

Franklin finally looked up, pain in his expression. "I know what he is."

Maddie's voice cracked. "I just wanted to help."

Beth's jaw tightened. "Then help me now. Testify. Tell the judge everything. What you knew. What you saw. That you were used. That he sent those photos to hurt me and win custody."

"I can't," Maddie said. "Not yet. If I do, he'll tell Mama everything. About Atlanta. About... all of it."

Beth narrowed her eyes. "You're still letting him hold your past like a leash."

Tears spilled down Maddie's cheeks. "I don't want to lose everything."

"You already did," Beth said, moving past her. "The minute you helped him hurt my son."

Maddie, overcoming the shock, stood tall and yelled back, "You hurt your son when you brought that pervert into your life! He deserves better than you and the little piece of shit that you call a home."

She turned without another word and walked out the front door leaving Franklin and Maddie in her wake.

Beth did not say another word; she looked down at the table. Franklin, lost and with no idea of what to do, reached out his hand to lay on top of Beth's. She moved as he approached and looked at him with eyes that condemned him, with eyes that said, "you may not have been a part of this, but you sat by and did nothing."

Franklin stood and left alone; Maddie had left walking on her own.

Beth picked up her phone and sent a simple message to Flex, "I need you, please."

Maddie walked like woman possessed through the little town of Tanner, past the empty firehouse and to a little house that she was beginning to know as her own. In the driveway sat a black pickup truck and she smiled. Denny was home.

She walked up to the front door and entered the code he gave her, 6969, his little joke.

She came inside and sat her purse down and called out, "Denny, where are you, baby?"

There was no reply, but as she walked to the back of the house, she heard the sound of music coming from the bedroom. Smiling she opened the door and said, "You will not belie..."

Her voice failed and her heart stopped; Denny stood beside the bed fully nude. He stood over another woman, a woman who was lying on the bed wearing black stockings with her hands cuffed behind her back. She was wearing those black stockings and red lashes from the small whip that Denny held in his hands and nothing more. The woman on the bed did not look surprised; her lips twisted in a sly smile that said she knew she had taken her man.

Standing there looking on, Maddie processed what was happening. Denny, her sister's ex, her lover, had another woman in his bed, and not just any woman, but the bartender that Denny was talking to the night he forcefully sent her home to service Judge Skinner.

Denny smiled, "Look at this, perfect timing! Take your clothes off and get in bed with my new friend!"

Maddie screamed inside, how could he! He was supposed to care for her; she did everything for him, gave up so much. "Who the fuck is this?"

"Told you, my friend, your new friend."

She walked over and slapped Denny, "You are cheating on me! You stupi..."

Maddie did not see it coming as Denny punched her in the belly. She doubled over and dropped to her knees, gagging. The woman on the bed screamed and slid off backwards, hands still cuffed struggling to get free as she ran to the bathroom.

Denny kneeled beside her, "Cheat. I did not cheat on you." His face was close enough for her to feel the heat of his breath and smell the bourbon that he was consuming. "You would have to mean something to me; you would have to be a person to me for me to CHEAT on you."

She tried to get the courage up to fight, but the confrontation with Beth, the shock of walking in on this left her defeated. She said lowly and full of shame, "I did everything for you; I gave up so much for you, did... things for you."

"Fucked my friends for me is what you mean." He grinned demonically at this and decided that now was the point to inflict the most damage. "You were just a tool, a piece of ass for me and my friends. You did your part and riled up your sister, got her so mad that she slapped me in public, you kept my hands clean working with the PI, and now I am done with you."

"What..." she looked up at him pitifully, the words striking her in a way that a physical hit could not.

"Sorry, can you not understand me?" He laughed and looked away into the bathroom then back at Maddie, "You mean nothing more to me than she does, you are both just pieces of ass to me. I can replace any of you whenever I want."

"You wanted me..."

Denny started pacing and laughing, his penis still erect and bouncing as he walked, "How could I ever want a woman that will fuck my friends on command-you are no better than any other prostitute working 1st Ave."

Tears rolled angrily down Maddie's face, "You lied to me, you son-of-a-bitch, I will tell ev..."

"Let me just go ahead and stop you right there." He walked over and picked up his phone, thumbed through it and then walked over and knelt behind her, his arms stretched around, and his genitals roughly pressed into her back. On the screen were pictures, pictures of Maddie blind folded with two men having sex with her and as he scrolled, she saw more, pictures of her having sex with Denny, pictures of her in her twenties, pictures of her when she lived in Atlanta and was caught by Denny stripping.

Her heart stopped, she did not know he had any of these pictures, she felt trapped, like her hamstrings had been cut leaving her stranded with no way to escape.

"You see, little bitch, little fuck toy. I own you." He stood abruptly and grabbed her by the hair dragging her backwards and towards the living room. The woman in the bathroom screamed as Denny let his inner monster out and he did to Maddie what he had done to Beth.

Maddie lay on the floor crying when he was finished. Her lips were split, her eyes bruised, but her soul was destroyed. She did not cry because of the assault, she cried because of the betrayal she had been a part of. She cried because she was alone, alone because her greed overcame her sense and she betrayed her sister.

On the couch a little boy slept. He had not stirred during any of the events and did not see or hear any of the violence or perversion as it occurred. He slept because on the counter sat a half empty bottle of children's cough medicine and a bottle of Lortabs, the medicine that he was given by his father so he could celebrate with a bartender that meant nothing to him.

Maddie looked at Jupiter and her heart broke all over, she did this, she was responsible. She thought this as she was being picked up and pulled across the floor. She was left on the garage floor where she finally lost consciousness and fell into her own hellscape of dreams.

After the fire was resolved and his shift over Flex cleaned

up and drove to pick up Beth. He called after the fire, and she asked him to please go to the attorney with her.

By noon, they were seated in the modest office of a family law attorney named Rachel Dane, a tough-as-nails redhead who'd once famously thrown her own ex-husband's possessions off the courthouse steps in full view of the local news.

The office of Rachel Dane was buried in a converted ranch-style house outside of Alabaster. Inside her office appeared to be chaos incarnate with books stacked everywhere, photos of protest marches and courtroom showdowns lining the walls. The kind of place that smelled of legal pads, potpourri, and lemon pledge.

Rachel sat behind a desk carved from a single log; it was stained a red so dark that it almost appeared black. She sat waiting, like a lioness on her perch. She held the newly unsealed documents in one hand and an open bottle of ginger ale in the other. She read the file in silence, then looked up.

Beth was shaking. "Can you use it?"

"I've seen worse," she said. "But not by much. Let me ask you a question, do you want to go nuclear? I mean it, if you do we go all in, I don't represent losers. I don't think you are a loser, am I right?"

Beth nodded.

"Then buckle up," Rachel said. "Because when we're done, he won't be able to step foot in that church without people seeing the stain for what it is."

Flex sat in the corner, arms crossed, foot bouncing anxiously.

"But, and I do mean but... we need corroboration,"

Rachel continued. "If there's any chance of this getting thrown out as hearsay or unrelated history, we need to connect the dots."

"I can," Beth said. "He threatened me. At church. Outside my car. In front of Jupiter."

Rachel nodded. "And you have a witness?"

"Jupiter."

Rachel shook her head. "He's too young. We need someone who is an adult. Someone who can say they've seen Denny's tactics. Someone he's used, manipulated..."

"Maddie," Flex said quietly.

Beth blinked. "She will not help; you should have seen her as she left. I don't know what or why she helped him, but she is involved."

"Then we make her help," Flex said. "She is our only hope in this and she will give in."

The next morning, Flex found Maddie sitting alone on a bench behind Wester's Coffee Bean with a coffee she hadn't touched still steaming between her hands. It was morning but already eighty-nine degrees, but she was wearing sweatpants, a hoodie, and large sunglasses.

She jumped as she heard him approach.

"You look like someone stepped on your grave," he said as he approached. "I'm not here..." He paused when he got close enough to see the revealed portions of her face and he dropped to his knees. His first responder instincts kicking in and takin over. "What the hell happened to you."

Maddie gave him a hollow look. "I... I fucked up."

Flex reached over to take off the sunglasses and shuttered as he saw her eyes. "Who did this Maddie?"

"To tell you the truth. I did. It was my fault." She turned away, jaw tight.

Flex gently put a hand on her knee, "Who did this Maddie?"

"I thought he cared about me. I thought that if I..." She could not speak.

"Jesus Christ, Denny?"

She could only nod.

"Give me a minute, let me call the po..." he was interrupted by her with a panicked expression.

"No, you can't! You don't understand, no one will! He will kill me if I call the police!"

He stood up and looked down, "OK, then help me understand."

He looked on for a minute and she nodded. He sat down in the parking lot on the already too hot asphalt, and he listened. He listed as she told a story about her past as a dancer, about her jealousness and relationship with Denny. She told him about the investigator and how Denny used her as a sex puppet for the pastor and Jenkins. She told him this like the devout at confession, and she wept.

When she finished Flex took a moment to think and then gently, "You know what he's done. You know what he's still doing. You've seen Beth fall apart trying to shield Jupiter from it. You helped him hurt them both, and hurt you. But you can help fix it."

"You think it's that simple?" Maddie whispered.

"No. I think it's hard. I think it's terrifying. And I think it's worth it."

She looked at him. "Why do you even care?"

"Because I love them," Flex said simply. "And because you do too. Whether you admit it or not and regardless of your actions. There is always a way Maddie, you just have to be willing to take the first step"

Maddie started to speak, but her phone buzzed. She looked down, and her face drained of color.

"What is it?" Flex asked.

She turned the screen toward him. A message from Denny.

"Hope the judge likes your pics as much as I did. You move; I move."

Flex read it twice, then looked at Maddie.

"He's already blackmailing you," he said.

Maddie nodded. "He took them without me knowing. From his phone. I thought... I thought he cared."

Flex exhaled. "Then let's end it."

"I don't know if I can."

"You can," he said. "But you have to choose who you want to be."

She didn't answer. But she didn't leave either.

The next day, Beth sat at her dining room table as Flex read the new affidavit Rachel had prepared.

"She's doing it," he said. "Maddie's going to testify."

Beth covered her mouth with her hands. Her

shoulders trembled with something between relief and grief. She tried to suppress the anger welling up in her, but failed as her faced turned red, "She owes it after what she pulled."

"She's scared," Flex added.

"So," Beth looked at him with suspicion, "so, fucking what? Do you think I care anything about her being scared? After what she has done? I have not seen my son in days, I had him pulled from me and I don't give a damn if she is scared or not, I want her to fix what she helped break!" Beth paced the house like a panther with heavy breath escaping with each step.

"Beth," Flex walked and stood before her, resting both hands on her shoulders, "Beth, he hurt her. She. He hurt her bad."

Beth took this in, "Denny hurt her?"

"I need you to sit with me." Flex guided her to the couch, and they sat. They sat and she listed to the recounted tale of how Flex found Maddie and the things Denny did to her. She still hated her sister, but the story brought back feelings that she thought were buried. The fear of being hit and the shame at being manipulated repeatedly. The way he made her think she was crazy and that she was the problem.

She thought this and the anger at her sister did not disappear, but something else joined the anger to become one, a new anger, anger directed at Denny for using someone she cared about to hurt her. She would never forgive her sister, but she could hate the man who she followed astray.

Beth stood and walked to the window. The

porchlight was still glowing, a halo of resistance in the early morning haze.

"We're going to win this," Flex said.

Beth turned to him, eyes still glassy. "What if we don't?"

Flex smiled. "We're just getting started."

Rachel Dane was a storm in heels.

By mid-morning, she'd filed the petition to vacate the Emergency Protection Order and submitted the sealed juvenile case alongside Maddie's sworn statement. It wasn't just procedural, after meeting privately with Maddie and getting her sworn statement, it was war. Rachel held something in common with Maddie and Beth, she was a survivor. She was almost killed by her ex-husband and this case brought with it all of the memories and anger of the past. It filled her with a passion to win, to help right a wrong. This passion drove her, and she would not stop until her mission was complete.

Inside her office, Beth sat beside Flex, barely able to breathe.

"She gave you the statement?" Beth asked.

Rachel nodded, sliding the document forward. "Three pages. Signed and notarized. She outlines how Denny manipulated her into hiring the private investigator, the photos, the messages. She also admitted to the Snapchats, the blurred lines, the judicial misconduct, and the coercion that followed."

Beth stared at it. "He's going to destroy her."

"No," Rachel said, steely. "he will not. We will use this, and her to destroy him and remove a stain from the bench."

Flex leaned forward. "What happens next?"

Rachel didn't smile. "We subpoena Judge Skinner's financial records, motion for an emergency hearing before a new judge, and drop this like a hammer. If we time it right, they'll both be caught flat-footed."

Beth rubbed her temples. "And Jupiter?"

Rachel's voice softened. "If this goes our way, you'll have him home before Sunday dinner."

Beth closed her eyes. "God."

Flex reached across the table and squeezed her hand. "He's coming home."

But just because Rachel was ready didn't mean the town of Tanner was.

By afternoon, the news had spread that Beth was contesting the custody order, armed with sealed files and a new lawyer. Rumors flared like dry pine in a firepit. Whispers drifted over cups of Wester's like wisps of fog on water, across the parking lot of the Piggly Wiggly, and down the pews of every weekday church luncheon.

Pastor Jenkins didn't hide his disdain.

He took to the pulpit that evening for a "special message," a half-hour sermon streamed on the church's Facebook page. He didn't say Beth's name, but he didn't need to. The congregation knew who the "fallen woman" was. The Jezebel corrupting the town with her "firefighter harlot" and "liberal attorney from Birmingham."

The comments section exploded.

Evelyn left a prayer hand emoji.

By the next morning, the video was flagged and pulled down, someone had reported it for harassment and targeted abuse. That someone was Maddie, who was laid up in a hotel in Hoover. She was afraid to go home and did not want her mother and father to see her, but by God she had enough of this bullshit!

Beth stared at her phone for a long time, then turned to Flex. "I think we just took the first stone out of Goliath's sling."

Beth dressed in muted blue; hair pulled into a tight braid for the emergency hearing, two weeks had passed, nothing moved quickly in the Alabama judicial system. Flex wore his off-duty uniform, black polo with the fire department insignia over his heart, pressed khakis, and the kind of steel in his jaw that made even lawyers look twice.

Rachel met them on the courthouse steps, her heels clacking like punctuation.

Inside, the courtroom buzzed. Evelyn was there, silent and severe, hands clenched around her Bible. Franklin had shown up, but stayed in the last pew, his face unreadable.

And then came Denny.

He walked in like he owned the place, charcoal gray suit, smirk like varnish, and Judge Skinner trailing behind him, dressed in a black suit. Both men looked like gangsters in slow motion walking across a movie screen.

When the court clerk announced, "All rise for Judge Sandra Woolley, presiding," everything changed.

Skinner froze mid-step, confused.

Beth leaned toward Rachel. "Who is she?"

Rachel smiled like a cat with cream. "Retired Circuit Court. Special appointment by the Governor."

Flex let out a low breath. "You're good."

"Damn right I am."

Judge Woolley was lean, silver-haired, and carried herself like she'd met men like Denny before and broken them.

She read the case file quietly, eyes scanning pages while the room held its collective breath.

Then she looked up.

"Mr. Keller," she said, voice sharp and cool. "Your request for emergency custody hinges on alleged misconduct by the child's mother, and a romantic relationship deemed inappropriate due to the presence of sexually explicit materials and creation of pornographic material in the home. Is that accurate?"

"Yes, Your Honor," Denny said, clasping his hands with mock humility.

"Do you have proof these materials were acquired legally?"

Denny blinked. "I, uh, they were sent to me by a private investigator..."

"Whom you paid?" she interrupted.

"No, your honor, someone else paid for them..."

"Thank you. That's all I needed."

She turned to Rachel. "Defense?"

Rachel rose, crisp and lethal. "We submit a notarized statement from Madison Keller, the defendant's sister-in-law, affirming Mr. Keller's directive to hire a private investigator to obtain damaging and sexually suggestive material with instructions to break and enter into my client's home if needed. We also submit sealed juvenile records unsealed under emergency ethics review, detailing prior patterns of intimidation and misconduct by Mr. Keller."

She placed the file on the bench like a gauntlet.

"Is Madison Keller here today?"

"Your honor, Miss Keller is not here today, she is in fact recovering from physical injuries inflicted by the Defendant." She turned and looked at Denny with disgust. "She will be prepared to testify if the Judge allows it at a full custody hearing."

Judge Woolley read a few more lines, then sat back. "Mr. Keller, in light of this new evidence, I am revoking your emergency order, restoring shared custody immediately, and scheduling a full custody hearing with family services oversight."

Denny's attorney tried to rise to stop him, but it did not stop Denny from standing and sputtering. "Your Honor, I..."

"You will be silent," she snapped. "One more

outburst and I'll hold you in contempt. You are lucky that I am allowing any custodial visitation at this point. I think that this is going to be an eventful few days. Bailiff, please escort Judge Jenkins to my office so we can discuss a few things in private."

LeRoy looked at Denny in panic as he felt his career, and possibly his freedom, slip away from him while he walked through the balustrade and behind closed doors.

Beth covered her mouth, eyes welling.

Jupiter was coming home.

After court, the crowd dispersed in uneasy silence. Evelyn said nothing as she passed Beth, just shook her head and muttered, "You'll regret this."

Franklin lingered.

When everyone else had gone, he walked up to Beth and placed a small, folded paper in her hand. It was a photograph of Beth as a little girl, sitting on his shoulders at the county fair. On the back, in his scrawled handwriting:

"Don't let them harden you. You're still that little girl."

She looked up to find him already walking away.

That night, the porchlight was still glowing, Beth sat with Flex on the swing. They looked down upon a little man coloring. Jupiter sat cross legged and leaned over in high concentration.

He paused and turned his head, catching them both looking at him. "Hey, why are y'all staring at me?"

"We missed you, baby."

"I drew you a picture," Jupiter said, pulling holding up the notebook. It showed their house, the porch swing, and three smiling stick figures again. This time, there was a dog, and a cape on Flex.

Flex knelt, "You made me a superhero?"

Jupiter nodded. "You're Fire Man."

Beth laughed through watering eyes, the days leading to this happy moment had been hard and she was struggling to keep the emotion held in check.

They sat on the porch long into the night before stepping inside for a late dinner of tomato sandwiches and dill pickle potato chips. They laughed together and Beth basked in the glow, this felt like family, and she wanted it to last.

After the last plates were put away, Jupiter curled up on the couch with a blanket and his favorite robot dog toy. Beth and Flex sat beside him, close but quiet.

"Tomorrow will be hard," she whispered. "Denny's not done."

"I know," Flex replied. "But we just proved he can bleed."

She nodded, resting her head against his shoulder.

And for the first time in weeks, the house didn't feel like a battlefield, it felt like home.

Beth lay in bed well past midnight, awake but still.

She could hear the ceiling fan clicking. The soft hum of Jupiter's new white-noise machine down the hall. The occasional sigh of the house, wood shifting, foundation settling, as if it too was trying to make peace with what had happened.

Her son was home. Her world was still intact, but the cracks in the walls remained.

She sat up and slipped out of bed, the cold air blowing through the AC made her shiver and she put on her heavy terrycloth bathrobe. The scent of his soap still clung to it, clean and faintly woodsy. She padded barefoot down the hallway and paused outside Jupiter's door. His soft snores broke her heart in the best way.

She stepped outside, letting the screen door sigh behind her, and stood on the porch, arms crossed tight across her chest. The porchlight was on, its glow steady against the night, painting long shadows across the yard.

Flex joined her moments later, stepping out of his truck where he waited, barefoot, hair a little wild from sleep. He didn't say anything at first, just leaned next to her against the railing, shoulder to shoulder.

"He's asleep," Beth said softly.

"Good," Flex replied. "He needs peace."

"We all do."

They stood in silence for a while, the breeze warm, carrying the scent of honeysuckle and distant cut grass. Somewhere in the distance, a train whistled low through the trees.

Beth glanced sideways. "You think this is the end of it?"

"No," Flex said without hesitation. "But it's a win. A big one."

She nodded, biting her lower lip. "I don't think my mother will ever look at me the same again."

Flex leaned his forearms on the rail, fingers tapping absently. "That's not about you. That's about her. You grew into someone she's too small to understand."

Beth looked down at her hands. "I never thought my sister... Maddie and I, we had so many late nights growing up. We used to whisper about running away, changing our names, becoming famous in some big city."

He looked at her gently. "You did run, and you made something better than fame."

Beth gave a dry laugh. "A beat-up house and a porchlight with a secondhand swing."

"Exactly," he said, turning toward her. "A home. You made a home out of ashes."

She didn't realize her eyes had welled until the tears slipped free. Flex caught one on his thumb.

"I want to be safe," she whispered. "I want to feel safe. And I want him, Jupiter, to grow up never questioning whether his mom fought hard enough."

Flex stepped closer, gently brushing her damp cheek. "He won't. And neither will you."

Beth leaned forward, rested her forehead against his chest. "Do you think we're broken?"

He shook his head. "I think we're scarred. And I think scar tissue's stronger than what came before."

They stayed like that for a long moment. Breathing. Quiet. Close.

Finally, Beth pulled back, a trembling smile on her lips. "You want coffee?"

"I want whatever keeps me near you."

She led him inside.

The kitchen was dim, only one light above the sink casting a golden hue across the counter.

As Beth filled the water tank on her Keurig, Flex sat on a stool, watching her move with a quiet kind of reverence. Her back was straight now. Her hands were steady. And even through the exhaustion, she radiated something new, something hardened and true.

She turned and leaned on the counter across from him.

"There's more coming," she said.

"Yep."

"Denny's not going to walk away quietly. He's a man who doesn't know how to lose."

Flex nodded slowly. "So, we teach him."

Beth studied him for a long moment, "You say 'we' a lot."

"I'm not going anywhere, Beth."

Her throat tightened.

"I can't promise it won't get worse," she said. "That they won't drag your name through mud again. That my family won't come for you too."

He gave her the smallest grin. "Beth. I've had beer

bottles thrown at me during a bachelorette party while I was wearing ass-less leather chaps. I can survive a few rumors."

Beth barked a surprised laugh, hand flying to her mouth. "You didn't."

"Paid for the transmission in my truck."

She laughed again, freer now. "God help me, I really like you."

Flex stood and walked around the counter. "Good. Because I really love you."

The words landed in her like a stone in still water, silent, powerful, and impossible to ignore.

She didn't speak. Just stepped into his arms and kissed him slowly, not out of desperation, not from sorrow, but from a place of choice.

Later, after the coffee cups were drained, Beth tucked herself into his side on the living room couch, and they watched Jupiter's drawing still hanging by the front door.

"Will you stay tonight?" she asked.

"I will, but here on the couch." He smiled and kissed her forehead, pulling her tight.

Beth closed her eyes and whispered, "Then don't leave, there is another storm coming, be with me when the storm breaks."

Flex kissed the top of her head again. "Let it come. I'll hold the line."

They sat there for the rest of the night, two lovers

who had never made love holding each other, each getting something that they both needed, both giving more than they took.

If this were a movie, this would be a pivotal moment, but this was no movie, this was real life. But, for the sake of argument we looked at the next moment like we were looking through the lens of camera, if there were one, it would slowly drift past the two lovers, into the darkness, beyond the fence, and down the gravel alley where a black car idled.

Inside, Denny sat with someone new.

Sipping from a travel mug, watching the glow from her porch with a dead, unreadable expression.

The man beside him, obscured by shadows, lit a cigarette and spoke through smoke, "Ready to make her disappear?"

Denny didn't answer.

He just smiled.

II

THE EMBERS SPEAK

B eth had just put Jupiter down for the night. The boy had nestled beneath his new spaceship quilt, tired from a day of trying to forget things his little brain shouldn't have had to remember in the first place. She'd read *Goodnight Moon*, not because he asked, but because she needed to say the words.

The porchlight flickered outside with a soft pulsing thrum, like a heartbeat. She stood there, arms crossed, staring out across the lawn. The shadows didn't comfort her tonight. They were watchers, tall and mute, waiting for something to go wrong again.

Then came the knock.

Three slow, unsure raps.

Beth turned, spine stiffening. She wasn't expecting anyone tonight, Flex was on a 24-hour shift. Then it hit her like a gut punch, was it Denny, was he here? She picked up a brass candle stick that she picked up at Wester's Coffee, just a knick-knack, but it was cut and had some weight to it.

She held it up high and cracked the door peeking outside with a foreboding dread of what might be waiting on the other side.

Maddie.

Beth opened the door but did not step aside.

Maddie stood on the porch in jeans and a sweatshirt that swallowed her shoulders. Her hair was pinned back sloppily, face pale except for a greenish bruise just beginning to bloom under her right cheekbone. She held a small duffel bag and a hoodie clutched in one hand like a shield.

"Maddie?" Her eyes lit up in surprise

"I..."

Beth's face regained its composure, the soft wrinkles that Flex loved so much, the ones in the corner of her eyes turned hard like metal stressed and ready to tear from the pressure.

"What? Why are you here? You here to set another fire in my life?!"

"I'm not here to fight," Maddie said, voice hoarse.

Beth crossed her arms. "Then what are you here for?"

"I'm... not ready to be at Mom and Dad's. And I can't go back to the house. Not tonight. Maybe not ever, and... I am broke, I cannot pay for a hotel any longer."

Beth's gaze hardened. "So, you figured I'd what? Let you in? Make tea? Pretend everything's okay?"

Maddie shook her head slowly. "No. I just didn't know where else to go."

Beth didn't respond. Didn't move.

"I know I don't deserve your forgiveness," Maddie continued, eyes shining. "I know what I did... what I helped him do... was beyond awful. But I'm scared, Beth. I don't have anyone else."

Beth's fingers clenched against her sides.

"You think being scared is a free pass? You think crying on my porch makes up for the fact that my son, my son Maddie, was taken from me because of what you did?"

Maddie's breath caught. "I never wanted him to take Jupiter. I didn't know that was the plan."

"But you knew what Denny was. You knew what I went through. You were there. You stood in the hospital room. You helped me cover bruises. And still, you gave him the keys to destroy me."

Maddie lowered her gaze. "I thought I was doing the right thing."

Beth's laugh was sharp and joyless. "Well, congratulations. You wrecked my life in the name of 'help.'"

Silence stretched between them, taut and trembling.

"I'm not asking you to forget," Maddie said quietly. "And I'm not asking you to let me off the hook. I'll testify. I'll go to the police. I'll sign whatever your lawyer puts in front of me. Just... not tonight. Tonight, I just don't want to sleep alone."

Beth looked down at the duffel. Then at her sister's bruised face.

She stepped back into the house and picked up a folded blanket that was in a pile of fresh linens. Beth then extended her arms, pressing the blanket into her sister's chest.

"You can sleep on the porch," Beth said flatly. "Stay here. You'll be safe under the light."

And with that, she shut the door.

Inside, Beth pressed her forehead to the wood.

Her shoulders shook, not from regret, but from rage and grief twisted too tight to unravel.

Behind her, the porchlight glowed steadily, casting a long silhouette across the deck where Maddie sat alone, knees pulled into her chest, hugging her sins beneath a borrowed hoodie.

Beth didn't sleep that night. Not really.

She dozed in pieces, her body heavy from days of stress, but her mind flared like dry kindling every time she closed her eyes. By 4:37 a.m., she gave up pretending and slipped out of bed. She made a cup of coffee strong enough to chew and sat at the kitchen table, staring at the folder Rachel had given her the day before. It was thick now filled with statements, affidavits, reports, and sealed documents that had been cracked open like old bones.

Jupiter still slept. She could hear the faint hum of his noise machine down the hall, the same static lull that had become her heartbeat these last few days. That sound told her he was home. It was the only thing that mattered.

Until this next fight.

Her phone buzzed with a text from Rachel Dane.

Today's the day. Noon meeting with the
Guardian Ad Litem. Judge Woolley
wants all parties heard before granting
formal reinstatement.

Beth typed back

We'll be there. Are they bringing Denny?

A pause that lasted only a few seconds but felt like an eternity while three little dots danced on her screen. Her stomach knotted and she knew the answer before it appeared.

Yes. He'll be present for testimony.
Maddie too, if she shows.

Beth didn't reply. She looked toward the porch, where the light still glowed faintly behind the curtain.

She stepped outside quietly. Maddie hadn't moved from the porch swing. Her knees were pulled into her chest; the blanket wrapped around her like armor. Her eyes were open, bloodshot and distant.

"I made coffee," Beth said.

Maddie didn't answer right away. "I couldn't sleep."

Beth didn't ask why. The answer was already written on her sister's face in yesterday's makeup and the swollen curve of her lip.

After a long moment, Maddie turned toward her. "Do you think they'll believe me?"

Beth leaned against the post, arms crossed. "It's not about what they believe. It's about what you're willing to say. Under oath. On record. All of it."

"I don't know if I can talk about everything," Maddie whispered. "Not... the Atlanta stuff. Not what happened with Skinner."

Beth's voice was low. "Then Denny still owns you. You are still his little slut."

That hit harder than a slap. Maddie winced. "You think I deserve that?"

Beth didn't blink. "I think Jupiter deserves better. And I think it's time you put him first."

They stood in silence, the soft chirp of a mockingbird starting its song too early.

Maddie finally nodded. "I'll go. I'll talk. But I don't want Mama or Daddy in that room."

Beth laughed softly, bitterly. "Don't worry. Evelyn's too busy praying for my soul and Franklin's too busy pretending none of this is happening."

Maddie looked up. "You still hate me, don't you?"

Beth's jaw tensed. "I don't know what I feel, Maddie. I feel everything at once. That's the problem."

Maddie lowered her head again.

Beth turned and went back inside, not slamming the door, not closing it softly, just letting it fall shut behind her like punctuation.

Later that morning, Flex pulled into the driveway in his truck. He was still in his station gear, navy blue T-shirt with a sweat ring at the collar, cargo pants wrinkled from 24 hours on shift. He looked exhausted. Still, he smiled when he saw her and that smile sent a jolt of electricity up her spine.

Beth opened the door before he knocked.

"You're early," she said smiling.

He stepped inside and kissed her forehead. "Couldn't sleep at the firehouse. Too much on my mind."

She wrapped her arms around him and buried her face in his chest for a moment. "You smell like B.O."

"Sorry, we were called out for a heart attack last night and I did CPR for two hours before EMTs arrived."

Beth pulled back slightly. "Oh my god, are you okay?"

He nodded and she noticed bags under his eyes that were not normally there. "But we're gonna need to be sharp today. You ready for this?"

Beth exhaled slowly. "Maddie's coming. She'll testify."

He blinked. "She said that?"

"Yeah. I'm not celebrating yet. But it's a start."

"I'll drive you," Flex said, gripping her hand. "And I'll sit in that courthouse until the sun goes down if I have to."

Beth nodded. "Let me get dressed. I need to look like I've already won." She walked away and Flex watched her go and caught the gentle rise of her rear as she walked, he snickered quietly to himself as he remembered an old pickup line, one that always made him smile, "Hate to see you go, but love to see you walk away."

At the Jefferson County Courthouse Annex, the meeting room was painfully beige, with low ceilings, buzz-flickering fluorescents, a chipped table with mismatched chairs, and the smell of old air-conditioning and nervous sweat. The Guardian Ad Litem sat at one end of the table, a composed woman in her early 50s with no patience for theatrics. Her nameplate read Marcy Duvall.

Rachel sat beside Beth, calm as a blade in a velvet sheath. Across sat Denny, smug in his tailored blue suit, hands folded like he was waiting for an awards ceremony. The woman seated beside him looked vaguely familiar, possibly a new attorney from Birmingham, young and sharp-eyed, but already wearing the stress of representing a man like Denny Keller.

Flex waited in the hall, not out of fear, but because Rachel said he would be a distraction, a target and he needed to mitigate that by staying distant.

Then came Maddie.

She looked like hell in the most honest way possible. No makeup. No false glamour. Her hair tied back in a plain braid. She wore jeans and a long-sleeved shirt despite the heat. Her face looked freshly washed, raw and unprotected.

Beth caught her breath when she saw her, with the mask off she could see not only the fresh damage inflicted by Denny, but the deep yellow bruises from old injuries trying to fade away like fog in the early morning sun. Her lip was split, swollen, and oozing a clear fluid, and something else, something that Beth had not seen because of the hoodie she wore when she walked up on the porch, her left ear lobe was split in half, the son-of-a-bitch had ripped an earring out of her ear.

She walked in and didn't look at anyone but Beth.

Then she sat down and faced the Guardian.

"I'm here to make a statement," Maddie said.

Marcy Duvall tilted her head. "Please begin."

And Maddie did.

She talked about the private investigator. About the photos. About the bar meetings. The fake documents. The threats. She paused once, describing the Snap messages that led to the judge, and then pushed through, voice tight but firm. She unflinching spoke about her body being traded for favors from the pastor and Judge, how she was prostituted out to serve Denny's sick needs.

Denny's attorney put on a show twice, threatening libel lawsuits. Rachel countered each time by silently mouthing "Bring it on" while waiving her hands in come hither motion. The Guardian listened to them all.

When Maddie was done, the room was quiet.

Even Denny looked rattled with a bead of sweat at the corner of his ears and running down his normally cool neck.

Beth said nothing. She didn't need to.

Marcy Duvall nodded once. "Thank you for your statement. I'll issue my final recommendation to Judge Woolley by close of business."

Maddie rose and left the room.

Denny lingered as Rachel gathered the papers.

He stepped toward Beth and whispered, "You think this changes anything?"

Beth didn't flinch. "I don't think. I know."

Outside the courthouse, Beth leaned against the stone banister and finally exhaled. The late-morning sun cut down in wide golden rays, making the world feel just a little more alive.

Flex handed her a bottle of water, and she downed it in one long gulp.

"That was brave," he said.

She shook her head. "That wasn't bravery. That was survival."

"No," Flex said, squeezing her hand. "That was the first spark of a woman setting her world on fire, to burn out the rot."

Beth closed her eyes and turned her face toward the sun.

"She, I, I am glad she did it, but it doesn't change anything, it doesn't change the fact that she used my son, and me to try and cash out." Beth paused, "I will not forget who she is now."

There was still a long road ahead.

But today, they'd taken the first real step toward reclaiming it.

That night, the sky cracked with thunder, though not a single drop of rain fell. It was the kind of night that made your hand stick to your arm when you touched it, a night with too much humidity to rest.

Beth stood on the porch, the storm just wind and noise for now. The branches of the sycamore shook like dancers in silhouette, and the porchlight buzzed faintly above her. The bulb had started to flicker again, a subtle stutter that reminded her of everything still unresolved.

Inside, Jupiter was asleep. Flex had read him *Green Eggs and Ham* before bed, doing silly voices and making the boy giggle until his chest hiccupped. Beth had watched from the doorway, her arms folded across her middle, afraid to interrupt the moment by simply being part of it.

Flex was good at this, gentle when it counted, serious when needed. Present in a way Denny had never been.

She hadn't told Flex about the letter yet. The one she found tucked under her shiny red door earlier that evening. No envelope. No return name. Just a folded sheet of printer paper, one sentence written in black ink:

We know what you are.

It hadn't scared her. Not in the traditional sense, but it wormed its way under her skin like a splinter too deep to see. *What did they know?* The past she hadn't shared? The things Denny made her do to survive? The dark moments that hadn't made it into police reports or court records?

The letter wasn't just a threat. It was a message:
You're still being watched.

She folded it carefully and slid it into the drawer beside the corkscrew, where things that could cut were kept, and walked back out onto the porch; arms wrapped around her ribs like armor.

Moments later, the door creaked behind her.

"I knew you were out here," Flex said softly, stepping onto the porch.

Beth didn't turn around. "The wind makes it hard to think."

"I figured you were having a conversation with your ghosts."

She smirked but didn't deny it.

Flex stepped beside her, standing shoulder to shoulder. "You want to talk about it?"

"No. I want to stay quiet for a few minutes. I want to listen to nothing."

He nodded and said nothing.

And for a while, they just stood there. Listening to the creak of old trees and the occasional groan of the house settling beneath its own memories.

Finally, she broke the silence. "Jupiter asked me today if he could bring a picture of you to school. He told his class you're a firefighter and his 'other best friend.'"

Flex grinned. "Other?"

"His main best friend is a robot on YouTube that eats spaghetti in space."

"Tough competition."

Beth glanced sideways. "He drew another picture, too."

"Oh yeah?"

She reached behind the porch swing, where she'd tucked a crinkled page. She handed it to Flex.

This one had a firetruck, their house, and three smiling figures again Jupiter, Beth, and Flex. But this time, there was another stick figure. A woman with long yellow hair, scribbled in red crayon tears and standing away from the three.

"She said sorry," Jupiter had explained solemnly. "So, I let her be in the picture."

Flex stared at it for a long time.

"Maddie," he said.

Beth nodded. "He forgives easier than I do."

"He doesn't carry all the weight you do," Flex replied gently. "Not yet."

She folded the paper and slid it back into her cardigan pocket. "She slept on the porch again last night."

"She going to testify at the full hearing?"

Beth nodded. "Rachel has the statement already. But it's not just her anymore."

"What do you mean?"

Beth walked to the edge of the porch, where the railing was warped from years of humid summers and freezing January nights. She turned and faced him.

"She called someone this morning. A woman who worked with Skinner at the county clerk's office. They used to flirt. Denny would visit her sometimes, Maddie said, when he was still 'courting her.'"

Flex raised an eyebrow. "That woman willing to talk?"

"She is now."

He exhaled. "So that makes three witnesses. Maddie, the clerk, and if the Lord's willing, the judge overseeing this, stays clean."

Beth nodded slowly. "Rachel thinks we'll have a full evidentiary hearing in two weeks."

"That's enough time for Denny to get desperate."

"He already is." She reached behind her again, this time handing him the letter from the drawer. "Found this today."

Flex unfolded the paper, read the sentence, and clenched his jaw. "He's still pushing. Still circling."

Beth leaned back against the porch railing. "You think he'll back off if we win custody?"

Flex looked up at her, face grim. "Beth. Men like him don't stop because you win in court. They stop because someone *makes* them."

She was quiet for a moment, absorbing that. The porchlight flickered again, twice, and then steadied.

"I need him out of my life," she said. "Gone. Not just from the courtroom. From everything."

"We'll get there."

"Will we?"

He stepped forward, close now, one hand on her elbow.

"We've come this far," he said. "You didn't break. I didn't leave. And Jupiter still draws pictures with hearts on them. That's not losing."

Beth leaned into him then, not a kiss, not even a hug, just the quiet presence of one body against another, sharing warmth on a warm Alabama night, warmth that still felt good, warmth that felt like an escape.

After a while, Flex whispered, "You ever think about what comes after this? After court? After all the noise?"

Beth pulled back slowly, searching his eyes. "I used to imagine disappearing. Selling the house. Starting over. Maybe move to West Virginia"

"You still want that?"

She thought for a long beat. "No. I want to *own* it. Not the house. The story. I want the people in this town to stop whispering about me and start seeing the truth."

"They will," Flex said. "But you have to believe it first."

She nodded.

Behind them, the porchlight flickered one more time and finally went dark.

The house was quiet again. Jupiter hadn't stirred since his bedtime. Flex had double-checked the front door and turned off the flickering porchlight. Beth had suggested they replace it soon with something brighter, solar maybe, but he suspected she didn't want to change it too much. That glow, however dim, had become something sacred. A relic of survival.

Beth sat on the couch with a cup of sleepy time tea cupped between both hands. She didn't drink it. Just held it close like it had a pulse.

Flex came out of the bathroom, barefoot, a towel slung over his shoulder. He'd stayed again, unspoken but understood, and was now wearing the same soft T-shirt he always reached for when he wanted comfort but didn't want to appear like he needed it.

"She out there again?" he asked.

Beth nodded slowly. "Haven't heard her move."

"She's stubborn," he said. "Like someone else I know."

Beth cracked a small smile but didn't meet his eyes. "I left a bowl of soup out there. It's probably cold now. Probably the only cold thing in Alabama right now."

Flex sat beside her. "You don't have to take her in."

"I know."

"You don't owe her anything."

"I know that, too."

He let the silence fill the space for a while before asking gently, "So what now?"

Beth finally looked at him, eyes heavy but alive. "Now I survive tomorrow. Then the day after. Then, however many it takes to bring Jupiter back for good."

"He's already back," Flex said. "Physically. But I know what you mean."

They sat quietly for a few minutes. The TV played something they weren't watching, the glow of a forgotten cartoon humming against the far wall. Jupiter's crayons were still scattered across the coffee table, tiny explosions of color against the grain of the wood.

Beth set her tea down on a small leather coaster that was embossed with a straw broom and the words Witches Stack, a small souvenir from a trip to Salem Massachusetts.

"I want to tell you something," she said, voice quiet. "And I need you to hear all of it."

Flex turned toward her, posture straightening.

"I wasn't always strong. Not even close. I used to think love was what you endured. That if a man was cruel, it was because he was broken. If I just gave enough, forgave enough, he'd stop hurting me. I believed that for years."

She exhaled hard.

"But now... I see it differently. Love doesn't ask you to

bleed. It doesn't break your bones or your spirit or your sense of truth. You don't, no..., you cannot fix someone to make them love you."

Flex reached for her hand, and this time she let him hold it.

"I've been afraid of trusting you," she said. "Because if I do, and something happens, I don't know if I'll recover."

He brought her hand to his lips and kissed her knuckles.

"I'm not going anywhere," he said.

"You might not have a choice. If this goes badly, if Denny finds a new judge, or twists Maddie again, or if something new comes out, I don't know how to protect you from it. I don't know how to protect Jupiter from seeing me fall apart again."

Flex leaned in closer, his forehead touching hers. "Then don't fall apart alone."

That broke something in her. Not in a painful way. It was the kind of break that lets a dam give way to healing. She leaned into him, her fingers curling into his shirt, and for a long time neither of them spoke.

They held each other and allowed the warmth from each other's breath caress their skin.

Eventually, Beth pulled away and stood. She glanced toward the front door. "I should check on her."

Flex nodded. "I'll stay here. In case..."

She shook her head. "No. If she's going to say anything honest tonight, it'll be without an audience."

Beth opened the door slowly.

Maddie was still there, curled on the porch swing

beneath the blanket Beth had handed her earlier. She was awake, staring at the sycamore tree like it might speak to her.

Beth stepped onto the porch and leaned against the column.

Maddie didn't speak. Didn't even flinch.

"I won't pretend this makes us sisters again," Beth said flatly. "And I'm not ready to have you in my house. But I'm not going to let you rot out here, either."

Maddie turned her face, just slightly. Her lips were chapped, and her voice was a rasp. "I don't expect you to forgive me."

"Good," Beth said. "Because I don't."

Another silence stretched between them.

"But I also don't want to hate you anymore," Beth added. "That takes too much out of me."

Maddie's eyes shimmered in the porchlight. "I don't want you to hate me. I hated myself. I thought... I thought if I could just be what he wanted, I'd feel safe again. Or powerful. Or... something."

"You thought being near him made you matter," Beth said.

Maddie nodded, slow and shameful. "But all it did was make me disappear."

Beth swallowed hard. "You don't get to do that anymore. If you're going to testify, if you're going to make this right, then you must stop hiding in the shadows of men like him."

"I want to."

Beth turned and walked back inside, not offering a goodbye. Just a choice.

When the door clicked shut, Maddie exhaled, long and shaking. She looked away into the distance and snapped her head around when the old cast iron porch light came back on. Beth would not leave her in the dark.

It was still broken. Flickering once, twice.

But it wasn't going out.

12

BENEATH THE DUST

The days since the meeting with the Guardian Ad Litem passed with the day to day events filling a normal life. Normal being viewed by the person looking, but life moved along with groceries being purchased, trips to Veterans Park, work, and time spent with family.

Thursday evening was like any other, any other that did not involve the ongoing drama of custody and a crazy ex-husband. Flex was away with a portion of the Tanner Fire Department, on loan to the small town of Guin, AL, to deal with a small wildfire that had overwhelmed the local volunteer teams. He was due back in the morning, with the blaze under control and the remainder of the night spent looking for hot spots that had potential to start the inferno again.

She was excited to receive a Facetime call from Flex when he had a break. He chatted smiling with the occasional interruption from one of his team jumping in front of the lens making smiley faces. She liked the men he worked with, while the town was condemning him, they stood by his side, going so far as to tell the Chief that if he took any punitive action against Flex they would walk off the job, along with all the Firefighters in surrounding cities.

While the town was condemning Flex, his teammates were saluting him. Their very own "axe swinger" was what he was called. Beth was still not completely at ease with his past, but his actions with her outshone his past.

She fell asleep not long after the call, content and safe in her home and eagerly awaiting his return. Even with Denny on the prowl, she felt safe just knowing that Flex, her Flex, would soon be back.

She awoke from startled and covered in a sheen of sweat around 2:00am. The dream that she was enthralled by had started pleasant but ended dramatically.

In the dream Flex had taken Jupiter and she to dinner, a nice Italian mom and pop restaurant in the Five Points district. They enjoyed the dinner and laughed when Jupiter looked shocked when the waiter offered to bring out complimentary tiramisu to the happy couple and added that they baked the lady fingers in house. This made Jupiter's eyes open in disbelief, and he spoke with a half-eaten breadstick in his mouth asking if they used real lady's fingers.

Afterwards they stopped for coffee at Westers Coffee Bean and enjoyed a cappuccino with Vanessa as her daughter's Trinity and Alyssa colored with Jupiter. The trip to the coffee bean ended with Vanessa closing shop to take the girls to go see a new movie and Jupiter excitedly asking if he could go along. After handing off forty dollars Beth said goodnight and told them she would leave the porch light on when they dropped him off after the show.

Beth and Flex left walked around the park and made their way to the safety of the faded yellow house with the glossy red door. Just a few steps inside the house and after the door closed Flex caught her by the hand and pulled her into him, looked deeply into her eyes and kissed her with the passion reserved for someone you truly love. The type of kiss written about by poets that made the skin dance with electric excitement.

After the kiss he stood back and pulled off his shirt, a well-worn shirt with the slogan, *Live Long, and Prosper*, he truly was a nerd. The shirt hit the floor and her hands moved to his smooth chest and she moved one finger down the line separating his abs until the finger caught in the waist band of his pants, resting with gentle pressure.

His hands moved down her back and he lifted her up by the hips and she instinctually wrapped her legs around his waist as he walked her to the kitchen, setting her gently on the counter. Their eyes stayed locked as he pulled up on her shirt, removing it and tossing it without regard. With one deft flick of his fingers her bra was unclasped and with the same motion removed leaving her sitting on the counter with her breasts moving as she breathed deeply in anticipation.

He moved forward and then pressed his bare chest to hers and leaned down for another kiss, and the world changed. The kitchen window crashed as a brick was thrown through.

They both jumped at this sudden violence and looked out to see Denny standing there with another woman, the new lawyer that he hired, her blond hair wild in the wind. His face twisted into a satisfied grin as she held a bottle with a rag on the end and Denny held a zippo lighter, he rolled his thumb across the lighters wheel and held the flame to the rag that immediately went up in flames.

With a dark smile and a swing of the arm, the lawyer sent the Molotov cocktail flying through the window. Flex moved to shield her as it hit the tile floor with a boom, and the kitchen went up in flames.

This is when Beth woke up. It took a few moments to realize she was dreaming and another hour before she could go back to fitful sleep, but as she slowly slipped into unreality again, she swore she could smell the scent of burning pine.

The kitchen was warm with the scent of cinnamon toast and burnt crust. Beth hovered near the toaster, the cord still hanging crooked where Jupiter had yanked it last week pretending it was a firetruck's water hose. She hadn't fixed it. Maybe part of her didn't want to. The fray in the cord reminded her they were still in recovery, not healed, but holding and still working.

Jupiter sat at the kitchen table, a halo of bedhead spiraling from his crown, dragging a red crayon in looping circles across a fresh sheet of construction paper. He was humming something tuneless but sweet. Just hearing that made Beth feel like she could breathe again.

"Eggs or toast?" she asked, trying to sound casual.

"Can I have cereal?" he asked without looking up.

"Only if you eat the banana with it."

"Can I draw a face on the banana first?"

"Deal."

Small things. Silly things. This was what mattered.

Flex had not returned from his tour in the forest, but he sent a text that morning saying he would be home "before dinner" and she'd nodded, her eyes could not conceal the excitement she held for seeing him back with them again. She missed his smile, and

Now she stood in her kitchen, breathing easier than she had had in weeks, but still bracing for the next shoe to drop, because peace never lasted long in Tanner.

She poured coffee and added her favorite hazelnut cream, transforming the dark black coffee into a smooth caramel color. She took her first sip quickly and let it burn her tongue a little. The house was quiet except for the scratch of crayons and the distant hum of the air conditioner kicking on. Maddie had slept outside again but did not knock on the door, but as most morning since that first fateful porch confrontation, Beth had found the blanket folded neatly on the porch swing, alongside an empty bowl of soup and a single scrap of paper that said, *"Thank you."*

She smiled at this little fragment of paper, it didn't

mean anything was healed, but maybe this little smile and moment of happiness could be the beginning of a long path to reconciliation.

The doorbell rang, and Beth's spine straightened like it always did now, muscle memory. Fight or flight, but when she opened the door, it wasn't Denny, or Evelyn, or some veiled threat tucked in an envelope.

It was Rachel Dane, in person and on her front porch. Wearing a red power dress with a pearl necklace draped lazily across her chest and carrying a worn leather bag filled with manila folders and yellow legal pads

"Thought you hated mornings," Beth said, surprised.

"I do," Rachel replied, stepping inside without waiting. "But I've got news, and caffeine can wait."

Beth shut the door behind her and walked into the kitchen, poured a second cup coffee and followed Rachel into the living room, where Jupiter had already stretched out on the rug and was coloring a spaceship with two flaming booster jets.

"Caffeine never waits." Beth quipped as Rachel smirked

Rachel sat, crossed her legs, and dropped a folder on the coffee table like a gavel. "Guardian Ad Litem made her recommendation."

Beth's breath caught. "And?"

"She's requesting Woolley grant full physical custody to you. Joint legal, at least for now, but Jupiter stays with you. Permanently."

Beth closed her eyes. Her body didn't know how to react, like every system in her was holding its breath.

"But," Rachel said, "there's a catch."

Of course, there is, Beth thought.

"She's recommending a final evaluation period, four weeks of supervised visitation for Denny. Court-appointed supervisor. Location-neutral. That way, he can't claim total alienation. It's a compromise."

Beth opened her eyes. "So... he still sees Jupiter?"

Rachel's voice softened. "For now. But only in controlled environments. And if he so much as blinks wrong, we lock it down. Also... they are recommending counseling for Denny, along with parenting classes."

Beth nodded, slowly, eyes glassy. "I'll take it."

Rachel reached out, placing a hand over hers. "Beth, this is a win. I've seen uglier battles that don't get this far. You're doing it. You're getting your son back."

Beth nodded again, but she couldn't speak. Not yet. Her hands were shaking too badly.

Rachel stood, smoothing her skirt. "We'll prep for the final custody hearing in four weeks. He's on the ropes now. We keep the pressure."

Beth watched her go, the door clicking shut behind her.

Then she turned back toward Jupiter, who was holding up his newest masterpiece.

"Look, Mom! It's me and you and Flex riding in a rocket ship!"

Beth smiled and wiped a tear with the back of her hand. "Looks like we're going somewhere new."

The sun had climbed just high enough to make the air heavy, that sticky kind of heat that clung to skin like guilt. Maddie sat on the front steps of Beth's house, ankles crossed, hoodie sleeves tugged over her hands like she was trying to disappear inside herself. The blanket she'd used the night before lay beside her, folded again with military precision, a silent ritual of remorse.

Beth stepped onto the porch, cradling a coffee mug that read "TANNER ELEMENTARY Tigers Never Quit." It was chipped on the rim, but she liked it that way. Imperfect. Familiar.

Maddie didn't look up. "I thought about knocking."

Beth didn't answer right away. She leaned against the railing, the same one she ran her fingers across while her son was missing from her home, the same spot she'd stood watching storms, watching silence, watching her life split down the middle.

"I would not have come to the door," she said finally. "I thought about changing the locks to make sure you could not get in."

"I wouldn't blame you."

Maddie's voice was rough, too much crying, not enough sleep. Beth watched her sister sit there, looking less like the girl she used to play dress-up with and more like a ghost that hadn't figured out how to fade yet.

"I need a favor," Maddie said, eyes still downcast.

Beth laughed softly, a bitter edge at the end. "You're really not great at reading the room."

Maddie finally looked up. "It's not for me. Not directly."

Beth sipped her coffee. "Go on."

"I want to not be afraid when I sleep," Maddie said.

Beth stepped down the stairs and stood directly in front of her sister.

"You want comfort?" she asked. "You want to be near someone who won't hit you or sell you out? That's rich, Maddie. That's really something."

Maddie didn't move.

"I'm not asking for your grace," she said. "I know I burned that. I just... I don't have anyone else. Not anymore."

The words hovered there between them. Not accusations this time, not denials, just weight. Just truth.

Beth didn't answer. Instead, she walked past her sister, down the driveway to the edge of the lawn. She stood there for a long while, staring at the neighbor's mailbox like it held the secret to forgiveness.

Maddie didn't follow. She stayed seated, clutching her own elbows like she might come apart if she let go.

Finally, Beth turned.

"You stay outside, out of my sight, and you keep quiet. You help the lawyer when she asks and keep your head down when she doesn't, and most importantly you testify."

"I will," Maddie said quickly. "All of it. Even the worst parts."

Beth nodded once. "You can sleep on the couch."

Maddie blinked fast as she processed what she heard, and Beth didn't miss the way her shoulders dropped like a weight had slipped off her back.

Maddie was not expecting this response, she was expecting to take a verbal lashing and reminded that her sister thought of her the same way she thought of herself. That she was garbage.

Beth climbed the stairs and brushed past her, setting the blanket back beside Maddie's duffel.

"I'm not letting you in because I forgive you," she said without turning around. "I'm letting you stay because I'm tired of being the only one in this family with a conscience."

And then she stepped inside, shutting the door with a soft, final thud.

Maddie sat staring at the road and cocked her head to the side as a truck pulled up and Flex stepped out wearing blue shorts, thong sandals, and a white short sleeved button-down shirt.

He walked up and stood in front of her, "Still porch sitting?"

She looked down, "Yes, I... Beth said I could sleep on the couch."

Flex smiled at this, leaned over and gently patted her on the shoulder. He walked up the stairs and not turning said, "We can always crack a window and let some mosquitos in if you find yourself missing the porch."

She smiled as the door opened and closed. She reached up and wiped away a tear that had formed in the corner of her eye.

The porchlight, still on from the night before, blinked once.

Then steadied.

Rachel Dane never rushed. She prowled, elegant, composed, and deliberate like a woman who'd seen too many courtrooms and buried too many good women. Her office, buried behind a dusty Mexican restaurant on the edge of Alabaster, still smelled faintly of potpourri, coffee, and dust.

It reminded Beth of the librarian's office when she was a child, the day Evelyn made her go into the office and explained that she was giving back her library card because she could not take care of other people's property. The day that she left her favorite book, *The Halloween Tree,* under the backyard tree and a thunderstorm drenched it through and through.

Beth sat across from her, Flex beside her with one arm resting along the back of the worn leather sofa. Maddie sat near the window, quiet, her hoodie pulled up and resting at the top of her eyes like armor. It was the first time she'd stepped indoors with Beth since the reluctant offer on the porch. She hadn't said a word since walking through the door; she just sat and waited.

Rachel dropped a manila folder on the coffee table like it was a loaded weapon. "We've got more than smoke now," she said. "We've got a full-blown fire."

Beth didn't even blink at the metaphor but vividly remembered the dream the night before. She was too tired for irony.

"What is it?" Flex asked, leaning forward.

Rachel pulled a document from the folder. A scanned financial report, thick with annotations.

"This," she said, "is Judge LeRoy Skinner's personal bank account, or one of them. You'll notice here", she pointed, "a cash deposit of ten thousand dollars, made two days before the Emergency Protection Order was filed."

Beth's mouth went dry. "From Denny?"

"Circumstantial, but yes." She pointed at another document, "This is the financial record of one of Denny's companies. This is a withdrawal from Denny's construction company Keller Development. The memo states that it was to pay a contractor. One that doesn't exist on the state registry. I have a friend at the DA's office digging deeper, but we're already into criminal territory."

Flex whistled low. "He bribed the judge."

Rachel gave him a thin smile. "Men like Skinner don't do things for free. Especially not for Denny Keller."

Maddie finally spoke, voice soft but steady. "He talked about it. One night. Said the 'old crew' was going to fix everything. That it was just like college all over again."

Rachel arched an eyebrow. "The pastor?"

Maddie nodded. "Pastor Jenkins. He, Denny, and Skinner were all roommates at Birmingham Southern. Denny called them 'The Three Kings.' Said they ran the school their senior year."

Beth leaned back against the cushions like she'd been punched in the chest.

"They still run this town," she said.

Rachel's fingers steepled. "Maybe. But not for long."

"What's the next step?" Flex asked.

"I motion for a full judicial review and press charges with the ethics commission. If we're lucky, Woolley uses it to subpoena church records, sermon transcripts, the works."

Beth shook her head. "He'll hide it. Denny will make sure nothing sticks."

Rachel smiled again, more predator than lawyer. "Let me worry about what sticks."

She turned to Maddie. "We'll need you on record about the bar meetings. What was said. Who paid who."

"I can do that," Maddie said. "I want to."

"And the photos?" Rachel asked gently.

Maddie hesitated, eyes down. "They exist, and he used them to keep me in line. But I didn't know he'd share them. I didn't know he'd send them to Beth."

Beth didn't speak. She just studied her sister for a long moment, then turned to Rachel. "Is it enough?"

"It's close," Rachel said. "But I'm still missing one thing."

Flex raised a brow. "What?"

"A reason," Rachel said. "Why this judge, this pastor, this developer, why all three of them are working so hard to destroy a woman who just wants to raise her kid in peace. What are they protecting?"

Beth felt the chill in her spine return. That quiet dread she'd been trying to keep at bay.

Rachel leaned forward. "I think this goes deeper than custody. I think there's something they're all afraid of getting out."

Maddie opened her mouth like she was going to say something, then closed it again.

Rachel saw it. "What?"

Maddie's voice was barely a whisper. "There's a box.

In Denny's safe. He called it his 'insurance.' I asked once what was in it, and he said, 'Only open it if you want to know who really runs Tanner."

Beth turned pale. "Where is it?"

"At his house," Maddie said. "In the office. Floor safe under the desk."

Flex was already standing. "Then we get it."

Rachel held up a hand. "Not without a warrant. Not if we want it to hold up in court."

"Then get the warrant," Beth said, her voice sharp. "Get it now."

Rachel nodded. "I'm on it."

She turned to Maddie. "And if you've got any more secrets, now's the time."

Maddie looked up, and for the first time, her eyes didn't waver. "I'll tell you everything. I'm done being afraid."

By evening, the sky was the color of bruised peaches, pink bleeding into deep blue, heavy with September heat and secrets. Flex stood at the bottom of Beth's porch steps, watching the wind shift the trees like something unseen was stirring.

He was relaxed in jeans and an old navy T-shirt with a faded Tanner Fire Department logo stretched across his chest. He looked tired, like someone who had stayed too long in other people's nightmares. But his jaw was set, and his eyes were sharp.

Inside, Beth stood by the sink, barefoot, her hands

buried in suds she didn't remember creating. The dishes were already clean. She was scrubbing them anyway, each plate a ritual, each cup a distraction.

Maddie sat on the porch swinging again, a pillow in her lap and a legal pad in her hand. Rachel had told her to write down every name, every meeting, every transaction she could remember. The paper was already a patchwork of crossed-out thoughts and arrowed corrections.

Jupiter was asleep early, exhausted from playing hard. Beth had let him run ragged, hoping the motion would keep his mind from spiraling. He hadn't mentioned Denny in two days. But she knew it was coming. Some questions took time to grow teeth.

She dried her hands on a dish towel and stepped outside.

"I need to talk to you," she said to Maddie.

Her sister looked up, wary but open. "Okay."

Flex looked at both women and understood that they needed privacy. He went into the house and closed the door.

Beth didn't sit. She leaned against the porch rail, arms crossed, the porchlight humming above her, the faint buzz, a reminder that no moment was ever truly quiet in this house.

"I don't know what comes next," Beth said. "I don't know if we win in court. I don't know if we burn everything to the ground and still find our lives charred on the other side."

Maddie looked down at her notes. "I don't either."

"But I know this," Beth continued. "If you walk into

that courtroom and back down... if you let that man, go unpunished..."

"I won't." Maddie interrupted, her voice was firmer than expected.

Beth blinked.

Maddie set the pad aside. "I won't. Not because I think it fixes what I did. Not because I expect you to forgive me. But because someone must put a match to that man's lies. If it's me, fine. If it ruins me, well, fuck it."

Beth stared at her for a long, taut moment. "You really mean that?"

Maddie nodded once. "I'd rather go down doing the right thing than keep surviving doing the wrong one."

Beth finally sat, just on the edge of the swing, arms still crossed. "I hate what you did."

"I do too."

"I don't know if I'll ever be able to trust you again."

"I don't blame you."

Beth exhaled, a long, worn-out thing. "But Jupiter... he drew you in a picture."

Maddie's lip trembled.

"He said, 'She's sad, but she's coming back.'"

Maddie closed her eyes, swallowing hard. "That kid always saw more than we gave him credit for."

They sat in silence for a few moments, the porchlight between them like a referee.

Then Beth said, "Yes, yes he did."

Maddie nodded. "I know it may not matter, but... I love you and I am so sorry."

Beth rose silently, looked at Maddie, face showing no emotion, and went inside.

As she stepped into the kitchen, she found Flex leaning against the fridge, arms crossed, watching her like he could read her thoughts.

"She'll sleep lighter tonight," he said.

"So will I," Beth replied.

They didn't kiss. They didn't even touch. But the energy between them was electric, like two wires just barely not touching, knowing if they did, the whole house might catch fire.

Beth rubbed her arms. "It's coming, Flex. I can feel it. He's got something left. Some big move."

Flex stepped closer, voice low. "Then we hit first."

She looked up at him. "How?"

"I've got some friends. Retired guys. Volunteers. They've been asking questions. About Denny. About Keller Development. There are rumors going around. Quiet ones."

Beth tilted her head. "What kind of rumors?"

Flex's mouth thinned. "Money moving through churches. Unbuilt projects. People disappearing from contracts. Rachel's looking into it, but it smells dirty."

Beth nodded slowly. "That box. Maddie mentioned it. His 'insurance.' It's in the house."

"Safe in the floor," Flex said. "Under the desk."

Beth looked at him, eyes heavy but steady. "Can we get it?"

"Not legally," he said. "But if we wait for a warrant, he'll move it."

Beth crossed her arms again. "I'm so tired of waiting."

Flex didn't answer right away.

Then he stepped forward and took her hand. "You don't have to do this alone."

"I know," she said.

"But you still think like you do."

Beth didn't deny it.

"Let me take this one," he said. "Let me be the one to make a mess."

"You'll get arrested."

"I'll wear something cute in court," he said with a grin.

Beth barked a short, unexpected laugh. "You're crazy."

"I'm crazy about you."

It wasn't a joke, even if it sounded like one.

They stood there for a moment longer. Two people on the edge of something dangerous and necessary.

Then the wind picked up again. A sharp gust slammed the screen door open against the house.

Beth turned toward it.

The air smelled like burnt pine from the fires a county away, and a coming storm.

The air inside the suite at The Black Lantern Inn was thick with bourbon and anger. Denny stood at the window, one hand braced against the frame, the other gripping a crystal tumbler half-full of Bulleit rye. The room was all polished wood and red velvet, the kind of place meant to impress, not comfort.

Behind him, Marina Voss sat stiffly on the tufted

settee, her legs crossed tightly, one stiletto heal resting on her calve, and her tablet closed on her lap. Her dark red dress clung to her like paint, intentional but not revealing. Not yet.

"He actually granted it," Denny said without turning. "Supervised visitation. Like I'm some kind of... predator."

"You *are* under review," Marina said, measured but not unkind. "The Guardian Ad Litem made her report based on the statements, your sister-in-law's, the PI's connection, the financial trail."

"She's not my sister-in-law," Denny snapped. He turned, eyes sharp, wild. "She's a slut I tolerated because she could fetch favors."

Marina didn't flinch. "Be that as it may, the Guardian's recommendation carries weight. We expected something lighter, not a full restriction."

Denny threw the contents of his glass into the trash and threw the glass against the wall. It shattered, sending fragments of crystal across the floor.

"I will not be chaperoned around my own son. That's a leash. A public one. Do you know what that does to a man's name in a town like this?" He stepped toward her. "Do you?"

"I know what it does in *any* town," she said.

Denny smiled, the kind that never reached his eyes. He walked slowly to the edge of the settee and lowered himself to his knees in front of her.

"You know what you're good at, Marina?" he asked, voice like syrup on a blade. "Reading the room. Reading me."

Marina said nothing, her spine straightening.

He set both hands on her knees and slowly pushed them apart, the hem of her dress sliding higher with the movement. "You knew exactly how far you could go before I got angry. And you knew when to back up and play quiet."

His hand slid up her inner thigh, fingers splayed.

"You're smarter than Maddie ever was."

From the corner, a deep voice interrupted.

"Well. That's my cue to leave."

They both turned as Pastor Jenkins stepped out of the shadowed doorway, adjusting the lapel of his suit coat.

Marina immediately pulled her dress down and stood, smoothing the fabric. She stood and walked over to a desk in the corner. Denny watched her hungrily as she stopped, put both hands on the desk, arched her back and looked back suggestively.

Denny, still kneeling, barely looked away. "Do it."

Jenkins tilted his head. "Do what?"

Denny rose, straightening his cuffs. His face was calm now, but with fire still burning in the hollows of his eyes.

"Deal with the Guardian Ad Litem. I want her discredited, removed, disbarred. I don't give a damn how. I will *not* stand supervised visitation with my own son."

Jenkins smirked. "That'll take more than a sermon and a handshake."

Denny poured another drink, eyes on Marina's thighs as she slid them together back and forth while still leaned over the desk. "Then start praying harder."

Jenkins walked out the door as Denny approached Marina. He slid his hands up her thighs as he knelt behind her. His head moved forward, and she let a slight moan escape her lips.

Outside, thunder rolled low in the distance, and the scent of rain mingled with something older, something sharp, acrid, and wild.

13

COALS IN THE FIRE

The Mended Bridge wasn't fancy. No white tablecloths or soft jazz piped through speakers. Just an old fishing cabin turned into a mom-and-pop bistro with reclaimed wood beams and a patio that overlooked the slow sweep of the Mulberry Fork River. It was not a busy place, but the patrons there smiled when you looked their way. It was the kind of place that felt stitched together by memory more than money. Beth liked that, she liked the hush of the place, the weight of it.

Flex was already waiting on the patio when she pulled in, still in his station boots but with his shirt changed into something cotton and wrinkled but still accentuated his physique without attempting to show off. He stood when he saw her and smiled, it was just a small thing, but she felt it bloom in her ribs.

"Hey," he said, pulling her into a full hug. "You look amazing, sorry I couldn't shower, the Chief was on a rampage and had us polishing brass on door hinges. I was excited when you said you had time to meet me tonight."

Beth stepped back, smoothing a hand down her blouse, suddenly hyper-aware of how many times she'd changed before leaving the house. "Thanks for asking me."

Flex pulled out her chair. "Wasn't gonna let you eat alone tonight. Not after the week we've had."

They sat, ordered sweat tea with lemon, and let the silence settle between them like a warm blanket instead of a wall. Across the patio, an older couple shared fried catfish and coleslaw, passing hushpuppies like love notes. Beth smiled at this; there was just something wholesome about old love that melted her heart. It reminded her that not all unions involved threats, manipulation, and violence.

"So," Beth said, picking at the corner of her menu. "What's the story behind this place?"

Flex smiled. "Used to be a bait shop when I was a kid. Owner was a Carolina transplant and moved here so he could fish in the river every morning, and make catfish stew by noon. His daughter turned it into a restaurant after he passed. Still uses his spice rub. Story goes that she never changed the menu, just put new paint on the walls and started dropping scented splash guards in the urinal trough instead of mothballs, which is great because now moths are free to use the restroom."

Flex tried to keep a straight face on his dry joke but cracked a smile. They both laughed and she wondered how he got so good at dad jokes without being a dad. Seeing him smile and watching the way his strong jaw sent a flush through her body. She unconsciously rubbed her thighs together creating a moment of sensuality running through her core that embarrassed her a little. She flushed and Flex saw this, he kept his eyes locked on hers in a genuine manner of caring. Inside he wanted to allow his eyes to devour her form, to look and study each curve of her body, to see her breasts rise and fall with each breath, but he wanted more. He wanted her to feel the same way he felt about her, not carnal, but spiritual.

Beth glanced around in an effort to change the topic and allow the flush to leave her face. "It feels... held together. Like somebody still cares."

"Yeah," Flex said, eyes catching hers. "Like somebody still thinks it's worth saving."

Beth looked away, her fingers tightening around the napkin in her lap. "I'm not always sure I'm worth saving."

The words slipped out before she meant them too. She froze, ready to retract, to armor up, but Flex didn't flinch. He just leaned in, resting his elbows on the table like he was settling into something sacred.

"You are," he said simply. "Even on your worst day." This led to an impish grin, "Not saying you have bad days though."

Beth tried to smile. It didn't quite land. "Some days I feel like I'm made of cracks."

Flex shrugged. "So? That's where the light gets in. Also, I don't think you need to be saved, you are doing pretty good on your own. Besides, I only save cats in trees, not damsels in distress."

She laughed then, quietly. It felt good in her chest. Real.

Dinner came, fried catfish with lemon butter and greens for her, a fried pork chop sandwich for him with a side of slaw, fries, camp beans, and greens. Beth's eyes got wide when she saw his spread and Flex caught the look.

"I know what you are thinking, and the answer is yes, I eat like a garbage disposal." He leaned over again, and she met him in the middle exchanging a brief kiss.

"Well, you need to fuel up," she added, "You never know when you will need to burn some calories." She again blushed at this and chided herself for acting like a twelve-year-old girl crushing on a boy.

They ate without rush, without the weight of expectation. It wasn't a where you needed to interview and decide if the person sitting across from you was acceptable. It was also not the comfortable nonchalant evening of a couple that knew everything about their partner. It was something in between, something growing. She thought this and looked over the table, all sweetness aside, it had been a long time, and she wanted to devour more than the catfish.

After dinner Flex had to return to the station to finish his shift. "I get off at 9:00am tomorrow, coffee and beignets from Westers?"

She agreed and gave him a full chest hug, then pulled him in with a passionate kiss. Her hand had slipped to the back of his head and grabbed a handful of his short hair not letting go. Flex, in response, moved his hand to her lower back and lifted her up, toes barely dragging the ground.

This occurred under a full Alabama moon, by a Creekside restaurant on a cooling September day. This moment was a defined moment in their lives; this was a moment that the smoldering coals of their passions caught new life and blazed.

He arrived at 9:30am in gray sweat shorts, Vans, and a tight-fitting blue t-shirt carrying a white cardboard box with an elegant gold embossed *W* on the lid.

She was waiting on the porch with two cups of coffee while Maddie played with Jupiter in the backyard.

He walked to her, and she allowed him to lean down, and they exchanged a brief kiss. They sat and laughed over coffee; she made a show of wiping white powdered sugar off his nose and he feigning offence.

Beth carried the empty coffee mugs into the kitchen, glancing through the window at Maddie and Jupiter in the backyard. Maddie was crouched low, tracing lines in the dirt with a stick while Jupiter arranged pebbles like they were tiny soldiers. Every so often, Maddie would point, and Jupiter would nod solemnly, moving a rock or stomping a stick into place.

It was almost... normal.

Beth leaned on the sink, watching them. Maddie's hoodie sleeves kept slipping past her wrists, and she'd push them back without thought, revealing faint yellow bruises along her forearm. But her face, her face was open in a way Beth hadn't seen in years, bent toward Jupiter with full attention.

Jupiter said something and Maddie laughed, a sound light enough to startle Beth. She had to bite down on the inside of her cheek at how much it reminded her of summers before everything went wrong.

Maddie glanced up toward the window and caught Beth watching. For a moment, neither looked away. Maddie's mouth formed a quick, almost shy smile before she turned back to the "battle" in the dirt.

Beth stayed there a few beats longer, torn between wanting to step outside and join them and wanting to keep this fragile scene untouched, afraid any move she made might shatter it.

She returned to the porch to sit with Flex and shook his shoulder, a little, as he appeared lost in early morning thought.

They laughed and enjoyed their company as a blue Ford Bronco pulled up and a man stepped out. "Hey guys."

Beth looked at Flex cautiously. He noticed her angst and replied, "How's it going?"

The stranger walked to the other side of his vehicle opened the door, Beth stiffened at this, and he removed a camera. "I was driving by and saw the big Sycamore; I grew up with one of these in my front yard and wanted to see if you would mind me snapping some pictures?" He made a big flourish with his hands, "I fancy myself a photographer."

He laughed at this, and Beth relaxed a little, she

turned to look at Flex who was not wearing his normal jovial smile. She noticed his jaw was clinched.

She thought for a moment, "Sure, I guess that would be ok."

"Thank you!" He made an exaggerated bow and walked through the gate. "My name is Alex Minter. I specialize," he held up his hands and made quotation marks with his fingers at this, "in natural photography. Even been in a few magazines, but mainly just take pictures for social media to collect the likes."

Beth and Flex watched him as he took dozens of photos of the tree. Flex intently looked for any sign of maleficence or pictures taken of them together. There were none.

When he finished taking pictures they exchanged pleasantries and as he left, "I have a release form if you don't mind, in case I do actually get to publish this I want to make sure I have the rights."

Beth looked curiously at him, "OK."

He walked to his SUV, put the camera up and took out a small folder. Walked back to the couple and on top of the folder was a release form. She glanced at it and signed offering it back.

Alex then took the top paper, leaving the folder and said, "I appreciate it, beautiful tree, also, you have been served."

He turned, walked to his vehicle waving as he drove away.

Rachel didn't waste time.

Beth had barely texted her a photo of the injunction letter before the lawyer called back.

"Meet me at my office," Rachel said. "Now."

When Beth arrived, Flex came with her. He insisted, not out of suspicion, but because he knew she'd been pushed enough times already. Maddie stayed behind with Jupiter, the arrangement silent but understood.

Rachel's office looked different in the early morning light, less cluttered, shadows stretching long across the wall like something reaching for the desk. She held the letter in one hand and tapped it against her palm as they walked in.

"This is a surgical move," Rachel said without preamble. "Somebody knew exactly how to cripple your case without going after you directly."

"Denny," Beth said flatly.

Rachel nodded. "Denny, with help. Probably the judge. Maybe the pastor. This kind of motion isn't boilerplate, it's aimed."

She tossed the letter onto the desk and leaned forward. "They want to freeze the hearing until they can 'investigate' the Guardian Ad Litem. That buys them months. Months for Denny to push a new narrative, months for his people to dig up dirt on you, months to wear you down until you either settle or break."

Beth's throat burned, but she kept her voice steady. "We're not giving him months."

"No," Rachel said. "We're giving him days. I'm filing a countermotion tonight to have the injunction denied as frivolous. If Woolley is smart, and she is, she'll want this out of her docket before it makes her look like she can't control her own courtroom."

Flex leaned forward. "And if Woolley's not smart?"

Rachel smiled without humor. "Then we'll make her look like she's protecting a deadbeat dad over the welfare of a child. Either way, I'm not letting this stand."

Beth felt something loosen in her chest, not relief exactly, but the weight shifted enough to breathe. "What do you need from me?"

"Stay clean," Rachel said. "No contact with Denny, no public outbursts, no social media comments, nothing they can twist. And if Maddie's going to testify, she needs to stay sober and credible. One slip and they'll burn her on the stand."

Beth nodded. "We'll keep it tight."

Rachel's eyes flicked to Flex. "And you, if anyone comes sniffing around about your past, direct them to me. Don't engage."

Flex gave a short nod. "I can do that."

Beth glanced at him, wondering if he really could.

"Also," Rachel uncharacteristically paused, "this means that unsupervised visitation is off the table, you will have to let Jupiter go to him."

Beth stood up like a spring, "NO, WE CAN'T, HE WILL."

Rachel held her hand up daggers in her eyes, "Don't interrupt, and don't do anything stupid, this is my world, my war, and I am the general. Do as I say and we will get you through this."

They left Rachel's office as the lunch traffic began to move. The sky was that washed-out blue that comes right before the clouds overdevelop, the air heavy with the promise of rain.

Flex walked Beth to her car, pausing with his hand on the door. "You know I meant what I said this morning," he told her.

"About what?"

"Not letting you do this alone."

Beth searched his face, seeing the quiet intensity there, the same look he wore when a fire had gone from bad to worse. "I know."

"And when this breaks open," he said, "it's going to get ugly. I'm not walking away when it does."

She didn't answer right away. Instead, she reached up and brushed her fingers lightly along his jaw. "I'm counting on it."

A few miles away, in the back room of a dimly lit VFW hall that had long since given up hosting bingo nights, Denny Keller sat at a round table with Pastor Jenkins and Judge Skinner. The table was littered with beer bottles, an ashtray, and a single manila folder.

Marina Voss stood near the doorway, arms crossed, her phone in her hand but her attention fixed on the men.

"You pulled it off," Denny said to Skinner, tipping his beer toward the judge. "Guardian Ad Litem's tied up, and the court date's as good as dust."

Skinner smirked. "Bought you time. What you do with it's up to you."

Denny leaned back in his chair, his smile slow and mean. "Oh, I know exactly what to do with it."

Jenkins chuckled, leaning forward, his gold watch catching the light. "Just remember, this isn't just about the boy. This is about making an example. People forget who runs Tanner, they get bold."

"They won't forget," Denny said. "Not after I'm through."

Marina finally spoke up. "And the Guardian?"

Denny's eyes flicked toward her, then back to the men. "Discredit her. Quietly, publicly, it doesn't matter which. Just make it so when she walks into court, nobody believes a word she says."

Skinner raised his beer in a mock toast. "Consider it done."

Jenkins leaned back, his voice low and almost reverent. "You take the mother's voice, the Guardian's voice... all that's left is yours. And once you've got that, the judge's pen is just a formality."

Denny smiled like a man picturing a house already burning. "Exactly."

From outside, thunder rolled across the darkening sky.

In Tanner, the storm was already on the ground.

After dinner, they took two to-go cups of sweet tea and walked the gravel path down toward the old wooden bridge the restaurant was named for. The boards groaned under their steps like they were telling secrets.

"I used to come here with Jupiter when he was a toddler," Beth said, her voice soft. "We'd throw leaves in the water and pretend they were boats. Sometimes we'd race them to the bend."

Flex smiled. "You ever win?"

Beth shook her head. "The river always wins."

They stopped halfway across the bridge, leaning against the railing. The sky was bruised lavender, the river catching what little light remained and holding it like breath.

Flex reached into his pocket and pulled out a small smooth stone. He handed it to her without a word.

Beth turned it over in her palm. It was warm from his pocket. Worn smooth like a worry stone.

"I found it last week," he said. "At the base of a tree out past the fire line. Don't know why, but it made me think of you."

Beth looked up, something sharp and soft in her eyes. "Because I'm shaped like a lumpy bumpy ball?"

"No," Flex said. "Because you survived the burn and came out smooth. No edges left to cut yourself on."

Beth looked back at the river, her eyes wet but not spilling. She didn't say thank you, she didn't need to, she knew that he understood in a silent moment a story was told.

They stood that way for a long while, side by side in the fading light. She let herself lean slightly into his shoulder. This time all the way in, she let her full weight lean into him, she allowed him to support her full weight as she let go with the tension in her body and the damn holding back the tears that fell like rain in the Alabama sky.

The tears fell just a moment before the rain fell from the storm.

The drive back from The Mended Bridge was quiet, but not in the way silence usually meant tension. It was a gentle stillness, like the air after a summer rain. Beth watched the road ahead, her fingers grazing the stone Flex had given her, still resting in her palm. He didn't press her with questions. Didn't fill the space with unnecessary words. He just drove, one hand on the wheel, the other resting open between them on the console.

She placed her hand in his and felt his rough but gentle hand.

He didn't startle or look over.

He simply curled his fingers around hers, like he'd been waiting. The warmth in his touch filled her body with tension, not the tension generated by the fear she knew so well, but the tension of longing, of desire.

The porchlight was on when they pulled into the driveway, burning soft and steady next to the glossy red door. It did not flicker tonight; it held a steady light that welcomed them home. The house looked calm in the evening hush, wrapped in that faded yellow paint and the sleepy hum of cicadas rising up from the grass. A quiet house. A safe house. A home.

Jupiter was at Vanessa's for a sleepover with her youngest son. Maddie carried him over with a permissive text which meant tonight was... unclaimed.

Beth stepped out first, the gravel crunching under her boots. She waited for Flex to come around the front. He didn't speak when she offered her keys, just unlocked the door like he belonged there, like they both did.

Inside, the air was cool and smelled faintly of lemon oil and detergent. She had left a lamp on in the corner, casting a soft amber glow over the living room. Beth slipped off her shoes and allowed her toes to curl into the rug. Flex stood just behind her, not moving too quickly. Not assuming.

"You want tea?" she asked softly.

He shook his head. "I want to stay in this moment."

Beth turned to him. There was something in her chest, a tremble, a hum, like a second heartbeat that wasn't hers.

"You sure?" she asked.

"Are you?" he said, voice quiet.

She took a breath. Not just to breathe, but to choose.

"I think I've never been surer of anything," she said.

The words didn't ignite anything, they *unlocked* something. Gently, slowly, he stepped forward, brushing his knuckles along her jaw as though memorizing her shape. She leaned into the touch, her eyes half-closed, the weight of a hundred sleepless nights finally slipping from her shoulders.

He kissed her, soft at first, barely there. A promise.

Then again, firmer this time. Real, passionately, and with the hunger of a starving man.

Beth rose onto her toes, arms around his neck, and Flex gathered her in like she was both delicate and vital. She felt the heat of his chest against hers, the steadiness of his breath, and the subtle tremor in his hands as they traveled the line of her spine.

He didn't rush. He didn't push, he caressed and memorized every inch of her body like a blind man reading a brail bible, filling him with hope and a desire of what was to come.

He held her like a slow dance.

Like something earned.

They made their way down the hallway, familiar as a childhood memory, bumping elbows and laughing under their breath as they navigated shadows and doorframes. His shirt came off with a tug and landed somewhere near the laundry basket. She pulled hers over her head, heart galloping, not from fear, but from the realization that she was no longer afraid.

Flex paused in the doorway to her room.

Beth took his hand. "Come in."

She turned on the bedside lamp, not because they needed light, but because she wanted to see him. All of him. Wanted him to see her. No hiding this time. No sheets pulled to the chin. No dimmed shame.

Just skin and truth and two people finally meeting in the middle.

He touched her as if every inch had a name worth learning.

Her hands mapped the shape of him, the scar on his shoulder, the curve of his ribs, the slight callus on his thumb. She had imagined this once, early on with newly purchased batteries, but imagination had never felt like this.

Their bodies met slowly, wrapped in warmth and weight and the soft, unhurried hush of something sacred. Beth arched under him, gasping once; more from surprise than pleasure. The surprise of still being whole. The surprise of not having to flinch.

Flex whispered her name like it was prayer.

She held his gaze, her eyes glassy but unbroken. "Don't look away," she whispered.

"I wouldn't dare."

The rhythm they found was less about friction and more about presence. About being fully known and still wanted. About reclaiming something that had been taken.

And when it was over, when they were breathless and tangled and still, she felt his fingers brush the small of her back, slow and steady.

"You, okay?" he asked.

Beth nodded against his shoulder. "Better than."

Outside, the porchlight flickered once, just a blink, as if acknowledging the shift, and then steadied.

Beth smiled into his skin. For the first time in a long time, she didn't feel like she was surviving something.

She felt like she had arrived. They drifted to sleep in each other's arms, held in the embrace that lovers shared since the first time Adam and Eve discovered the joy of sin.

Beth woke slowly, her breath hitching at first, not from fear, but from disorientation. The world around her was soft and pale, the late morning light filtering through the blinds in hazy ribbons. The air in the room was warm and still. Beside her, Flex slept on his stomach, one arm draped across her waist, his breathing deep and rhythmic.

He was real.

His presence filled the room like cedar and safety, like something she didn't know she'd been holding out for all these years. Her hand found the curve of his bicep, and she traced the tan line there absently, memorizing the shape of him in peace.

There was a comfort in the quiet. A kind of lull she didn't trust yet, like the calm before the world came calling again. But for now, it was just the two of them, the weight of the past paused somewhere outside the glossy red door.

She slid out of bed carefully, not because she feared waking him, but because she wanted to carry the silence with her, hold it as sacred a little longer.

In the hallway, the house felt like it had exhaled overnight. The floorboards didn't creak. The kitchen didn't buzz with old refrigerator sounds. Even the porch light had gone out for once, finally giving in to the sun.

Beth stood at the kitchen sink with her coffee, watching the sycamore tree sway. She could hear birds, the occasional bark of a neighbor's dog, and Jupiter's crayon box tumbling off the dining table where he'd left it yesterday.

For the first time in months, the house didn't feel like a cage.

It felt like it could breathe.

She smiled into her mug.

Behind her, soft footsteps. Flex's arms wrapped around her waist, his skin still warm from sleep.

"You didn't sneak off to make me breakfast, did you?" he mumbled into her neck.

"Wouldn't dream of it," she replied, leaning back into him.

"I'd settle for coffee," he said, pulling gently away. "But only if I can make the toast. I'm pretty sure you are an accomplished bread burner." He smiled widely at this.

"I do not..." she started and returned his gesture.

"You do." He grinned. "I saw the smoke alarm twitch in anticipation."

She rolled her eyes and bumped his hip as she stepped aside.

While he moved to the counter, Beth checked her phone. A text from Rachel lit the screen:

Need to talk. Something's moving. Call me.

Beth's stomach tightened, her eyes lingering on the words.

Flex looked up from where he was buttering toast. "Something wrong?"

"Rachel. Wants to talk."

He nodded slowly. "You want me to step out?"

"No. I want you to stay."

She called. Rachel picked up on the first ring.

"Hey," Beth said, voice steady.

"I won't keep you long," Rachel replied. "But we got a problem."

"Of course, we do."

"The Guardian Ad Litem, Marcy Duvall, there's noise that she's being pressured. Someone filed a complaint to the BAR to question her impartiality. Anonymous. Untraceable. But it's aimed at halting her recommendation."

Beth's throat went dry. "Can they do that?"

"Not easily. But if the court decides to pause the hearing until they 'review' her ethics, it stalls everything. It puts you right back in limbo."

Beth closed her eyes. "That son of a bitch."

"I'm digging," Rachel said. "I'm not backing down. But you need to be ready. They're escalating."

Beth opened her eyes slowly and glanced at Flex. He had stopped what he was doing, toast forgotten, just watching her with a calm, focused stillness.

"Thanks, Rachel," she said. "Call me when you know more."

She hung up.

Flex didn't speak right away.

Then: "Denny's not letting go."

"No," Beth said. "He's not."

They ate in silence, but it wasn't cold. It was just quieter now, like the house had started breathing again but knew it might have to hold its breath soon. The fire from the night before still burned and after they shared silence Flex lifted her in his arms and carried her to the shower carrying on and stoking the flames from the night before.

Later that afternoon, Beth stood barefoot in the front room, folding laundry while Flex lay on the couch reading a paperback with the cover bent backward. Jupiter's pillow fort still took up the far corner of the living room, half collapsed and stitched together with two mismatched blankets.

Everything looked lived in.

Everything looked normal.

And then came the knock.

Not loud. Not frantic. But firm.

Beth stiffened.

She went to the door and Vanessa stood there with Jupiter. He looked afraid and her normal olive skin was pale.

"I am just bringing Jupiter back...can we talk?"

Beth motioned Jupiter in with her arm, and he walked slowly to Flex. She walked on the porch with Vanessa. "Sure, what's up?"

She handed over the phone, the old phone she gave to Jupiter to play games and watch videos. "I... I saw this last night." With a flick of her thumb, she opened the phone and a text from an unsaved number appeared.

Beth looked up at her and back at the phone. There was a video of Maddie standing with Denny.

Maddie, "I am sorry, I want to come back, I..."

Denny, "I don't know if I can trust you now, what with your sister and all."

Maddie, "I need to look out for me, just, no hitting."

Denny, "I don't know, you said some bad stuff about me, to keep me from my son."

Maddie, "I can fix that."

Denny, "Well, come in and let's talk. I am always open to new possibilities."

The video ended with Maddie going inside.

Vanessa cleared her throat, "Why would someone send that to Jupiter?"

Tears welled up in Beth's eyes. The feeling of completion from the night before was not replaced with a hollow emptiness, the emptiness of betrayal. She knew who sent the video, it did not come from Denny, it came from Evelyn, it came from her mother.

The world started to spin and as she started to fall, she heard Vanessa shouting for flex and the last thing she saw was the porch light flicker on and off. The lamp seemed to be a part of her now, the house part of her circulatory system and as she dropped, the house seemed to fall with her.

Darkness.

14

THE PRICE

Beth had done her best to make the morning normal for Jupiter. Pancakes with extra blueberries. His favorite T-shirt, the one with the cartoon Rocketship, fresh from the dryer. She even tucked a tiny note into his backpack pocket, the kind of thing she'd been doing since kindergarten: *I love you to the moon and back.*

She was up before he was packing the small suitcase she purchased the night before with clothes that she knew would never come back. The game, Denny's game, would involve making her struggle every day. Little things like making Jupiter's clothes disappear served one purpose, bleeding her financially, penny by penny. She wondered if he did this believing that with enough pain she would come back to him.

Maddie was up early as well, feeling the tension in the air and keeping true to her word to stay out of Beth's way. She needed to speak to Beth, but she didn't know how to tell her about her evening with Denny. So, she sat on the porch, picking at a worn flat cushion until Jupiter was awake and moving.

Beth succeeded at making the morning feel normal for her little man, but normal felt like a cheap suit on her today. It hung wrong, fit too loose in the places she needed protection, too tight where the air wouldn't come in.

Jupiter sat on the couch with his knees tucked up, eyes on the muted cartoon playing across the TV. He wasn't laughing, and he hadn't really laughed all week. He was withdrawn at school and sat coloring by himself instead of playing with his friends.

Beth crouched beside him, brushing the hair back from his forehead.

"You're just going for the weekend, buddy. I'll see you Sunday night."

He nodded but didn't meet her eyes. "Will Flex be here when I come back?"

Her throat tightened holding back the bile that suddenly wanted to force its way out her. "If you want him to be."

They both jumped as a knock sounded at the glossy red front door.

The knock at the door was too loud, even though it was just a knock, and to them both it sounded like battering rams at a castle gate. She stood slowly, every muscle in her body taut. She peeked through the window next to the door and saw Denny's truck idle at the curb. He stood in the doorway in jeans and a clean white button-up. She had a moment of internal dark humor and thought to herself, he looked like he was auditioning for the role of "decent father" in the new to Broadway production of *Dad in the Streets, Demon Behind Closed Doors.*

She took a deep breath and squeezed her hands together tightly, she did not know when they started to tremble. Releasing the air in a slow deliberate exhale, she grabbed the door knob and twisted, revealing the smiling face of Jupiter's father. This smile was not the smile of good humor, or well wishes, but the smile of a small and mean hearted child that killed his first frog. She held back a tremor at the sight.

"Morning," he said, a little too bright.

Beth didn't return the smile. "Jupiter's ready." She said this matter of factly and in a manner that can only be conveyed by a seasoned elementary school teacher.

Denny's eyes flicked past her to the living room, lingering on his son for a moment before he stepped inside just enough to take the backpack from Beth. "Got his toothbrush in here?"

"Everything he needs until he is back Sunday at 6:00pm.," she said evenly as she blocked his path.

"Oh yea, well you never know, traffic can be bad, cannot control that, we will have to see."

She was speaking before head to time to finish his final word, "And you remember that we have a court order, with court ordered times of visitation, and we have a final hearing coming up. Do not make me call the Sheriff."

They stood there for a second too long and the smile on his face cracked a little as she could feel the anger begin to well up in his eyes. Those eyes screamed "How dare she," "She needs to get back in line."

Denny broke the silence with a smirk that didn't reach his eyes. "You know, court might say a lot of things, but weekends with me are still mine, you know, according to the court orders."

Beth's hand clenched at her side. "Don't make me regret following them."

He shrugged, clearly enjoying the small victory of walking into her house without an invitation. "Let's go, champ."

Jupiter slid off the couch and padded toward the door. Beth dropped to her knees, pulling him into a hug so tight he made a small grunt.

"I love you, Jup. Be good. Call me if you need anything."

"I will." He clung for one extra heartbeat, then pulled back, shoulders slumped. He reached over to grab the little suitcase and Denny held out his hands.

"Oh, no, no need for that. We are going shopping; it is time for you to be treated right son."

Jupiter looked up at his mom, with a look of distress, he was in the middle and did not know what to do. His face flushed and she could see tears starting to well up in his eyes.

"It's ok, you leave it if you want to."

"He wants to, now let's go champ. This old place has had you cooped up long enough"

Denny ushered him out and put him in the backseat of his truck. Beth stood in the doorway until the truck's taillights disappeared down the street. Only then did she realize she'd been holding her breath.

Behind her, the porchlight gave a single, faint flicker.

Beth didn't even take off her shoes when she got back inside. She went straight to the coffee table where her phone sat, picked it up, and pulled up the video Vanessa had shown her.

She watched it again, once for the words, once for Maddie's face, and a third time for the spaces between; where hesitation could hide, where choices were made.

Maddie wasn't outside on the swing when Denny arrived, she had gone to the gas station for a pack of cigarettes, the recent events had reignited her love of Marlboros.

Beth paced around the back yard, back and forth, waiting. Waiting for her sister to return, when she came back into the house she found Maddie in the kitchen, bent over the counter with a half-eaten bowl of cereal, scrolling through her phone like the rest of the world didn't exist.

Beth set her phone down hard enough to make the spoon in the ceramic bowl rattle.

"You want to explain this?"

Maddie froze, eyes dropping to the screen, where the paused image of her and Denny glowed under the kitchen light.

"Beth..." Maddie started, but Beth cut her off with a sharp wave of her hand.

"No. I don't want soft words, or excuses, or any more *I didn't know*. You knew what you were doing standing there with him. You knew what he's done to me, to Jupiter, FOR FUCKS SAKE MADDIE WHAT HE DID TO YOU! And you still..."

"I wasn't..." Maddie tried again, voice rising in panic.

"You weren't what?" Beth's voice cracked like a whip. "Weren't selling me out? Weren't making nice with the man who's dragged me through hell so you can go back and get what you deserved? I let you back into my house, back into my life!"

Maddie's face flushed, her hands curling into fists on the black countertop. "It wasn't like that! I went over there because I needed answers..."

"Answers?" Beth barked out a humorless laugh and with eyelids open showing the red tinged whites of her eyes all around her pupils, eyes that had shed too many tears. "You could've asked me. You could've asked literally anyone except *him*."

"Beth, I..."

Beth moved forward, inches from her faces and said flatly, "Get out."

"What?"

"Get out of my house and get out of my fucking life you snake. You deserve what he will do to you."

Maddie's voice dropped along with her eyes, low and shaking. "I didn't trust anyone else to tell me the truth about why he's pulling Mom into this."

Beth blinked. "What?"

Maddie looked up finally, her eyes shining but hard. "He's been talking to her for weeks. Feeding her crap about you keeping Jupiter from his *real family.* Making her believe you're the problem, not him."

Beth's stomach turned cold. She pictured Evelyn, her mother, sitting in the living room with Denny, sipping coffee, nodding like every word out of his mouth was gospel.

"And you thought cozying up to him was the way to fix that?" Beth's voice was raw now, almost hoarse.

"I thought if I could get him talking, I could find out what he's planning," Maddie said, but her voice wavered. "I didn't know he was recording. I didn't know he'd twist it and send it to Jupiter."

Beth's arms folded tight across her chest. "You didn't know a lot of things. But you should have known well enough to stay the hell away from him."

Maddie flinched like she'd been struck.

"Beth..."

Beth stepped back toward the doorway, her voice dropping into something cold and final. "I am going to my room. I will be out in ten minutes. When I come back you will be gone."

She left the kitchen, leaving Maddie sitting alone, tears again in her eyes with the sounds of the settling house creaking and the refrigerator humming. This sound would be the soundtrack of her soul breaking and the last shred of the slim chance of redemption gone, lost to the black hole of miscommunication and betrayal.

She did as Beth demanded, she left and wandered around on foot. She caught the glances of several women hiding their mouths and pointing at her. The story of her sexual indiscretions did not remain hidden in this little town, and she was getting a full dose of the attention that she had brought upon Flex.

She walked and mulled this over, trying to ignore the stares of the women. The walk led her to the town square where she sat on a cast iron bench, her hand brushing the petals of the chrysanthemums planted around the side and back of the bench. The touch was soothing, and she lost herself in the events of the past few weeks.

When the fragile old lady sat down next to her, she did not notice. "Darlin."

Maddie jumped and pressed both of her hands to her chest. "Oh my, I am sorry, I did not even see you sit down."

"I understand darlin, you were just caught up in your own. I thought I recognized you, you're Evelyn's daughter Maddie, right?"

"I am." The mention of her mother brought back the tension that the mums had erased.

"Look here darlin, I just saw you and had to stop and say hello."

A smile formed on Maddie's lips. "Awe, how nice. Thank you"

"No thank you necessary darlin, and I also wanted you to know that Jesus will forgive you."

Eyes wide in surprise, "I am sorry, what?"

"Jesus will forgive you dear. I have heard about the... well the harlot things you have been doing with all those men, and I wanted you to know that Jesus will forgive you. All you have to do is ask. Remember Mary Magdalene was a whore and Jesus loved her just like he loves you."

With this said and Maddie's mouth hanging open, the old lady patted her on the leg, stood, and smiled waving as she walked away.

Five minutes passed before air pressed from her lungs could form words, before the shock in her face changed to anger. The words were simple, "Bitch." With that out, she stood and marched down the street on a new mission.

The late afternoon heat clung to Maddie like a second skin as she stood at the curb outside Denny's place.

She hadn't planned this visit, she'd left Beth's house without saying a word, walking until her pulse stopped pounding in her ears and she learned the joy of Southern Baptist forgiveness.

Now, she was here, standing in front of the man that was attempting to, no that is not right she thought, the man who had torn her family apart by driving discontent and betrayal between them at all angles like a woodsman driving a wedge into a log.

The Keller house looked the same as it always had, trim cut short, driveway spotless, the American flag on the porch fluttering lazy in the breeze.

From the outside it looked clean, almost sterile. It looked like every house in every magazine that had been staged to present the real American dream, the dream of how your home should look if you were truly happy, if you were truly good.

It looked like perfection, but that perfection had a dark spot inside. In this home a cancer lived.

She knocked once. Then again, harder, hard enough to break the skin on her knuckles leaving white tufts of skin raised on her hand.

The door swung open and there he was, barefoot in jeans, a gray T-shirt stretched over his chest, damp hair like he'd just come from a shower.

And he smiled.

The same smile that used to make Beth go quiet in the bad years. The one that said he was already three steps ahead.

"Well," Denny drawled, leaning one arm on the doorframe. "If it isn't the prodigal sister-in-law. Here to switch teams again?"

Maddie's hands balled into fists at her sides. "Cut the crap, Denny. I want to know why you dragged my mother into this."

Denny's brows went up, like she'd just asked him about the weather. "Your mother called me. Said she was worried about Beth, and more so about Jupiter."

"You fed her lies," Maddie snapped. "Made her think Beth's the bad guy. Why?"

He shrugged, the picture of casual charm. "Because I don't like losing, Maddie. And your mom? She's smart enough to see the bigger picture. The way things should be. The life that your sister could have had if she had just kept in her place. Hell, she was even willing to give up on

Beth if you would have taken the spot, but like your sister, you couldn't keep your whore mouth shut!"

Maddie stepped inside without being invited, the air-conditioned chill raising goosebumps on her arms. "You used her. She was your wife, and you used me. You sold me like I was just a toy."

He laughed. He actually laughed at her anger. "Everyone's a toy Mads, even better, everyone is a weapon if you hold them right."

Maddie's stomach turned, but she forced herself to stand her ground. "I saw what you sent to Jupiter. The video. You think twisting things is going to win you back? All you're doing is burning every bridge left standing."

Denny's eyes narrowed, just slightly. "You came here to scold me, Maddie? Or did you come here because part of you still like being on my side? Part of you still wants what I have to give you." He made a mocking gesture and rubbed his hand across his crotch.

"Don't flatter yourself you piece of shit."

He stepped closer, his voice dropping low. "You want to talk about family? Then let's talk about loyalty. You've already proven you'll turn on your own blood when it suits you. Now you're wondering why Beth still looks at you like a snake, you wonder how I could toss you to the dogs to be fucked like the bitch you are. I wouldn't spit on you if you were dying of thirst, you are trash."

Maddie swallowed hard, but she didn't look away. "Maybe."

"Maybe what?" He grinned sarcastically at this.

"Maybe I am a whore, a piece of shit, a goddamned

snake, but I am still better than you. One day your money will run out and the people that you buy will be gone. When that happens, I hope no one is there to see it. I hope that die alone and miserable left with nothing more that the hateful memories of your like to keep you cold."

That gave him pause, just for a heartbeat.

Then he grinned again, cold and sharp. "If you're done playing the penitent sister, you can show yourself out. I've got plans tonight." He picked up a tumbler full of bourbon and shook it at her.

She turned toward the door, her hand on the knob before she looked back. "You keep drinking the way you are, Denny... one day you're not going to wake up from whatever plans you've made."

He smirked. "Guess we'll see."

Maddie stepped out into the fading light, slamming the door behind her. She heard a small voice through the door, and it made her heart jump, and she paused. She heard the sweet sound of Jupiter, "Why were you and Aunt Maddie fighting Daddy?"

"Son, sometimes, you just have to keep trash out on the curb. I have a lot to teach you."

More was said through the door, but the words faded to whispers and Maddie stood there, arms wrapped around herself, the anger she felt melted by the sound of innocence in the den of inequity that was his father's home.

Night had settled thick over Tanner, the kind of deep Southern dark that swallowed edges and blurred lines.

Cicadas hummed in the trees, steady and relentless.

The Tanner Fire Department was still on that night. Leaving the men with a slow shift, the kind where the radios crackled only with weather updates and the occasional call from a neighboring county. Most of the crew had already retreated to their bunks after eating their weight in spaghetti or found ways to kill time in the day room with the sound of spinning foosball athletes and the smart assed comments that comes with the game.

Flex sat alone in the small office just off the engine bay, the dim desk lamp casting a warm pool of light over the cluttered tabletop. His laptop screen glowed with an open browser tab, a real estate listing.

It wasn't much, a small one-story house, faded white siding, and a pond out back that caught the light like a mirror. Off to one side was a crooked wooden playground set, the kind a kid could lose hours on without noticing the sun had moved. It was not a mansion, but it had the look of home, and it had a little bit of land, 3.14 acres to be exact.

He zoomed in on the listing photos, imagining Jupiter running across that grass, Beth laughing on the porch, her hair catching the wind. Visions of tomatoes growing and fish being pulled out of the pond made the hair stand on his arm.

With a few clicks he filled out the request to view the listing and he smiled. His life had changed so much over the years, and this was one of the few times that he felt true and it was because of a woman that he had only known for a few months.

Flex reached into his pocket, fingers curling around the familiar shape. He pulled out a small, polished teakwood box, the grain deep and rich in the lamplight. He hesitated for a moment before flicking the lid open.

Inside, nestled against black velvet, was a rose gold ring shaped like vines with extended leaves and in the center sat a simple moss agate stone cut in the shape of a kite. Simple. Elegant. The kind of ring that didn't just say *marry me*, it said *I see you. I choose you.*

In some circles, this would have been seen as costume jewelry, but it meant more to Flex, from the moment he saw it he thought about what it symbolized. Vines growing, becoming more established over time until the roots run deep and holding strong through the different seasons of life.

The stone, that simple agate stone cut and shaped like a kite impressed him with the heights that real love could reach while being firmly grounded, the combination of the earth stone transformed into a flying instrument weighed heavy on his heart and he purchased it immediately, knowing exactly who he wanted to wear the ring.

He stared at it for a long time, the weight of the choice pressing heavier than the gold itself.

A quiet laugh escaped him, though it was laced with disbelief. "I must be crazy," he said to the empty room. "Barely know her, but... feels like I've known her forever."

He sat there another moment, thumb brushing the curve of the band, before snapping the lid closed. He set the box on the desk beside his phone and wallet, left it there with the rest of his personal items.

Then he pushed the laptop shut, stood, and walked out into the cool concrete cavern of the engine bay.

The firetruck waited, gleaming under the fluorescent lights. Flex grabbed a rag from the tool bench and started wiping down the chrome bumper, his reflection fractured in the shine.

The ring stayed in the office, silent and waiting.

Inside his house, Denny sat slouched on the leather couch, the blue flicker of the TV washing over his face. A canned reality show droned in the background, laughter and obnoxious applause spilling into the quiet like static.

His hand rested around a heavy tumbler of bourbon that sat on the small round table near his chair, the glass dripping beads of sweat in the leather coaster that separated the glass from the table.

Jupiter sat on the far side of the room on a tan leather couch, small knees pulled to his chest, eyes on the screen but not really watching. The boy's thin voice had asked for water earlier, and Denny had waived him toward the kitchen without looking up.

The bourbon, along with the zanies that he took earlier, was hitting him now, turning his blood thin while making his mind slow and thick. His eyelids dipped. The glass tilted in his grip, sloshing amber liquid toward the rim. He caught it before it spilled, chuckling to himself.

"Still got it," he muttered, though the words slurred together.

From the kitchen came the soft hiss of oil heating in a pan. Denny had decided, half an hour ago, that cheese sticks would make the night better. He'd poured the oil into a deep skillet, flicked the burner to high, and left it while he "rested his eyes."

The bottle of Gentleman Jack he'd been working on all night sat open on the counter beside it.

Jupiter glanced toward the kitchen doorway, his small brow furrowing. "Dad, something's burning."

Denny waved a lazy hand, his gaze never leaving the TV. "It's fine, bud. Just the oil. I got it. Just go on to bed, we, can, I, tomorrow..." A small line a drool rolled out of his lip as Jupiter walked away to his bedroom, head down but casting looks back at the kitchen trying to remember everything that he learned from Flex and Sparky.

Jupiter walked to his bed and then turned and went back. He remembered seeing his mom being thrown into the wall, bleeding and falling onto the floor, he remembered, and it left him shivering. With tiny shaking hand, he reached up and turned the door lock and climbed into his bed. He was sleepier than normal and was having trouble keeping his eyes open. His final thoughts before drifting off were of how much he hated the taste of the nighttime medicine his father made him drink; it was yucky and made the room spin.

In the kitchen the oil was already smoking, thin tendrils curling toward the ceiling like searching fingers.

The bourbon's sharp scent hung in the air, weaving into the smell of hot grease creating a sickly-sweet aroma.

Outside, a faint wind rattled the flag on the porch.

And miles away, at the faded yellow house with the glossy red door, the porchlight flickered once, twice, like a warning pulse keeping beat with a dying heart.

Beth was at the kitchen table, bent over a mug of tea, when she noticed it.

She stared at the light for a long beat, a prickle running up the back of her neck creating a sensation of dread that only a mother can feel or understand.

At Denny's house, the oil popped sharply.

In his chair, Denny lurched slightly, his glass slid in his grip again.

This time he didn't catch it.

The bourbon pooled dark on the carpet.

The kitchen already thick with smoke gained a new light from the fire that erupted from the overheated pan of oil.

The porchlight at Beth's steadied.

The alarm at Fire Station 2 screamed.

The storm had chosen its path.

15

WHEN THE LIGHT GOES OUT

"Shuttap, fuhks!" Denny screamed as he came back to consciousness. The screaming fire alarm cut through his drunken stupor. He turned and his face paled as he saw the yellow orange flames leaping out the skillet.

He jumped and stumbled to the kitchen, staring dumbfounded at the fire. He looked to the counter and took hold of first thing he saw, a dishtowel that Maddie had purchased when she was making this house "home".

He slapped at the fire with no effect and was almost ready to give up when with a final fling the towel hit the bottle of bourbon, sending it flying. As it flew, the brown liquid splashed out, adding new, horrible life to the flame. The bottle rolled and spilled liquid until it came to a rest at the pantry door that was not used to store food, this was Denny's pantry, and it contained the tools needed to keep the shakes from his hands and reality just out of reach.

Denny stumbled away and was overcome by the

smoke. He collapsed in the walkway that joined the kitchen to the living room. There was no great moment of clarity for Denny, he simply lapsed back into unconsciousness as he slumped to the floor, his head striking the wall much like the head of his wife in years past.

Upstairs, Jupiter slept. His mind was dulled by the cough syrup that his father required him to drink. The cough syrup that removed the responsibility of being a father and allowed Denny to drink his own mind away without bother.

Flex finished his cleanup and settled in to relax and let the final six hours of his shift fly past. He had been leaning against the scarred desk in the small office off the engine bay, boot heel hooked over the rung of a chair, mind still drifting back to the little white house with the pond. The laptop sat open, the real estate listing staring back at him like an unanswered question. Beside it, his wallet, his phone, and the small, polished teakwood box. He'd placed the box there earlier, meaning to tuck it away before the shift ended, but he'd left it, close enough to touch, far enough to pretend it didn't exist.

The dispatch radio voice came crisp through the overhead speaker, the voice of the speaker stating the facts straightforward with no emotion:

"Structure fire. Residential. 742 Riverbend Lane. Flames visible. Possible occupants inside."

Then the bell, that sacred sound that sent all men,

and women, in his procession into work mode. It was a jarring sound to outsiders, but to this group it was a call to action, a call to put themselves in harm's way for the chance to save another life.

For half a second, his brain didn't connect the address to his memories.

Then it hit.

Riverbend Lane.

Denny's house.

Flex's body moved before his thoughts caught up.

Boots hit the floor.

Gear bag yanked open.

Adrenaline began its climb.

"Let's go, let's go!" The captain's voice boomed across the bay as the rest of the crew spilled from the day room, sharpening from lazy banter to battle-ready in the span of a heartbeat.

Flex shoved his arms into his turnout coat, fastened the clasps with practiced speed, pulled his helmet down tight. The ritual of preparation was muscle memory, but this time, the edges felt sharper, like every strap and buckle knew where he was headed.

The teakwood box sat on the desk, forgotten but watching.

The truck was rolling before the bay door was completely open and, the siren split the night, echoing off the storefronts and the low brick walls of Tanner's quiet streets. Red strobes spun across the pavement, turning houses into flickering snapshots. Flex sat forward in the passenger seat of Engine 2; eyes locked on the dark ribbon of road ahead.

Nobody spoke. Not because they didn't have words, and not because the crew didn't know every detail. They knew *who* lived at 742 Riverbend, Denny's name was a persistent background chatter at the station. It was the name of the man who went after one of their own.

The captain leaned forward from the back seat. "We'll be right behind you when we hit the yard, Flex. You take lead on interior if we've got confirmed victims."

Flex just nodded. His jaw was set hard enough to ache.

Miles away, Beth was rinsing her tea mug in the kitchen sink when the sound of sirens began to rise. At first, it was just a hum you heard when driving towards an area full of cicadas, low and consistent, but it grew louder, rolling closer, the pitch rising until it was pressed right up against her windows.

She dried her hands on the dish towel, moving toward the front door without quite knowing why.

Two engines tore past her street, lights cutting through the darkness, reflecting red in her glossy front door. She stood there for a long breath, watching the taillights vanish into the curve.

And then, without warning, the porchlight above her flickered.

Once.

Twice.

Then out.

She stood there in the dark when a prickle started at the base of her neck and crawled upward, gripping her scalp. She didn't know how, but she knew somewhere deep in the marrow of her motherly bones she knew. She knew exactly where those trucks were headed. And she knew who was inside.

She took three steps forward; bare feet stepping on the painted floor of the porch and rested one palm on the distressed wood railing and leaned her body into the wooden porch column. She stood and made manifest her intuition with a whisper, "Jupiter..."

The heat hit before the truck even stopped.

Orange light flickered in the thick black sky, rising over the rooftops like a false sunrise. Smoke moved low, snaking across the yard, curling around the mailbox, the fence, and the flag that hung limp against the porch rail.

Flex was out of the cab before the air brakes finished their sigh. His boots thudded against the asphalt, the smell already clawing at his throat, burning oil, melting plastic, something acrid and chemical under it all. He didn't need to see the house number. The shape of the front steps, the trim cut in neat lines, the perfectly painted door, all of it was burned into his memory.

The flames glowed in the windows of some rooms, while it was dark in others, the fire had not spread throughout the house. If Jupiter was inside there was hope, but he had to act.

The flames had already chewed their way through the kitchen windows, glass shattered out onto the porch. A dull roar swelled with each fresh breath of oxygen the fire pulled from the night. The siding bubbled and peeled like old wallpaper on the corner of the house.

Neighbors had gathered in the street, their faces pale in the glow, voices rising in frantic fragments. He was only able to focus on pieces of the panicked words.:

"I saw him go in earlier..."

"...saw a kid playing in the back yard..."

"...back door's locked..."

Flex didn't hear the rest as he advanced towards the inferno. His helmet light caught on the figure of a woman waving both arms wildly toward the porch. "He's still in there! The little boy's in there!"

Every muscle in his body tightened at once.

"Flex, mask up! We'll run the line!" the captain barked, yanking the charged hose into position.

Flex's gloved hands worked without hesitation, face mask sealed, airline connected, regulator hissing to life. The first lungful of filtered air felt too slow, too thin, but it was enough and with it the small film of moisture that started to form on his visor slowly started to retreat.

He charged toward the porch, boots hammering wood already hot enough to steam in the night air. The front door hung crooked on its hinges, one corner scorched black, the brass knob hissing where the heat licked it.

Inside, the smoke was a living thing. It moved in waves, dark and heavy, pressing low like it wanted to pin him to the floor. His light caught nothing but swirling smoke and ash until he dropped to a crouch where visibility was better.

The kitchen was to his left, fire climbing the walls, licking across the ceiling, dripping molten bits of light onto the floor. His mind processed without thinking that this was where the fire started. Somewhere deeper in the house, faint and muffled against the cacophony, he thought he heard coughing.

"JUPITER!" His voice boomed in the mask, swallowed almost instantly by the roar of the fire.

Behind him, the crew pushed through the door, hose line snaking across the charred floor. Water hissed as it hit the heat, sending up clouds of steam that blurred everything into shifting shadows.

Flex pushed forward. The living room couch was tipped at an angle, one cushion half-melted, the TV screen spiderwebbed in heat cracks. Beyond it, down the hall, the faint sound came again, not coughing this time, but a small, choked sob.

He didn't think. Trained muscle memory took over as

he continued to walk in a low crouch to avoid the roiling black smoke so dark that it seemed to absorb the orange glow of the fire. He moved towards the sound, silently praying that the small boy who captured a part of his soul was ok, that he would not fail the woman he loved.

Halfway down the hall, something heavy shifted to his right, a slumped figure against the wall, head down, one hand dragging along the scorched paint. The professional side of him was exalted at finding someone alive, but the creature part of him was angry that it was Denny and not Jupiter.

Flex's beam caught his face just long enough to register glassy eyes, sweat pouring, lips forming words that didn't reach over the noise. He held his hand against a gash that was cut deep into his forehead, blood poured black down his face, a sick color formed from the heat of the fire and the smoke and soot in the air.

Flex's first instinct was to grab him and shove him toward the door. But he stopped and shouted "Jupiter!"

Denny looked at him with eyes glazed and mouthed nonsense words that would not have been intelligible even if there were no fire.

Flex shook him, "WHERE IS JUPITER?!"

Denny's eyes cleared for just a moment, and he pointed towards the stairs.

Flex didn't waste the breath to answer. He yanked Denny by the collar, dragging him toward the light of the front room. "Get him OUT!" he shouted to the crew through his radio, two firefighters peeled away to drag Denny toward the safety of the porch and front yard.

Flex moved to bound up the stairs when chaos boomed more ferociously. The pantry filled with Denny's spirits added new sustenance to the fire as the shelves holding the liquor dropped spilling a tsunami of liquid under the door, a burning torrent of blue flames licking the floor.

The hose team went to take action and steam billowed on contact with the water. A black rain started to drip from the ceiling as the steam mixed with soot and smoke. This false rain smeared Flex's visor, and he wiped it away while continuing to move.

The stairs were carpeted, and the heat of the fire had started to make the nylon fiber melt, his boots made a sucking sound as he went up, the visibility was almost zero as the smoke filled the higher parts of the home.

The hallway at the top of the stairs had five doors, he threw them open and looked inside seeing two empty bedrooms, a bathroom, and a closet. The last door, the bedroom door at the end of the hall, was locked. Flex hit it once with his shoulder, nothing. The second time, the frame splintered. The door flew in as two of the hinges gave way leaving the door at an odd angle held only by a screw still in the casing on the bottom hinge and smoke billowed in like a flood.

In the far corner he saw a bed, curled in a ball on the bed under a spaceship quilt, was Jupiter. In the amount of time that it took Flex to make this out the visibility was gone, smoke rushed in to fill this new space created by the open door.

"Jup! Hey, hey, buddy, it's me," Flex's voice was muffled through the mask, but urgent.

The boy's head jerked up from the quilt, eyes wide and wet. His small hands gripped the fabric so tightly his knuckles were white.

"Flex?" His voice was thin, scratchy, barely audible over the roar above them and immediately lost to heavy coughing.

"Yeah, it's me. We're going home. Come on."

Flex crossed the room in three strides, sweeping the quilt away and tucking Jupiter under one arm. The boy coughed hard, his body jerking with each breath. Flex pressed his gloved hand to the back of Jupiter's head, lowering both of them closer to the floor where the air still had some visibility.

The hall was a tunnel of acrid smoke now. The heat rolling up the stairs was so intense that Flex could feel the inside of his suit start to steam. His helmet light cut a narrow path through the rolling darkness, enough to see the glowing outlines of the door frame ahead.

They made it down the hallway to the stairs and Flex's heart stopped. The fire from the kitchen had started its carnivorous feast up the stairs. He inhaled deeply and moved down the stairs still holding the oxygen starved and unconscious boy in his arms. The hose team was working on a retreat with radio chatter competing with rational though. He made it halfway down the stairs before a violent crack echoed from the kitchen.

The pantry, fueled by the stockpile of liquor that Denny stored sat underneath the stairs. The added fuel to the fire accelerated the burn weakening the structure of the stairs. As Flex made his way, the sixth step lurched beneath his boots, and he dropped.

As Flex fell into the abyss his oxygen tank caught the step above suspending him. Jupiter, still under his arm, started to burn, the flames rolled over his body and licked at his young skin.

Robert, a longtime member of the team, rushed up the stairs and pulled the boy from his arms and turned, radioing "MAYDAY" as he moved. Flex heard this and started to scream as the flames in the void under the stairs roasted his body.

His screams grew louder and reached a crescendo when, thankfully, unconscious took him. His last sight before the hungry darkness carried his waking mind away was the boots of two firefighters rushing up the stairs towards him.

Beth was still awake, sitting at her kitchen table, the porchlight steady overhead, hands clenched around a mug she couldn't drink from. The fire trucks screaming down the street had unnerved her. She didn't know if she was cut out for a life with a man who constantly put himself in danger, even if it was for the benefit of others. She sat, and she waited, phone in hand for a response to a text message that Flex did not receive. A response to a text that was sent to a phone that sat on a desk next to a small teakwood box that contained the hope of lasting love.

When her phone rang, she quickly grabbed it, happy to hear the voice of the man she loved telling her that the night was routine and it was just another cat.

However, the call was not from Flex, it was from Vanessa.

"There is a fire down the street, it is Denny's place..." She said more, but the words were lost to Beth.

She didn't remember grabbing her keys. Didn't remember the drive. Just the rising scream of sirens in the distance and the way her chest had tightened until it was almost impossible to breathe.

By the time she reached Denny's Street, the night was ripped apart by red strobes and the deep, thunderous cough of water pumps. The house, the torrid house Denny had purchased in his continued attempt to torture her, was nothing but a black-limned skeleton wrapped in orange. Flames clawed out through what used to be the kitchen window, the roof sagging in on itself like a broken ribcage.

She slammed the car door and ran, heart pounding, vision narrowing. The air was a wall of heat and smoke, tasting of ash and burnt oil.

"Beth! Beth, stop!"

Vanessa's voice. A hand on her arm, tugging her back as she strained toward the yellow tape. "Where's my son? Where is he?!"

"He's here, he's here, look!"

Beth spun. A paramedic was kneeling beside the ambulance, a blanket-wrapped Jupiter clinging to him like a lifeline. His face was streaked with soot, but his eyes, her eyes, found her instantly.

"Momma!" He screamed through the oxygen mask held over his little mouth.

She fell to her knees, arms wrapping around him before the first responder could even stand. He clung to her, sobbing into her neck, his body trembling in her grip. She could feel his heart hammering against her chest.

"It's okay, baby. I've got you. I've got you." She kept saying it, over and over, until she realized she was shaking as hard as he was.

"Ma'am," the medic placed his hand on her shoulder, "we have to get him to the hospital." This is when Beth saw the burns on his arms and legs, the missing hair on the back of his head.

Her heart broke for her little man, and she held him until the E.M.T.'s lifted him onto a gurney and started rolling him to the ambulance, she in tow.

The sound changed, the fire's roar dimming under the hiss of hoses, and Beth looked up, searching for one face.

She did not see Flex, but she did see a group of

Firefighters standing in a circle with another team of paramedics working on someone laying on the ground. She saw an ambulance backing up and the team loading a man into the back in a frenzied rush.

As she stepped into the back of the ambulance with Jupiter, she caught the sight of a badly burned face that rolled in her direction. The face, though badly injured, was clear to her. She looked out of the back windows as the ambulance doors closed to see her love, injured, possibly dying being loaded.

The lights strobed on that face as she caught glimpses between the medic's urgent hands. She longed to rush out and be by his side but could not bring herself to leave her beloved little man alone.

While the paramedics drove away, she saw another sight. Denny, uninjured and yelling at police officers, she saw him push one of the officers and saw him being taken to the ground.

Beth saw all of this as tears filled her eyes, washing out all of these scenes with a serene filter, like she was looking out at the world from underwater. She made this connection and a long howl of emotion escaped her lips, and she felt like she was underwater, like she was drowning.

Miles away there was no commotion. The cicadas still hummed their unceasing call and wind still rustled leaves that were starting to dry as a new season approached. The little house with faded yellow siding, worn porch, and glossy red door sat quietly as always. Next to the door the wrought iron porch light still hung, secure to the wall with a light bulb still burning.

While the scene of chaos took place farther away the house sat. At the moment that the anguished howl escaped the lips of Beth the light blinked rapidly and went dark as a puff of smoke came out from the base of the lamp. It was dark and would never light again, its functionality gone like hope ripped from the soul of a mourner.

16

SCARRED HEARTS

The fluorescent lights in the pediatric ICU hummed overhead, too bright, too white, reflecting in the polished floor like they were trying to erase the shadows from the night before. They couldn't, not for her, and not for him.

Beth sat in the molded plastic chair beside Jupiter's bed, her shoulders curved forward, hands cradling his small fingers. His skin was warm but fragile under her touch, wrapped in fresh gauze from mid-thigh to ankle. His chest rose and fell in shallow, careful pulls of air beneath the transparent mask that covered his mouth and nose. Each hiss of oxygen felt like a lifeline.

A children's cartoon played soundlessly on the mounted TV, bright colors moving in jerky rhythm. He hadn't opened his eyes since they wheeled him in last night, but the nurse had told her that was normal, that his body needed the rest more than anything.

The door opened quietly, and a man in a white coat stepped in. His hair was pressed flat on one side; the kind of detail that told Beth he'd been here through the night. The badge clipped to his coat pocket read *Dr. Lansing*. He stopped at the foot of the bed, eyes soft, voice even.

"Mrs. Keller?" he said gently.

Her head came up fast. "Weston," she corrected out of habit.

"Mrs. Weston," he amended with a small nod. "Your son is stable. The burns on his legs will need skin grafts. We'll schedule the first in a few days once we're sure his lungs can handle the anesthesia. He's young, strong, and if all goes as expected, his long-term mobility should be fine."

Her hands tightened over Jupiter's, as if sealing that future in place.

The doctor's tone shifted, weight pressing down on each word. "I also want to make you aware... when he arrived, he was groggy. Incoherent. His reaction was not in line with anything given to him by the paramedics. He kept mentioning something about 'sleepy medicine' his father gave him." He paused, looking at her face. "We ran a toxicology screen. His blood tested positive for opiates."

Beth's breath caught, the air in her lungs turning solid.

"We've reported it to the authorities," Dr. Lansing continued. "DHR and law enforcement will open a joint investigation. I know this is difficult to hear, but it's important you're prepared."

Her vision tunneled, not from shock, but from the kind of rage that makes the body go utterly still. She looked down at Jupiter's sleeping face, at the faint smudge of soot still clinging to his hairline. He was here. He was breathing.

She knew without being told that Denny, the man she once loved, had drugged her son so he would not be in the way. She immediately knew deep down to her core that if he had not been drugged, he would have left the house when the alarm sounded. She knew that the son-of-a-bitch had almost killed her son and in doing so hurt the man who did love her.

"Ms. Weston, this is going to be a long hard process. We have counseling resources that we encourage you and your son to take advantage of. He will need you more than ever."

With a professional smile the doctor turned and left, he stopped outside to give instructions to the nurses before moving on to more patients.

She brushed her thumb across the strip of clean skin between the mask and the bandages. "You're safe now, baby," she whispered, low enough that only he could hear. "No one's ever going to do that to you again."

The ICU felt colder than the pediatric ward, as if the air itself was afraid to linger too long in the rooms here. Every door was a glass panel framed in steel, every heartbeat inside measured by blinking lights and steady beeps. The sanitary smell of cleaning supplies barely masked the other aromas, the special scents of patients struggling for life, the smell of cancer in the air. The misery of the occupants creating a miasma of grief that felt tangible to all those who walked past.

Beth walked slowly, her shoes making no sound on the tile. She had to keep one hand pressed to the wall as she passed each room, like she needed the building to steady her.

When she reached *Room 14*, she almost didn't look in.

Flex lay in the bed like someone had stolen the life from him and only left the shape behind. White sheets covered him from the waist down, but the rest...

She had thought she knew what fire could do to the body. She had been wrong.

His skin was a patchwork of raw, angry red and glossy, blistered stretches. His arms, arms that had once wrapped around her and made her feel like nothing could reach her, were mummified in gauze, tubes and wires snaking in and out like roots feeding a dying tree. A thick collar of white bandage circled his neck, disappearing beneath the oxygen mask strapped over his mouth and nose.

The monitor beside him ticked out a rhythm, soft and indifferent.

Beth stepped inside, the door whispering shut behind her.

She sat in the chair by his bed and reached for his hand before stopping. Only the tips of his fingers weren't swaddled in white. She touched them lightly, like he might break under her.

"They say you can hear people," she whispered, voice trembling. "So, hear me now, Flex. You went into that fire for my son. You went in knowing whose house it was.

You..." Her voice caught, breath hitching before she forced the words out. "...you brought him back to me."

Her eyes roamed his face, searching for some flicker of the man she knew. The room's quiet was heavy, interrupted only by the hiss of oxygen and the faint beep marking his pulse.

She stayed like that for hours, talking when she could, holding her silence when she couldn't. Nurses came and went, adjusting drips, checking vitals, but none of them spoke to her beyond what was necessary.

By the time the sky outside the window began to lighten, her hand was still resting on his, and she was still waiting for him to come back to her.

Three days blurred into each other like colors left too long in the rain. She leaned on her new friend Vanessa, who came to the children's hospital and sat with Jupiter so she could spend time with Flex.

She only left the hospital long enough to go home, shower, and bring back special treats for Jupiter. When she went home to shower, she would always stare in awe at her little porch. Every time she returned it would be filled with flowers, little toys, but more importantly, one of Flex's firefighter brothers would be on the porch sitting in the swing. They were taking shifts sitting and waiting so she would not have to return home alone.

These men sat in vigil, and each time she arrived they recited the same sentiment, a little differently each time, but the same, nonetheless. Each time they told her that she was family to them, they would help her any way that they could, and they would shed a tear when she updated them on Flex. One of these trips left a mountain of a man, Bruce, a sobbing heap with arms like oak trees wrapped around her.

In between rooms, and trips home, she dealt with investigators. She spoke to multiple DHR agents, the District Attorney, and detectives. All assuring her that Denny would go to jail, that she was safe now, justice would be served.

These visits left her cold, the idea that justice could be served was ridiculous. She felt deep down that Denny would find a way to beat the system, that he would be back and his reign of terror for her and her son would continue.

She always smiled and thanked these investigators, but her false smile faded quickly once their backs were turned.

Beth slept in the chair when she could, her neck aching from the angle, her back sore from the stiff cushion. Every morning, she brought fresh coffee into the ICU, though most of it went cold before she remembered to drink it.

Jupiter's condition had stabilized in the pediatric burn unit across the street. His little voice had been hoarse when she visited, lungs still struggling against the damage, but he had squeezed her hand and asked for Flex. She told him the truth: "He's sleeping, baby, but he's fighting hard."

Beth would sit with her son until the medication carried him away to sleep, and she would pass the precious reigns to Vanessa. Then make her way to the next bedside vigil. Flex was never alone, when she arrived one of his faithful team members would step out, the hospital lifted the visitation rule for him so that "the hero" would always have someone by his side.

It was just after midnight on the fourth night when she heard it.

A low, raspy sound that wasn't the hiss of the oxygen.

Her head snapped up.

Flex's eyes were open.

Not all the way, just slits rimmed with red, but they were on her. Eyes that were focused, present, knowing.

"Hey," she whispered, her voice shaking with relief and fear all tangled together. She reached for his fingers again, this time holding them without hesitation.

He blinked slowly, lips parting under the mask. The nurses had prepared her for this moment, they told her to speak softly, to keep his mind anchored when he woke up. They told her not to be surprised if he drifted in and out. She was also told that he might not wake up, with sixty percent of his body burned, his chance of survival was slim, that it was a miracle that he was still alive.

With obvious effort, he lifted his right hand an inch off the bed. His voice, when it came, was shredded and wet, "Marry me."

Beth's breath caught. "Flex..." Her eyes burned instantly. "I..."

"I do, say that, say I do." His lips twitched into something almost like a smile beneath the mask. "Life's short... figured that out the hard way."

She shook her head, tears spilling freely now, half-laughing through the ache in her chest. "You're supposed to wait until you can get down on one knee."

He gave the faintest shrug, his eyelids fluttering. "Consider this... the floor version."

She leaned forward, pressing her forehead gently to the bandage above his brow. "Yes. Yes, I'll marry you."

His breath shuddered out against the mask, a small exhale that might have been relief. His hand slackened in hers, but his eyes stayed on her for one long, final heartbeat before slipping closed again.

The monitors kept their rhythm. The machines kept breathing for him. But Beth knew, deep down in the place that had warned her about the porchlight, that he was already drifting somewhere she couldn't follow.

The next sunrise came and went.

Flex didn't open his eyes.

The doctors said it was the body protecting itself, that the pain from the burns alone was enough to send a man under for days, but Beth knew better. She had seen the way his gaze lingered the night before, the way his voice had sounded like it came from a place already half gone.

She stayed anyway, because she loved him. She stayed because he had run into fire for her.

The days bled into one long unending toil of seeing her loved ones suffer and smiling at outsiders. Going room to room, updating well-wishers, and listening to prayer offers. She had to speak to security to prevent her mother, father, and sister from entering either room. The lines of family had been destroyed, she would never be able to sit with them again, whichever way this new season in her life went, it would be without the people she thought she could depend on.

Through the soft tread of nurses, the beeping of monitors, the shifting light from the blinds. She held his hand when they changed his dressings, whispered to him when Jupiter was strong enough to speak to him through Facetime.

On the morning of the sixth day, the room was quiet, too quiet. The machines still hummed, but the air felt thin, as if some invisible door had been left open.

Beth was dozing in the chair, her fingers still threaded with his, when the steady tone of the heart monitor gave a single high-pitched note.

Then another.

Then the long, unbroken sound she would hear in her sleep for years to come.

A nurse moved quickly, pressing buttons, calling for the doctor.

Beth didn't move.

She just held his hand tighter, her tears sliding down and spotting the crisp white sheet.

"It's alright," she whispered, even though her voice cracked on the words. "You saved him. You saved us both. I love you."

The doctor confirmed what she already knew.

Flex was gone.

Beth bent over him, her forehead resting against the bandages on his shoulder, letting the sobs come unchecked now, ugly tears that choked her. The true tears of loss.

When the choreographed dance of the medical team ended, with orders given, and the funeral home called to retrieve his body, the room fell to silence.

She stayed there for one last minute, feeling the cooling stillness of the man who had run into fire for the people he loved. Her hand stayed on his, memorizing the weight, the shape. She tried to remember it as it was before the burns, but like the scars her son would carry, she would carry the scars in her heart of her love's final days.

In the quiet of that sterile hospital room, she made him a promise, one she'd keep for the rest of her life.

"You showed my son how a man could be good, strong, loving. I will make that count, I will let your light carry on through him."

END

Porchlights and Promises

EPILOGUE

Beth sat on the porch of her faded yellow home. She watched her son sit at a small desk she set up for him to craft outdoors during his recovery. He had already endured six skin grafts since that fateful September night, and the wounds that can heal did so in an almost magical way. They both still felt the loss of Flex and Jupiter asked questions about him frequently. She never denied him the chance to talk, but it tore her apart each time.

She stood and walked over to see what he was coloring, it was a vibrant picture of something that he had seen, two fire trucks, ladders raised, with an American Flag suspended between them. It was the sight he saw on the day of Flex's funeral. A well-attended, beautiful ceremony was held. Jupiter saw the funeral from the back of an ambulance; special steps were taken to keep the environment sanitary so he could see his friend being laid to rest. The firefighting family made it happen.

She recalled the moments after the funeral the chief took Beth aside and put a small box in her hand. Inside she found a rose gold band ornamented with leaves and in the center sat a moss agate cut in the shape of kite. He told her that it was found with Flex's belongings, and he was sure it was for her. She had not told anyone about the proposal, and it took every remaining ounce of self-control she still retained to not fall to her knees weeping.

She rubbed his short hair that had regrown during his recovery. With a kiss on the top of his head and a scruffy look given back, a look that screamed, "MOM STOP" even though he did not say it.

It was time to get back to work on the house. As she went in Beth looked over at the new porch light that the guys at the station had installed for her. The old wrought iron lamp could not be repaired, no matter who tried it would always short out. The new light was more utilitarian, an off-the-shelf option from the local hardware store. It was ugly, but it served its purpose.

The picture stirred up memories, and as she walked through the house events of the past few months bombarded her. The loss, the arraignment and holding of Denny, LeRoy, and Carlton. It had started with the arrest of Denny for child endangerment and the charges snowballed from there. Now the FEDS were involved and per the words of her attorney Rachel, "Denny is fucked five ways from sideways." She still wondered if he would be able to get off, but she felt more at ease every day.

She thought briefly of when Vanessa stepped between her and her sister, the day her family showed up demanding to be a part of her life. Evelyn demanding forgiveness, her father stood silent witness. When Maddie got aggressive, rumors were that she was drinking heavily since the fire, and pushed Beth, Vanessa stepped in and punched her. Vanessa then told them all to "respect Beth's boundaries and to not ever let her find out they had done otherwise." Followed by, "Also, you are all banned from my coffee shop." Beth smiled at her friend, she was a hot mess, but solid.

On the black kitchen countertop sat a small box, it held some decorations from Easter that she had been delaying packing away, her back hurt these days, but today was the day. She carried it out back to the new shed that the boys from station 2 built for her. As she entered the room she caught a glimpse of the old wrought iron porch lamp, the one that could not be repaired. She could not bring herself to throw it away or recycle it. So, it sat and every time she walked into the room it broke her heart and made her smile at the same time.

The box of Easter decorations went into a tidy bin for decorations, firefighters like things in their place and they built cubbies for everything. She turned and just before she made it to the door she paused, she swore that out of the corner of her eye she saw the old light flash.

That was, of course, impossible. Even though it still had a bulb in the socket, it was not wired, and of course, a porch light not wired and with no power will not turn on. She told herself that as she walked out and closed the door. When the door clicked, she said out loud to no one, "These hormones really have me messed up." She said this as she stretched her back and rested her hand on her stomach and then smiled as she felt the baby kick, some lights never really go out.

ABOUT THE AUTHOR

Terry W. Wester is a writer, producer, and Southern storyteller with his pulse firmly rooted in Alabama's landscape and its hidden histories. As the co-writer and producer of the *Broken Ashler* series, he channels his intricate experiences, including years of involvement with the Scottish Rite, into narratives that crack open the rituals and moral shadows of our world.

Drawing on his time as a 33rd degree Mason and Deputy for the Orient of Alabama, Terry's writing blends authenticity with emotional courage, asking tough questions about loyalty, authority, and light in the dark. When he's not writing or producing, you can find him behind the counter of his cigar shop, dreaming up his next Alabama-set drama, or pursuing yet another dusty story waiting to be told.

He lives with his family in Alabama, where *Porch Lights and Promises* is his debut, as Southern, as heartfelt, and as real as the porch light that never fades.

https://shelbyliving.com/fraternal-light/
https://www.imdb.com/name/nm16277057/

instagram.com/author_terry_wester
facebook.com/AuthorTerryWester

ACKNOWLEDGMENTS

Special thanks to my family, friends, and early readers who believed in this story before it ever found the page. And to every soul who's ever stood on a porch in the dark, searching for the courage to knock.

Mikel Wilson, Thank you sir. You made a difference.

Jacqulyn Ward Tripp, I don't think editors get enough credit. I hope to keep you correcting my mistakes!

www.ingramcontent.com/pod-product-compliance
Lightning Source LLC
Chambersburg PA
CBHW070215260626
47160CB00002B/559